NOV 2 5 1977

Ludwig
Little boy lost

LITTLE
BOY
LOST

LiTTLE BOY LOST

a novel by

JERRY LUDWIG

4F

DELACORTE PRESS/NEW YORK

Published by
Delacorte Press
1 Dag Hammarskjold Plaza
New York, New York 10017

Library of Congress Cataloging in Publication Data

Ludwig, Jerry.
Little boy lost.

I. Title.
PZ4.L9464Li   [PS3562.U29]   813'.5'4   77-24185
ISBN 0-440-04796-X

For Barbara
who always believed
it could happen.

And the cat's in the cradle,
And the silver spoon.
Little Boy Blue
And the Man in the Moon.

When you comin' home, Dad?
I don't know when.
We'll get together then.
We're gonna have a good time then.

—HARRY & SANDY CHAPIN
"Cat's in the Cradle"

LITTLE
BOY
LOST

Robert Kennedy was a pain in the ass. Brenner remembered the first time he saw him. Standing up on the trunk of a cream-colored Lincoln Continental convertible, rolling slowly through the crowds in Watts. He was wearing a fifty-dollar shirt with the cuffs rolled back. The campaign sun had bleached the hair on his arms platinum. And his shirttail was hanging out the back of his pants. It took three of them to keep him standing on his feet; an ex-FBI man and the javelin thrower, what's his name? Johnson. Rafer Johnson. They each held on to a leg and big Rosy Grier clutched Robert Kennedy's belt.

The crowds loved him and so they pulled and tore at him from all sides and their yells were punctuated by a rhythmic smacking sound as the car crept slowly forward and upraised hands would strike against Kennedy's outstretched palms. He was smiling. But his body shuddered under the staccato impact of a thousand instants of contact.

Ganzer was with Brenner that day. Crowd control. No one in those days would admit the possibility of anything happening. Not in L.A. So it was good duty, like policing a Santa Claus parade. But that didn't stop them from getting uptight as a tall, fierce-looking young black came leaping out of the crowd when the car was almost at a standstill. He threw himself across the hood of the Lincoln, but then he only waved to Bobby and grinned happily, showing big empty pink palms. Peace! And the black man sprawled with his back against the windshield and began to chant loudly to the throng blocking the advance of the convertible: "Make way for Kenne-dee! Make way for Kenne-dee!" And the people obeyed their self-appointed Moses: the sea of faces parted and a path appeared allowing the car to pass.

"You see that? You see that!" Ganzer complained. "The son-of-a-bitch doesn't want to be protected. He wants to be loved!" A pain in the ass.

5:01 . . . oh, Christ.

Faint traces of daylight were starting to ooze in through the green curtains. Green, gold and brown, Brenner thought. The national colors for motel rooms. Was there a federal law against a nice light bright yellow? Or blue. How about baby blue? Sky blue? No. show me a motel and I'll show you green, brown and deep gold. Doesn't show the dirt. And that's what it's all about.

Some of the guys detailed to RFK wound up voting for him in the primary. Not Brenner. He was a registered Republican that year and Nixon was his man. Not that he ever followed politics that much, but Nixon was a California guy. Up from the ranks, hometown boy makes good then falls on his face and tries again. Got to hand it to the guy, Brenner thought then. Shows how wrong you can be.

So. The ladies. Yeah. The foxy ladies that used to hang around the candidates. Workers. Bandwagon riders. Hustlers. Crusaders. The guys on special duty would compare notes. There was the Gene McCarthy bunch: granny glasses and baggy sweaters and no laughs. Nixon's camp had the drum majorettes. Blonde and blue-eyed with good bods but nothing doing. Like the girls in the suntan-oil ads. Smiling. Handing out leaflets, wearing straw hats with red-white-and-blue bunting. Salute the flag and forget about scoring.

But Bobby's bunch . . .

Yeah.

For Brenner it was being a kid again and walking into a candy store. There they all were: a whole ballroom full of them.

In the dawn-brightening motel room, Brenner smiled as he remembered. A whole ballroom. Crowded. Everyone loves a winner and their man had taken it. Easy. Take it easy . . . everything easy.

Time. What time is it now? 5:11. Sounds like a train schedule. The 5:11 arriving on Track 58. Click! 5:12. But who's counting?

A pair. A sensational pair. Brenner couldn't remember her face, but he could recall her knockers as if it was yesterday. A chesty lady. There were two large matching buttons pinned to the too-tightly-fitted beige turtleneck: "RFK All the Way." She was clapping her hands and jumping up and down, bouncing with glee, because up on the crowded little stage Bobby had appeared and was waving to them all. He said something about ending the

■ 3 ■

divisions in America, ending the violence. Brenner looked up at the stage. Behind the swarm of politicians and photographers, right behind Bobby, there was a white plaster frieze on the wall. A touch of hotel elegance. Two matching angels playing their harps. Bobby grinned and made victory signs and the whole place shook with the cheering and when the stage was empty Brenner went back to trying to hit on the girl in the turtleneck with the two big buttons. And that's what he was doing when he heard the first faint sounds. Dry twigs snapping . . .

It was a cartoon. Huge Rosey Grier was sitting on top of this little dark guy. He'll squash him, Brenner thought. God. The noise and the shoving and the shitty kitchen smells and then Brenner saw an open place on the narrow passageway floor where Bobby was laying on his back. And Brenner couldn't believe it. Bobby didn't look hurt, just surprised. His eyes were open, unblinking. Then, as Brenner took a step closer, the eyes were closed. For a long instant. Another step, now they were open again. Brenner thought of a black-and-white drawing he once had seen in the window of a Mexican restaurant near Olvera Street. It was a picture of Christ, wearing the crown of thorns. But it was the eyes. The artist had done one of those optical illusion tricks. If you looked at it this way, the eyes were closed, but from over here they were open. Closed. Open. Closed. The arms outstretched in the darkness . . .

A slash of light was peeping in through a parting of the motel curtains—across Brenner's face. He could get up or just continue to lie here thinking about something that happened in the middle of another night nine years before. He glanced over at the stand beside the bed.

Time. 5:23. Oh, hell. Close enough.

Brenner reached behind the luminous dial on the white

Westclox and pushed in the button on the alarm set for 5:45 that hadn't had a chance to buzz in days. He swung his legs out from under the sheet onto the carpet. The green carpet. The beach dampness of Santa Monica just outside the door had seeped in sufficiently during the night to make Brenner shudder slightly. He snapped on the light.

The nightstand was dark mahogany, a formica top pretending to be grained wood. Beside the motel telephone there was a clip-on holster with Brenner's .38 Police Special and a worn black leather display holder with the silver-and-gold badge shining up at him. Brenner reached for the first cigarette of the day. Marlboro. The cowboy's smoke. He inhaled and coughed. The way his father always did. Brenner hadn't thought of that in a long time: asleep as a kid on those dark winter mornings, coming half-awake to the reassuring sound of his father moving around the kitchen of the old house, making his breakfast, coughing and clearing his throat. First cigarette of the day. Like father, like son.

■▄■▄■

There is a banner flying over the main street of Reno, Nevada, boasting it is "The Biggest Little City in the World." The chic citizenry of Beverly Hills, California, would consider that hopelessly déclassé not to mention laughably rural; nevertheless, there is an invisible banner proclaiming their environs "The Richest Little City in the World."

No less than Liechtenstein or Monaco, this is a principality unto itself. Those that are here cherish a simple belief: Everyone wants to be here, but we are the chosen few.

Along Beverly Drive from Wilshire to Santa Monica Boulevards is where everyone comes out to play. The more exclusive shops and restaurants are on neighboring streets;

so are the avenues given over to orthodontists, psychiatrists, dermatologists, cosmetic and orthopedic surgeons who combine with the accountants, lawyers, agents and business managers to make life in these regions the unblemished experience it can be. But on Beverly Drive in these few streets, everyone crowds in to look at everyone else. Here is where Beverly Hills' primary rule of order is displayed: If you've got it, flaunt it; if not, then fake it.

Beyond Santa Monica Boulevard, Beverly Drive becomes a real-life backlot. Cape Cod, Monterey and Regency homes co-exist with English Tudor cottages, Spanish ranchos, Colonial estates and French châteaux. Mia Farrow used to play jacks on the pavement here; or at least that's the word given out by the leather-skinned harpies wearing muumuus who materialize on the weekends to sell "Maps to the Movie Stars' Homes." The mélange of mansions parts briefly at Sunset Boulevard to make way for a landmark: the Beverly Hills Hotel. Howard Hughes kept a bungalow here year round, guarded by a platoon of Mormons; and the Polo Lounge remains the de rigueur watering hole, each afternoon luring a colorful cross-section of hondelers, hustlers, entrepreneurs and dreamers.

But it is a few blocks north of Sunset Boulevard that Beverly Drive takes a strange turn. Where Coldwater Canyon starts its run for the Valley—at the cream-stucco-and-red-Spanish-tile firehouse—Beverly Drive slips inconspicuously off to the left past a small park. Next comes an orange grove, right here in the city. And then houses again —but with a difference: the same confusion of styles, but smaller. Almost miniaturized. Like Disneyland, everything suddenly seems five-eighths of reality and a purist glancing quickly at the street signs will pierce the secret.

For the street signs are no longer white with black lettering, but dark blue with white letters; even if it still says "Beverly Drive," you are no longer in Beverly Hills but back in the city of Los Angeles.

Some people live here because it is quiet and convenient; others only because it is confusingly close to Beverly Hills. Although their children cannot go to Beverly Hills Schools and they do not qualify for the low property taxes or the high security police protection provided by Beverly Hills, there is reflected glory. The residents of these streets can claim kinship. And many pretend to outsiders that they are part of the world of the white street signs; only their postman knows the truth. But what dream was ever measured by the amount of truth it contained?

The street lamps continued to glow across the sleeping houses as the night sky brightened into a chalky white. Soon morning would be here, but for now the cul-de-sac just off Beverly Drive still belonged to the creatures of the early hours. A coyote crept down from the wilderness that surrounds the canyons of Beverly Hills and Los Angeles.

Searching for a stray cat but willing to settle for a few overripe plums, the coyote nibbled at the fruit tree in front of a house that had been designed for show: amoeba-shaped chunks of flagstone walled in with white mortar, oversize picture windows covered by perpetually drawn white curtains, forming great sightless eyes staring outward; the sharp, graceless lines of the nouveau-riche School of Modern Architecture.

Now the coyote looked up, suddenly alert at the sound of running footsteps. A dawn jogger, in maroon sweatsuit, trotted by and the coyote melted away into the dark foliage. The jogger continued away up the street, unaware that he had interrupted anything.

And inside the house . . .

There was a giraffe on the wall. Bobby Montrose had

seen a real giraffe once when Pete and Billy's father took him with them to the Griffith Park Zoo. The giraffe there was even taller than the one on the wall and he ate the branches off a tree.

Bobby got out of bed carefully. His mommy and daddy didn't want noise early in the morning when they were sleeping. There were a lot of toys in his room but they all made noise. So he decided to go outside and play. He opened his door very quietly.

His feet didn't make any sound because he was wearing Dr. Denton's. Light blue zipper-neck pajama tops snapped to bottoms that had rubber-soled feet. Bobby's hair was blond and long and silky-fine. His eyes were blue and he had the kind of chubby-cheerful face that made strangers smile at the sight of him. The police report would later describe him as "four years old, approximately 3½ ft. tall, weight 37 lbs. with no identifying marks."

Bobby padded into the kitchen and collected four chocolate chip cookies from the cupboard. Then he reached up to open the side door and went outside. The sun was beginning to shine.

"That's you, isn't it?" Jeannie, a cute red-headed part-time waitress, who always had questions for Brenner, was standing next to his booth at the Pancake House.

Brenner was alone in the booth, sipping his third cup of coffee from the bottomless carafe on the table. The hostess was off conferring with the cooks, the other waitresses were loading the salt and pepper shakers and there were hardly any other early-bird coffee drinkers in the restaurant yet.

Jeannie was holding out a folded page torn from a newspaper. She was nineteen, in her sophomore year at Santa Monica City College and taking a crap course in abnormal psychology that she found fascinating. "Look at you," she teased, "the only one staring at the camera."

Brenner had seen the photo that ran the day before on the front page of a West Los Angeles weekly advertising throwaway. Usually the stories in that paper were timeless and pointless, devoted to ground breaking for new supermarkets and "16 Exciting New Ways to Prepare Zucchini." But the manhunt for the West Side child rapist had riveted the attention of their readership, too, over the past weeks; and his capture was big news. The streets were now once again safe.

Four columns across the top of the page. The six men of the special squad of detectives who had worked the case, standing behind the Skipper, Ben Ramirez, who sat at a press conference table heaped with files, folders and microphones. The other guys were all looking down at Ben, who was pointing at a chart; Jeannie was right, only Brenner was looking out of the page.

Brenner examined himself in the photo. Early thirties. Medium height, weight. Ordinary even features. Dark eyes. Dark hair, cut not too short, not too long. Wearing his good dark suit that only came off the hanger for funerals and weddings and there hadn't been any of those lately. Objectively viewing himself, Brenner had to admit that he looked like the kind of man witnesses have the most difficulty describing. A face that smiled easily, though not too much. Someone who didn't betray emotion; most of the time you couldn't tell by looking at him if he was mad or glad. And he liked it that way. The caption under the photo identified him as (left-to-right) Det. Sgt. Edward M. Brenner. Above their heads on the page was a thick black headline: SEX FIEND CAUGHT.

"They say the guy is a psycho." Jeannie wanted the inside scoop. Brenner leaned back with the steaming cup of black coffee in his hand.

"Surprised?" he asked.

"No. But it says he had a long record."

"Don't they always?" The man they had arrested and charged was recently released from a jail term on a related offense. But that was in another state.

"Did the Department make a psychological profile on

him?" That's what she was interested in. Brenner smiled and nodded. It was now standard procedure in these cases. A shrink plus a computer would put together a word picture of the criminal being sought. Kind of an up-dated version of "Twenty Questions." Given this fact, added to this kink and that quirk—who are we looking for? Animal, vegetable or mineral? It never seemed to be of much use in catching anybody. But, after the fact, it was fun to see how closely the profile checked out. Lots of fun. The guys in the squad room kidded about it: Parker Brothers was bringing out a new game for Christmas: "Catch the Creep."

"We worked up a terrific profile in class last week," Jeannie was enthusing. "On Adolf Hitler. Told you everything. All kinds of weird things."

"Everything you ever wanted to know about Adolf, but were afraid to ask?" Brenner laughed. Clue No. 1: He tap dances at Berchtesgaden. Clue No. 2: He and Eva Braun like to play dress-up with each other's clothes in the bunker. Question: Who is he? Right! A. Hitler, the Beast of Berlin.

But it wasn't for laughing as far as Jeannie was concerned. "I bet it helped, psyching him out. How'd you find him?"

"Police work." Brenner winked confidentially. "Intensive police work." She didn't really want to know; she wanted to believe it was scientific sleight-of-hand or Freudian magic. That made the catching of all Bad Guys possible, the righting of all wrongs inevitable. She didn't want to know how the job really got done.

Five-year-old Vickie Weston was playing in her front yard on a quiet middle-class West Los Angeles residential street. A man pulled up in a car and asked her if she wanted to go to Disneyland. Vickie was found several hours later in an apartment construction site a few miles away. A woman walking her dog heard whimpering sounds and discovered the semiconscious child.

Vicki had been badly beaten and sexually abused. The child had bite marks over much of her body and one undeveloped breast had been almost severed. She was suffering from acute shock and was barely able to speak; the sight of a man—any man—sent her into hysterics. Police women and Vickie's mother could only get the essential facts: a white man. With a blue car.

Fortunately, a witness was found who had seen a blue car driving away from the construction site. A compact. Either a Valiant or a Falcon. Mirrors on both front fenders and a distinctive skiing decal on the rear window. The police investigation focused immediately on the car; within the next few weeks, hundreds of blue compacts were pulled over to the curb and countless drivers with mirrors on their fenders were questioned, regardless of the color of their cars.

Responding to the outrage of the community, the special six-man detective task force was formed and assigned exclusively to the case. Their efforts centered on the ski decal, checking sporting goods stores that sold the decals and trying to trace customers who had bought them. The work was slow, difficult and unproductive. A routine request to Criminal Investigation and Information in Sacramento asking for the names of known sex offenders•living in the vicinity resulted in four huge cartons of files being dropped on the squad room floor. "And," Ramirez shook his head, "these are only the registered sex offenders. If it's a first-timer or anyone else who's managed to stay off our books, then we're still up the creek."

One sensational crime often seems to provoke another— and another. While the search for Vickie Weston's attacker went on, a man broke into a house one night in a different section of West L.A. and kidnapped a nine-year-old girl from her bedroom. She was molested but not beaten. Because of the lack of similarity, the two crimes were not thought to be related. A woman came out of a laundromat in midday on Westwood Boulevard and as she drove off a man sat up in the rear seat of her car. He forced her to drive to a secluded area where he raped her. Again, no apparent connection, but these crimes along with a sudden rash of daylight purse snatchings and "Hot Prowl" night burglaries had the police hopping and the community panicking. "It's a goddamn crime wave," Ramirez complained. "Every freak in town is doing his number in our district this month."

The crime wave ended in a telephone booth. A black-and-white patrol car spotted a man trying to force the coin box in a gas station phone booth with a tire iron. The officers brought the man in to the West L.A. station for booking. By that time, everyone getting arrested for anything was being questioned about the Vicki Weston rape.

Brenner and his partner, Norm Jonas, should have only spent a few minutes talking to Arthur Hauser. That's all it was worth. But they were due to go off-duty in another half hour so they killed a little extra time asking Arthur a few extra questions.

Arthur was a clean-cut young man with nice manners. He was from Illinois and had that awkward-sensitive James Dean look. Arthur was living out here now with a doctor who was an old friend of his family. He was kind of an office assistant and general handyman for the doctor. He didn't know why he got the urge to bust open the phone box; it just seemed easy. Arthur had a car—a green VW—and that should have been that. But Brenner and Jonas poked a little more and then, to their surprise, it began to come. Everything. Arthur Hauser copped out to everything. Both child attacks, the rape of the lady, the burglaries, the purse snatchings. Eleven weeks worth of investigating was over. This skinny polite kid was the whole West L.A. crime wave, all by himself.

What about the blue compact with the ski decal? It belonged to the doctor, who didn't drive it much. Arthur just happened to be out in that car on the morning he passed Vicki Weston's house. It was just luck he wasn't driving the green VW; as it was just luck that Brenner and Jonas had some time to waste talking to a phone-box thief about sex crimes. "Arthur William Hauser has been captured and charged," Manny Ramirez told the TV cameras, "as a result of intensive police work . . ."

Jeannie shook her head. Brenner was standing at the cash register holding out his check and three dollar bills. "Not today," Jeannie said. "It's on the house—if you sign for it."

She held out her ballpoint pen and the newspaper. Self-consciously, while the hostess and two of the other smiling waitresses watched, he autographed the photo. "We're going to put it right here," Jeannie pointed proudly at the top of the glass showcase.

Brenner told her that was terrific and thought that he'd have to find another place for breakfast from now on. He went outside to the parking lot. The Pancake House was located on palm-lined Ocean Avenue, just across from the entrance to Santa Monica Pier.

The sky was the murky color of a school blackboard that needed washing, and rolls of fog were slowly retreating out to sea. It was more June weather at the beach than late September. Hard to believe that it would clear up out here by ten o'clock. Automatically, as if the area was zoned for sunshine. Brenner heard the toot of a boat whistle, and sea gulls rose over the sport-fishing boat moving out with its morning cargo of amateur anglers, mostly retired talkative old men who lined the rails of the boat that only traveled a mile or so out to sea in search of fresh bass and companionship. Maybe Brenner would take Mike out on the boat this weekend. Rent poles, buy some bait. Teach his boy how to fish. Yeah, that might be a nice day.

▗▝▟▖

The wide white double garage door on the front of the house swung upward. From the street it was like the lantern jaw of a huge face suddenly breaking into a yawn. Inside the garage, the golden chariot came alive with a backfire of exhaust fumes and a roar of the great inefficient engine.

Harold Montrose settled behind the wheel of the Cadillac. A big man in a big car. He had a tanned, autocratic face with slate gray eyes, a well-formed nose and wide thin lips. A handsome face saved from prettiness by an innate sense of skepticism. He wore a three-piece custom-tailored suit, the vest a raffish plaid counterpoint to the conservative brown silk fabric of the jacket and trousers. It was part of the wardrobe that he had made in Hong Kong on a business trip two years before. Just a little juggling of the invoices had made the clothes, like the rest of the trip, a business expense and therefore fully deductible—not from his personal income statement but from the company ledgers. Montrose flicked a speck of invisible lint from his chest as he permitted the motor to idle.

He believed in warming the car before driving. The new manual said it wasn't necessary, but Harold Montrose had been trading in his Cadillac for the top-of-the-line model, loaded with extras, every other September for the last two decades of his forty-two years. And he always warmed the motor. He was a man who took good care of the machines that he owned. And for good reason. Machines properly cared for never failed you, which is

■ 15 ■

more than you could say for people, no matter how well you treated them.

Enveloped in a cocoon of Detroit's heaviest steel, Montrose felt secure. More casualties on the streets, highways and freeways each year than there had been in Vietnam. A man had to protect himself. Drive one of those tinny compacts or even a snazzy foreign sports job and you were taking your life in your hands. Ralph Nader was antibusiness, but he was right about most of the cars. Unsafe at any speed? Not the Cadillac. Built like a luxury tank. Hit me and you'll be the one who gets hurt!

Montrose was convinced that he heard a slightly more subdued rhythm to the rpm's now. Like Neil Armstrong aboard the spaceship Apollo, Montrose took command of the controls. The Cadillac surged backward out of the garage down the driveway. Then Montrose, who had glanced over his shoulder only once, suddenly stamped on the footbrake: He had caught a glimpse of movement—a flash of blue and red—in the rear view mirror.

The brakes screeched, the Cadillac bucked and came to a fitful halt beside Bobby Montrose.

The boy, still in his blue pajamas, didn't seem to be aware of the car. He was on his red tricycle, blond head down, intent on riding tight little circles on the pavement beside the driveway. Bobby looked up as he heard the muffled voice of his father calling his name. Harold Montrose was leaning across the empty passenger seat, yelling through the tinted glass window.

Bobby didn't understand what his father was saying or why he looked so mad. Maybe it was a game. Sometimes his father did that. He hollered very loud and his face would get red and then he would smile and say he was just fooling.

"Bobby! Get out of there! Go on! Get back in the house!" Montrose was shouting to be heard over the litany of morning stock quotations babbling from the radio. He was angry at Bobby for being so close to where he could have run him over; and angry because Montrose knew he should have been backing out slower and watching the driveway. But what was Bobby doing out here so early anyway? A wife that never wakes up and a kid who never sleeps! If he wasn't running late, he'd get out of the car and take Bobby by the hand and lead him into the bedroom and wake Claire up and give her hell! But he had to get to the office. He didn't even have time to roll down the electric window or turn off the AM-FM stereo radio. So he waved his arm in a sweeping motion, pointing at the house, and called louder: "Inside! Move! Get going, mister! Go play inside!" There, the little guy seemed to have the idea now. Bobby was smiling and waving back at his father.

Slowly now, Montrose backed out into the center of the deserted street and then started forward. He gunned the motor to make up for the wasted seconds. As the car raced off, Bobby was still sitting on his tricycle, still waving good-bye to his father.

". . . bouncing back from Tuesday's decline with a sharp midday advance in another hectic trading session." The voice on the radio didn't seem happy. Probably just some deep-voiced kid who didn't even understand what he was saying. People's lives were on the line, every day, and always that flat emotionless voice. "The market's rise came against a background of news that Wall Streeters considered to be on the negative side . . ."

Negative. Fighting in the Middle East. A 5.4 percent growth in the gross national product for the quarter, where experts had been promising 6 percent. And oil prices . . . new increases threatened again. But despite the tamperings and manipulations of Big Government, despite it all—the market was up. Montrose wondered what the big boys knew that he didn't? He pulled up to the red light and waited to make his left turn onto Coldwater Canyon.

A gun-metal gray Mercedes 540SL with the top down came sprinting past Montrose's view, moving toward Beverly Hills. He got a quick look at the driver. Gorgeous. Honey-blonde hair pushed back by the wind, oversize Bausch & Lomb sunglasses, a smile that held a secret. Where was she bound for at this time of morning? Too early to be going shopping. And that tanned face didn't spend the days inside an office. Probably coming home after an all-nighter in some lucky guy's pad up off the Canyon.

Montrose felt a stirring in his loins at the happy thought as he remembered last night. He had been dreaming. About that little Japanese girl on the business trip to Seattle. She had taken a string of small beads—maybe pearls—inserted them in his asshole and then slowly had drawn the string out. Incredible! Coming like Niagara. He woke up with a monster erection and realized where he was. Home sweet home. Harold Montrose listened to the slow deep breathing beside him in the king-size bed. Claire was sleeping, but he was wide awake. He touched himself and felt gratification. But why do it to yourself when she was right there?

Harold Montrose lifted the blanket gently and squinted into the darkness. The moonlight was shining dimly through the drapes. Claire's silk nightgown had crept up and he could see her firm little buns. One of her very best features. The first thing he had noticed about her years ago. He was on the Red-Eye Special to New York, flipping the pages of a magazine, when he glanced up and here was this dynamite ass waggling just above his face. A stewardess pulling down pillows from the overhead compartment. One of the great slow-motion memories of Harold Montrose's life.

Now he reached out and touched her cheeks. He started to push his hand through to her center, but Claire mumbled something unintelligible in the darkness and rolled away to the other side of the bed. Montrose moved after her; Claire's eyes were still closed and she was in a groggy sleep. She was on her back. Montrose, holding himself, reached for her again with his other hand. She stirred, dimly protesting. "Sleeping—honey, I'm . . ."

"Sure, baby," Montrose crooned softly. "I know . . ."

"Harold, have to sleep . . ."

"Love it. You know you love it." He was rising to mount her now. And again, she moved; eyes still closed, more thrashing in her sleep than consciously avoiding him. But her body turned away and he was facing her back again.

Harold Montrose lay there on the bed and he heard her breathing resume its previous rhythm. He felt his pulsing groin and looked at her buttocks. Then with a rush of frustration and anger, he grabbed her cheeks and spread them—shoving himself into her from the rear. Her face called a protest into the pillow and she tried to get away but this time he was prepared for her. He was much bigger than she was and he maintained his position with ease, keeping her face down on the mattress as he thrust his tempo to its conclusion. Then he rolled off contentedly onto his back on his half of the bed. For a long moment neither of them moved. He thought she was asleep again and he started to doze off. Then Claire got up and barefooted away like a sleepwalker. He heard her collide with the bureau near the bathroom door. "Son-of-a-bitch!" she said distinctly.

He smiled as she slammed the door and turned on the light and the faucet. He was sleeping soundly before she staggered back to bed.

Montrose's light turned green and he made his turn.

Just a few minutes over the Canyon and then onto the freeway. He would be downtown at his office before eight o'clock. He made it a point to be the first one there every morning; that way they all knew that the boss was a harder worker than any of them.

※※※

Caryl Ritchie clutched her housecoat closed over her nightgown as she came out of her house to find the *Los Angeles Times.* She knew just where to look for it; the delivery boy insisted on tossing the paper into the ivy, despite all the requests to throw the paper onto the porch.

Sure enough. There it was. Caryl picked up the paper and looked across the street. Inside, her boys were eating their cornflakes and Brad was showering. A few minutes ago, putting up the coffee, Caryl had glanced out her kitchen window and seen little Bobby riding his tricycle out in front of the Montrose house.

The tricycle was still there. But it was overturned. On its side. Wheels still spinning as if Bobby had dismounted just a moment before. But the boy was no longer in sight. Later, Caryl would estimate the time to be approximately 7:25 A.M. She went back inside the house to her family. And after her door was closed, the turning front wheel of the tricycle continued to spin . . . gradually slowing, until it came to a complete stop.

The sign flashed "Don't Walk" as the man stepped off the curb. He just kept going. He was a young man, or at least he used to be not long ago. Now he needed a shave, his hair was greasy and matted and there was something wrong with his left leg. He wore a stained green fatigue jacket with the U.S. Army patch over the right pocket. Cheap crumpled black pants that had a tear on one cuff, battered sneakers—and a foggy, faraway grin. He was holding a paper bag from which the neck of a bottle of Ernest & Julio Gallo's finest cooking sherry protruded. The car behind Brenner's honked, but Brenner and the ex-G.I. both ignored it.

It was the V.A. Hospital only a few blocks north. Veterans came and some of them never went. Old soldiers didn't all fade away. The funny thing was how they began to resemble each other: World War II vets, Korea and Vietnam survivors. The walking wounded who wander Santa Monica Boulevard in West L.A.

The man climbed the far curb and Brenner put the Chevrolet in gear again. Brenner continued rolling past the new-car showrooms and the body and fender shops, the taco stands, furniture stores and Thrift gas stations, then turned right onto Butler Avenue, just before the post office. The car was equipped with police radios but Brenner kept them turned off. He wasn't on duty yet.

The parking lot adjoined the two-story corner building, and raised metal letters embedded in stone identified the place as: " est Los Angeles Polic Station." Brenner locked up the blue Chevy on a wall lined with black-and-whites and walked toward the orange tiles that framed the front entrance and added a dash of color to the otherwise bland tan-and-brown structure.

Brenner stopped as he saw a tall, heavyset man in the stiff flannel uniform of a police sergeant lumbering out. He was carrying a dented Donald Duck lunch pail.

"They letting you out, Marty?" Brenner said.

"Bet your ass. Once a day, every day." Marty Ganzer was fifty-four years old and less than six months away from retirement as a thirty-year man. They had him finishing out his time working the Property Window and he hated it.

"Busy night?" Brenner asked.

"How the hell should I know? Stuck away on a goddamn shelf. But I guess I ought to feel honored. I've got the only window in the whole place." He flashed the evil grin that always delighted Brenner. Ganzer gestured at the building with his soggy cigar. "Look at it! A worthy addition to the beautiful West Los Angeles civic center. What you see before you is a prime example of the Watts School of Architecture."

The police station was one of the first to be built after the 1965 Watts riots. There was not a window anywhere; the entrance was concealed around a bend so that potential skirmishers could not ride by and take potshots. The inner building could be converted instantly into a barricaded fortress.

"Time was when a police station looked like a police station," Ganzer remembered. "The big round lights out front, swinging doors, people hanging around." Ganzer put the cigar back between his teeth. "Now we've got these clunky blockhouses. I walk in there and I feel like Henry Fonda in *Drums Along the Mohawk*. We stay inside and peek out at the hostiles. 'Put your rifle through the slit in the logs and hold out until the cavalry comes.'"

"You just don't like fluorescent lighting," Brenner said.

"What're you talking about? The magic sensation that it's always half past two in the morning and it's raining outside? I love it!" Ganzer flicked the ash off his cigar.

Once Ganzer had been his partner. When Brenner was a rookie, they'd assigned him to Ganzer's car. He learned a lot in a hurry and all the right way. But that was eleven years ago. Now Brenner was wearing the "soft" civilian clothes of a grunt detective and Ganzer walked like his feet hurt.

"How's Donald?" Brenner pointed at the lunch pail.

"All that gets me through the night." Ganzer loved coffee and brought two huge, hot Thermoses of his own brew with him each day. "I found a new mix. Mostly Viennese. There's a place in Farmer's Market that makes it up for me."

"Sounds good."

"Everything's good," Ganzer answered. He was divorced recently after twenty-six years of marriage, two grown kids, one of them married, the other in law school. "What about you?"

"Getting by," Brenner said.

"That's what it's all about," Ganzer agreed. He moved off, swinging the lunch pail. Brenner went in to go to work.

Claire Montrose woke up with a headache. It wasn't a bad one. Just a buzzing at the base of her skull as if someone was humming off key back there and occasionally rubbing rosethorns under her skin. She knew the feeling. It meant that the Seconal hadn't fully worn off. A medicinal hangover.

She swung her feet over the side of the bed and sat there looking at her toes. Pedicured, polished. Pretty my toes! The only part of her that felt pretty at the moment. At twenty-eight, Claire was grimly aware of the precise state of her charms. Properly made-up and wardrobed, she knew the effect she had on men; it was still the way it was when she was strolling the Friendly Skies of United. Hard-ons hidden by magazines, arousing any man she cared to—plus a few extra by accident. And women still gave her that look—the hungry, appraising one that told Claire they envied her equipment and how it was deployed.

But now it took more makeup to bring it off; not a lot, but a bit more. Her body was fine, kept firm by careful daily workouts at the health club. But the face. No one else noticed, but Claire knew what to look for; she had studied the faces of her mother, her aunts and her grandmother. So she could see the shadow beneath the jaw that hinted at a double chin still years away but coming. And, while the wide-eyed baby stare of innocence was intact, the tiny faint lines beneath the eyes in time would etch deeper. Since she was nineteen, Claire had been on guard against growing old. The mistake most people made was waiting until major work was needed. Then it was too late. The difference between before-and-after was too dramatic. Everybody knew and what good was it then? Claire had determined to avoid all that. Planning ahead, she had mentally projected her first face-lift for the age of thirty; unfortunately, she seemed to be right on schedule.

Claire stood up and yawned and shrugged her bare arms

through the filmy peignoir and shoved her pretty toes into puffy pink slippers. She shuffled sleepily out of the bedroom, paying no attention to the pile of clothes tossed on the floor in the corner. Harold's wise-ass way of getting to her, hinting that the wash had to be done. Since Doreen left it had been awful. Harold wanted Claire to get someone else, but he didn't want to pay. Even if you imported them from Colombia, they talked to other maids and caught on quick. Everyone wanted to be paid.

The kitchen was a mess. The dinner dishes from the night before, and even some from yesterday's lunch, were still soaking in the sink. Later, Claire thought. After coffee —after her head leveled off. She plugged in the percolator and switched it to rewarm. The happy bubbling sound of the coil working on the liquid began at once. The plastic orange juice container was out on the counter, left there by Harold. Look who's calling who a slob! He figured she'd sleep in and the juice would be warm by then, but she'd fooled him today. Woken up earlier . . . although she wished she hadn't. She sipped the cool, sweet frozen juice and tried to plan the day. She could stay home and clean, or—the agency cleaning crew would be coming tomorrow. And she did have something else she could do . . . she certainly did. If she wanted to. Again. The bubbling sound ended; coffee was ready.

Claire was on her second cup, sitting at the cute white ice cream table and chairs in the pastel yellow breakfast nook, gazing wearily out at the sunlit pool beyond the brick patio, when the thought came to her. Mildly at first, almost idly. The quiet, the lack of interruption . . . she listened and heard nothing. "Bobby?" she called. There was no answer. He must be playing someplace. In a minute she'd go find him. After she finished her coffee.

■ 25 ■

There was a door within a door. First the jailer locked the one behind them, then the steel door leading to the holding cells was opened. Brenner and Jonas had their plastic-coated I.D. cards with the mug photos clipped prominently to the breast pockets of their jackets, but they still had to sign in. The door clanged shut and they walked down the hall to a cage at the end.

Arthur Hauser looked like a Boy Scout. The gray pants with the letter P stenciled on the knees and the starchy shirt were both a little too big on him. He smiled his puppy dog smile as he saw them. "Hi—Sergeant Brenner, Sergeant Jonas. How are you?"

"Fine, Arthur," Brenner said. "Want to take a little walk?"

"Sure. Whatever you say."

The jailer was sliding back the barred door. Arthur Hauser waited patiently for the jailer's nod before stepping out into the corridor; he knew jailhouse protocol and didn't want to offend.

"Where we going?"

"Gonna talk some more," Jonas said flatly.

"Upstairs," Brenner explained. "So how's it going?"

"Couldn't be better," Arthur said. "Food here is a lot better than it was in Illinois. And everybody's nice."

On a lot of cases, you could bat your brains out and nothing. Harry Willinger had great hopes for this one. He had to pull a string or two to get assigned, promise a couple of favors. Not that he wasn't fully qualified; in fact, he knew that he was considered a comer on the D.A.'s staff. And this could be the one to do it for him.

The case had all the right elements. Sex. Violence. Gore. The kind of thing that the media picked up on heavily. The newspapers, of course, but Willinger had seen his name in the papers before, and while it was pleasant, the novelty was gone. You had to be realistic. TV was where it's at; those outside-the-courtroom interviews that wound up on the eleven o'clock news. Everybody listening to you, and "Prosecutor Harry M. Willinger" superimposed in white letters at the bottom of the screen. Establishing a name and connecting it with a face . . . representing the People in their quest for justice. And the People would want Arthur Hauser's ass to get nailed for what he had done. First step, of course, was to fend off the State of Illinois and their extradition request for parole violation; they'd just have to wait their turn until California was done with him.

Today was just a formality, but Willinger was particularly interested in seeing how the little girl behaved. It would be very important for the courtroom. Vickie Weston was the witness everyone would be waiting to hear. Willinger leaned against the counter of the police station's front desk with his attaché case open, sorting some papers, but really looking over them at Vicki. And her mother, Gloria Weston. Pretty, twenty-two, married young, not much more than a kid herself—but dark smudges beneath the eyes, put there by the past few weeks. Her life would never be quite the same again, but she was trying already to pretend that it was. They sat there together on the wooden bench opposite the counter, Vickie playing with a Barbi doll, her mother holding the special box that contained Barbi's wardrobe, handing Vicki various items of doll clothes, discussing the ensembles with her, playing the game.

Now the dark-haired detective was coming for them. Brenner. Willinger made it a point to remember the names. They were good boys. Jonas and Brenner. Jonas was the tall, balding one who did most of the talking. They handled it well. Gave Arthur Hauser his rights early, loud and clear, and kept him chattering. Got the whole confession on tape and without a trace of tainting. Willinger didn't think he'd have much trouble getting it admitted. But he didn't want to submit in transcript. Play the tape in open court. Much more dramatic. "Got him?" he asked.

"Ready and waiting," Brenner said.

Willinger snapped shut his attaché case, pocketed his gold-rimmed-frame glasses and walked up to the bench. "Vicki? Mrs. Weston? This way, please . . ."

Brenner led them down the hall and around a few corners. There was talking and typing and the clack of a teletype machine coming from the rooms they passed. Gloria Weston held her five-year-old daughter's hand and Willinger made conversation.

"What's the doll's name, Vicki?"

The child didn't answer.

"Barbi," Gloria Weston said. "She named her Barbi doll 'Barbi.' " Gloria gave a little smile and squeezed Vicki's hand.

"Doll's very pretty," Willinger said to Vickie. "Just like you."

It was quiet in the corridor. Brenner paused before a panel of one-way glass. The reverse side of the glass looked like a mirror, but from the corridor it allowed observers to watch everything going on in the Interrogation Room.

The walls inside were white and soundproof. Jonas was chewing Trident sugarless gum and leaning against the wall next to the mirror. Arthur Hauser had turned his chair at the table so that he could face Jonas; that meant he was also facing the mirror.

"Yeah, I remember reading about him in the papers," Jonas said.

"Well, he was right in the next cell from me. At Joliet. For a while." Arthur smiled. "Know what he used to say? People would ask why he killed all of them."

"Twelve people in three states, right?"

Arthur nodded. "And he'd say, 'They're not dead. They're at the ranch.' "

"What ranch?"

"That's what I asked him. He said, 'The ranch outside Albuquerque. When I get out of here, I'm going to go there and we'll all be together.' " Arthur began to laugh. "See he chopped up all those people but he believed they weren't dead. That they were all waiting for him out there and they'd all get together again."

"In Albuquerque," Jonas repeated, chewing methodically on his gum.

"Yeah. He was a psycho. They finally came and took him away." Arthur thought about it. "But you meet a lot of interesting people in prison."

It was very quiet in the narrow hallway. Brenner had the sound turned off so they couldn't hear anything Jonas and Arthur Hauser were saying. Just see them. Willinger stepped up to the glass like a lecturer about to point out the mysteries of a slide exhibit on Byzantine art. "Look inside, please, Vicki. And tell me if you recognize anyone."

Brenner watched the kid. She was fussing with the clothes on her doll and didn't seem to have heard the assistant D.A. Her mother was staring, unblinking, stunned at the sight of Arthur Hauser, sitting so close but separated from them, unaware of them, talking casually, wordlessly, just on the other side of the glass.

"Vicki, the tall man is a detective," Willinger said. "But do you know the other man?"

"Oh, my God," Gloria Weston whimpered softly, tears filling her eyes. But Vicki still was intent on her doll. Her small fingers moving feverishly, tugging at a sleeve of the little dress; now the sleeve ripped and the fingers stopped.

"Vickie . . .?" Willinger kept his voice warm, concealing any trace of impatience or anxiety. She had already identified Hauser from photos. So this didn't mean anything, but . . .

"Honey?" Gloria asked. And without looking up, the child answered in a thin voice.

"He's him."

"What did you say?" Willinger wanted it spelled out.

"That man. Who hurt me." Vickie looked at Willinger, then pointed at Arthur Hauser through the glass.

"Okay," Willinger said.

"And . . ." Vickie trailed off and stared down at her doll, touching the tiny torn piece of fabric. Gloria Weston kneeled beside her daughter. "What, honey? What?" she encouraged, her own voice shaky. Now Vickie turned her gaze toward the glass again and when she spoke her voice was low but very firm.

"And I want him to die."

"You—don't mean . . ." Gloria choked.

"Yes, I do. I want them to put him in the, you know, the gas chamber. Like they showed on TV. And I want him to be dead."

Under glass, Arthur Hauser, unhearing, began to smile at something Jonas was saying.

And Brenner studied the small, serious face of Vicki Weston. Five years old and she had gone way past anger to where the real hating got done.

Willinger thanked Gloria Weston for bringing Vicki and he patted the girl's shoulder. She was going to be a terrific little witness.

▪▪▪▪

This was the nerve center. A long room that was continuously noisy. But it was an odd kind of noise: all male voices mingling in a discordant chant, talking almost without stop and almost without passion. Not unfeeling or uncaring, but it was official policy to keep emotion out of it. And the men had long since discovered this was the best way to protect themselves. Be precise, polite—but just a little impersonal. Follow the golden rule as set down by Jack Webb: "Just the facts . . ."

Whenever anyone in West Los Angeles picked up a phone, dialed Operator and said, "Give me the police," the call was routed into this room. The men at this switchboard were plugged into the pain and confusion of an entire section of the city. They were the first to hear the panic and the hope, the rage and the horror.

Gilbert Garcia, born in the East L.A. barrio, was twenty-four, three years out of the Police Academy, six months with the phone lavalier around his neck. He calmed the callers, got the information as quickly as possible and sent the messages onward for action. Garcia was one of the bilingual men; he thought as quickly in Spanish as in English.

But the voice that came over the telephone now wasn't Chicano. Pure paddy. California Golden Girl. Garcia passed the time by imagining faces and backgrounds to go with the voices.

"Is this the police?" she said.

"Yes, ma'am. Officer Garcia speaking. Can I help you?"

"It's—my son. I can't find him."

"How do you mean, ma'am?"

"I've looked all over. All the places he plays and—he's not here."

Garcia knew the questions to ask now. Name of Caller. Address. Name of Victim. Had she tried phoning friends' houses . . . when had she seen him last . . . and while Garcia waited for the answers he entered the time: 10:27 A.M. In the blank space after Nature of Report he filled in: little boy lost.

It had become a predictable September day. Hot, arid and sunny. That was the weather yesterday. It would be the weather tomorrow. There are only two seasons in Southern California: the rainy season and the rest of the year. When the rains came it was always like a Biblical deluge and the City of Los Angeles stopped. Intersections flooded, streets and freeways became a Destruction Derby as cars hydrofoiled into each other in spectacular, skittering formations on a carpet of drenched gas fumes. But there was the bright side: After the rains, it was easy to see why people first came to California. Suddenly, everywhere, the lines and images were sharp. The smog was gone. The air was clean.

It never lasted very long.

This year the rainy season had started late and ended early. Since then, the long summer's heat had parched the earth and combined with traffic and industry to contaminate the air. In the hills bisecting Los Angeles, brush fires broke out with regularity aided by the efforts of the mischievous, careless or psychotic.

The people standing on the sidewalk near the house formed a tableau. They seemed nearly frozen in their positions: women who had started out for markets or shops, a man walking a dog, a housewife with a scarf over curlers. Some of them knew one another, but not many. The rest were strangers despite the fact that they all lived on the same street. It was the nature of California living. Everyone driving, nobody walking. The cars on the street were more familiar than the faces of the neighbors who lived five doors away.

But for a brief moment now, they were joined. They had emerged from their separate worlds to gather in unspoken commiseration that also contained an element of curiosity-seeking: Something bad, maybe even something terrible, had happened. The barriers of privacy and anonymity had dropped away. The people didn't wait for introductions. They simply spoke to one another. Quietly, in hushed tones. And their eyes remained focused on the Montrose house.

There were several black-and-white patrol cars and two unmarked cop cars parked in the cul-de-sac. Two motorcycle officers, jackbooted faceless spacemen in white helmets with blue-green Polaroid sunglass lenses where their eyes should be, stood talking not far from their powerful machines. Directly in front of the house, a station wagon with police markings on the sides was in use; the rear seat was filled with radio equipment, and the nasal, crackly police calls made a seemingly unheeded drone of sound. The tailgate of the station wagon was down and a large map of the area fastened on a wooden board was being examined by a patrolman and Frank Rybicki, a jowly, irritable thirty-four-year-old uniformed police sergeant, who suddenly grabbed one of the humming voices out of the air and reached for the radio microphone, acknowledging a call.

The metallic voice on the other end belonged to a motorcycle cop who had followed a fire road leading up into the hills close by; he was at the end of the road now and wanted to know what to do.

"Turn around and come back," Rybicki ordered curtly and turned back to the map. He looked over as the blue Chevrolet rolled up to the curb.

Jonas got out from behind the wheel and stretched, reaching for his jacket in the back seat. Brenner slammed the passenger door and moved toward Rybicki. "Guess it's all yours," Rybicki said in greeting. "Rest of the boys are inside."

"What's it look like?" Brenner said.

"Three hours ago, when we got the call, it looked like a lost kid. Now—you tell me?" Rybicki shoved the map board into the wagon and snapped shut the tailgate.

"Been over the territory?" Jonas asked.

"Fifteen guys on motors, working an ever-widening radius." Rybicki smiled thinly to emphasize the conversational use of manual jargon. "Patrol units have been looking in the bushes and talking to the neighbors around here."

"And?" Brenner said.

"The kid's still gone." Rybicki shrugged.

"See you, Frank," Brenner said. He and Jonas walked toward the big wooden front door that had been painted ivory to match the white stone of the house's exterior.

Rybicki watched them go inside and thought that probably this was all nothing. Probably the boy would turn up playing in a backyard somewhere around the corner. But the radio calls were continuing, there were other places for Rybicki to be and he was glad this wasn't all his problem any more.

"Let's go," he said to the patrolmen and waved at the two motorbike troops to take off.

The living room was very large and done all in white and gold. White ceiling, white walls, gold couches, white deep-pile carpeting, a pair of gold chairs, white grand piano and overstuffed toss cushions in alternating colors. The brick surrounding the fireplace had been painted white with a framed golden sunset hovering above. An ultra-modern free-form glass-top coffee table on a golden metal pedestal dominated the center of the room. On it, there was an enormous thicket display of dried flowers; golden-rod and white daisies, of course. Ben Ramirez knew the flowers once were real because his nose was tingling. He was a spring sneezer and didn't need this. The damn thing was so bushy Ramirez could hardly see around it. He got up off the couch, note pad in hand.

Ramirez was a deceptive-looking man. He didn't seem particularly big until you stood next to him. At fifty-three, he had the thick-featured countenance of a cherub who slept on his face. Ringing the crown of his ample brownish-graying hair there was an indentation that showed he recently had been wearing a hat; he would be wearing it again soon. Ramirez was one of the few men in Southern California who still wore a hat. It was a legacy from the old days. Ramirez had been the youngest member of the celebrated Hat Squad, a special crack group of Los Angeles detectives who years ago affected snap-brimmed Dick Tracy fedoras and rolled up an amazing arrest record. Most of the Hat Squad were gone now. Some of them became judges, police chiefs in various communities. But Ramirez was still here on the job.

The father had been doing most of the talking, asking questions instead of answering them. But now the mother broke in. "They're leaving!" she said. "Why are they leaving?"

Claire Montrose, in a pink housecoat, still no makeup, pointed outside where the mobile command post was driving off. She looked at Ramirez and at Jonas, who was near the white piano with his pad and pen poised; and then at Brenner, who was prowling the back of the room. She was on the gold couch beside her husband.

"It's procedure, Mrs. Montrose," Ramirez said. "It doesn't mean they're giving up the search."

"But all those men, they're leaving!" Brenner thought she should sound upset, but she didn't. Just scared and sort of spacy. "You haven't found Bobby yet," she said.

"They'll keep looking for Bobby," Ramirez assured her. "But after the first few hours, we add detectives to the search."

"And you're the head of detectives?" Montrose sounded like he was interviewing job candidates.

"For this division," Ramirez said.

Montrose seemed a trifle disappointed not to be talking to the absolute top man. "What happens now?"

"We make sure that every possibility is explored. For instance, is there anyone who would want to harm Bobby?"

"No." Montrose's answer was immediate and flat. Brenner stopped at the mantelpiece at a framed 11 x 14 photo of Claire. Studio portrait. Very pretty. He looked from the picture to the lady.

"Everybody loves Bobby," she was saying. "He's no trouble ever . . ."

"Anyone who would want to hurt you, Mr. Montrose? Or your wife?" Ramirez moved closer to where the mother and father were sitting.

"You think he was kidnapped?" Montrose sat up straight. "That's ridiculous. Bobby just . . ."

Ramirez thumbed back a few pages in his notes and

rattled it out fast: "You're the president of a plastics man-
ufacturing company, drive a nice car, make a good living.
Why not?"

Montrose was shaking his head, dismissing the idea. But
Claire held up a fluttering hand to still his movement.
"Maybe, Harold, you never know—the way people today
. . ." She didn't seem able to speak in complete sentences.

Brenner had arrived at the white piano. He ran his
finger over the surface and left a path on the undusted
wood. There was another framed photo of Claire on the
grand piano. An informal windblown, smiling shot. Also
very pretty. She had the kind of edgy, neurotic quality
that Brenner found a turn-on.

"All right," Montrose said, "maybe somebody thinks
we have some money. But don't they call or send a note
or something?" He was starting to get irritated as his
suspicion grew that they had sent him a platoon of clowns;
that's always the way it seemed to work out: he had to do
everyone's thinking.

"You got a recent photo of the boy?"

Montrose looked around to find who had spoken. It was
the dark-haired one in the off-the-rack blue checkered
sports jacket. "What?" he asked.

"A picture—of Bobby," Brenner repeated.

"Sure," Montrose said. Of course. A picture. Obviously.
But he didn't remember where the photos were kept.
"Claire!" he prompted sharply. The way she let things go
around here, it was a wonder you could find anything.

Claire rose from the couch, reaching her hand upward
to draw the folds of the pink housecoat tighter at her
throat, as if suddenly aware that there were strangers in
the room. She smiled nervously, briefly, at Brenner and
led the way to a white gilt-edged French pseudo-antique
desk. She sat in the uncomfortable-looking wooden chair
and pulled open the top drawer. A cascade of papers

bulged up to meet her hands: old department store brochures, crumpled receipts, rubber bands, a personal telephone book, old letters, blank envelopes, stamps, pencils —Claire's fingers began to burrow through the collection in search of Bobby's photo.

Ramirez had taken Claire's place on the couch near Montrose. His pencil hovered over the pad. "I asked you about, you know, enemies. You personally . . . ?"

"Me?" Montrose shrugged. "Anyone in business has some, but—like this—no."

Now it was the big balding cop, over at the piano. "You saw Bobby out on the street when you went to work?"

"That's right." Montrose got up so his back was to the questioner—Jonas—as he walked toward the built-in bar. "Told him to get inside, too early to be playing in the street."

Montrose poured Scotch from the cut-glass decanter into a tumbler with a gilt coat-of-arms. He smiled at Jonas and Ramirez—disarmingly, he hoped. "Since he learned how to walk, Bobby's been all over the place—into everything."

Why mention that he didn't get out of the car when he saw Bobby? Should've rolled the power window down! Or stayed to make sure the kid went inside. It would've only taken another minute maybe, but he was late and—Bobby understood. Why didn't he listen? Why did Montrose always have to check and double-check on everything, everyone? He sipped the ten-year-old Scotch and looked at Claire. Still digging through the mess in that desk.

"He was wearing blue pajamas?" Brenner asked.

She looked up at him. The words digested slowly as if being translated into another language. Then her head bobbed. "Yes—the kind with . . ." Her fingers drew a shape in the air. "With the little feet."

"When did you first miss him?"

"When I got up. Around ten."

"Up early," Montrose shot at her. Brenner turned his head to look at him, but Claire didn't.

"I—have trouble falling asleep at night. So sometimes I sleep in . . ."

"Till noon!" Montrose cut her off. "Look at you, still not dressed! If you'd been up . . ." Montrose cast his eyes down and his voice went tremolo. "Bobby'd still be here."

Brenner felt uncomfortable. The way he used to in the squad car days when he'd have to go referee the Saturday night husband-and-wife hassles. They'd both want him to decide who was right and no matter what he said it always seemed to end up with both of them jumping on him.

But this was different. This lady didn't want to fight. Nothing seemed to get her mad. Her fingers had been rippling ineffectually through the layers of junk in the desk drawer; now she just sat there like she'd forgotten what she started to do.

"He's a good boy," she explained to Brenner. Slowly, patiently. So he'd understand what Bobby's like. She looked at Brenner and he saw there were tears forming in her eyes. Brenner wasn't sure if she was aware of it. "He gets up by himself and plays . . ." There went the fluttering fingers again. "He'd just take some cornflakes and—play."

Brenner waited, but there wasn't any more. That seemed to be the best thing she could think of to say about the kid: He was a good kid. He didn't bother anybody.

"*I know!*" Montrose snapped his fingers. "Of course! I bet *I* know . . ."

They were all looking at him now.

"*Doreen.*"

Claire couldn't grasp it. "You think . . . ?"

Montrose turned to Ramirez. "Doreen Mason—our maid. *Ex*-maid. I fired her last week."

"Bad feelings?"

"On my part. I caught her stealing."

Ramirez flipped over to a new page on his pad. "Got an address on her?"

"Sure do." Montrose was moving toward the desk. "If she's doing this to get even—to punish us . . ."

Montrose shouldered in, ignoring Claire as he groped for a telephone book, found it and turned to the "M's." Ramirez' pencil was poised.

"That's Mason?" he asked. "M-A-S-O-N?" Montrose confirmed the spelling and showed Ramirez a page in the book. Ramirez began to copy.

"It's her," Montrose said. "Be just like her."

Claire was staring down at the open desk—and now her fingers reached out for a piece of paper lodged in the back of the drawer. She looked at it and then held it up to Brenner.

"Here's one . . ."

He took it from her. It was a bent, cheap 4 x 5 jumbo-size color photo. Bobby Montrose. In knee pants and polo shirt. The picture was a little out of focus, so the face of the boy was slightly fuzzy. But he was smiling.

Brenner closed the screen door behind him and walked up to the two plainclothesmen waiting in the Montrose backyard.

"Looks a little like my boy," Brenner said. He showed them the photo. "When he was that age."

George Hyatt, a lanky shit-kicker from Wyoming, took the snapshot and held it up for his partner, Ron Elgort, a funny fast-talking guy. Brenner strolled toward where Jonas was: at poolside.

The Montrose backyard originally was fair-sized. Now it was all swimming pool, cool decking and brick patio. There was a breeze blowing in from the Valley side. Hot air.

Brenner stood beside Jonas, squinting as the sun bounced light off the water into their eyes. "Really keep things in tiptop shape around here, don't they?" Jonas indicated the pool. Brenner knelt to look down.

It was a mess. The heater and filter obviously were off. And nobody had been tending the pool in a while. Some dead leaves were floating on the surface, and the water was an unappetizing slightly milky shade of turquoise. There was a residue of dark grease clinging to the top of the tiles circling the pool: suntan oil left behind like a bathtub ring by departed swimmers. Brenner could see the bottom of the pool. Totally empty, except for a black plastic toy snorkel lying on the pool floor amid a thin coating of silt.

No maid, Brenner thought. No pool man. Foliage looks shaggy, so probably no gardener. But a fairly expensive house. Maybe all front with not enough to back it up. There was the scraping sound of the sliding aluminum door being opened. "Okay, here we go." Ramirez' voice announced.

They gathered at the redwood table on the patio. "Got enough for everybody." Ramirez spread out a map of the area. "Reservoir isn't far from here—I'm sending scuba guys up. I want you fellas to divvy up this area, talk to everybody, see where it goes."

"What about the maid?" Brenner asked.

"Team's checking her out. Could be our best shot."

"Child molesters?" Hyatt suggested.

"The computer will have a choice selection—soon." Ramirez smiled at them. "Meantime . . ."

"We shag," Brenner said.

"You got it," Ramirez said.

■.■.■.■.

Kenneth Morrissey stood on the pedestrian island in the center of Beverly Drive at Olympic Boulevard.

He walked around the bronze monument. The southern-most frontier of Beverly Hills is guarded by ghosts, he thought. The shadows of the silver screen were etched in bas-relief: Mary Pickford of the sweet ways and tumbling curls. Beside her, the swashbuckling figure of Douglas Fairbanks (Mary and Doug! Together Again!). Harold Lloyd, the ingenuous Everyman in black-rimmed glasses and straw boater. Tom Mix, poised to lunge for his straight-shooting six-gun. Fred Niblo, director of *Ben Hur,* megaphone in hand. Rudolph Valentino, the gaucho who sent pulses galloping. Conrad Nagel, wearing the courtly cutaway, frills, boots and britches of a French fop. And, finally, Will Rogers, scratching his hand as if still per-plexed at the shenanigans that do go on.

Eight musketeers. Back to back. Above their heads, a coil of film rising to reach a star at the top.

Morrissey wondered how long the monument had been there. Certainly he had driven by it hundreds of times. The way the cars all around him were doing even now.

The movies. Where everything always worked out right. Morrissey hurried across the street with the green light. He was a slender, almost slight man with sensitive features, who looked far younger than his forty-one years. He moved like a tennis player. Morrissey wore a charcoal-gray suit and a white shirt with a bow tie. The attaché case he carried was of worn but originally expensive leather.

Morrissey approached the office building on the corner and went past a row of newspaper vending machines. The *Herald-Examiner* was just being delivered to the rack. Latest edition. Morrissey caught a glimpse of the front page of the *Herald* as the delivery guy took off. And he stopped.

Slowly, Morrissey came closer and through the scratched plastic window of the vending machine he saw the big headline: MIDDLE EAST FLARE-UP FEARED. And above it: BEV HILLS BOY MISSING.

The story that went with the streamer headline was below the fold in the page so Morrissey couldn't read it. Morrissey shivered slightly on the sunlit sidewalk and walked off, entering the building without buying the paper.

She was looking out the window through the filmy white drapes and saw them coming. They had been working their way down the street. Now it was going to be her turn.

Caryl Ritchie started for the front door. It rang before she got there. She opened it. The taller one was mopping his flushed face and balding head with a handkerchief. The other one showed her a badge and introduced them both. She invited them in.

"Would you like some coffee?"

"Well," Brenner joked, "we're not supposed to drink on duty, but . . ."

The kitchen was spotless. They sat on the comfortable chairs at the round white formica-top table. There was a swing set out on the grass in the backyard.

"My boys are both in school, kindergarten and second grade," she explained. "They'll be home soon. My little guy plays with Bobby—his chance to be big brother."

The cops smiled.

"Then Bobby is over here a lot?" Brenner asked.

"He's around everywhere—up and down the street." She sipped her sixth cup of the morning. "When we moved in last year—Bobby was the first person we saw. He was sitting on the curb while the moving men were unloading."

"Kind of like a goodwill ambassador?" Jonas liked the idea.

Caryl hesitated. But someone ought to know. "Like a stray dog," she said.

∎∎∎∎

The roses were blooming. Each morning at the end of the radio newscast the announcer would quote the Air Pollution Control District on ". . . the amount of smog expected in the Los Angeles Basin today." But Mrs. Bowman had her own method of gauging. The roses.

When she had first started the rose garden here in 1943 the flowers that grew were unblemished. Now, when the roses unfolded, she often found black singes on their petals. "Smog burn," the man from the garden shop had diagnosed. Apparently the smog wasn't good for the roses.

But the roses had become her way of checking on the APCD. Whatever was in the atmosphere would be reflected on her roses. So far this had been a fairly good summer, she judged, as she sheared off a virtually unmarred Churchill rose.

Mrs. Bowman dropped the rose with her gloved hand into the straw basket and pushed back her sun bonnet to look up at the two police officers.

Brenner guessed that she probably was past sixty. High cheekbones and a relatively untroubled life. She still looked good. But she must have been a beauty.

". . . if only they had beaten the child. Abused him in some way. Then we could have complained. Called you people."

"But they didn't," Jonas prompted. The mulchy soil was radiating waves of heat back up at them. Mrs. Bowman didn't seem to notice as she unhurriedly snipped another rose for her basket.

"Those parents," she said, "they didn't even know if their child was alive half the time. I'd give him crackers and milk. A snack." She pointed with the shears. "The woman up the street would feed him lunch."

"That's—well, sad," Brenner said. "But not a . . ."

"Not a crime." She finished for him. "There, you see? I told you."

Mrs. Bowman touched a small wooden stool. "Bobby used to sit here—ask me questions. About that chicken."

There was a red clay planter shaped in the form of a pudgy chicken. Daisies were growing in the planter, but the unblinking ceramic hen stared straight ahead.

"Bobby wanted to know, 'How'd the chicken get like that?' "

"Yeah." Brenner smiled. Kids saw things we missed, asked things like that. But there was a kid missing now. "Thanks for your time," he said.

They started away and Mrs. Bowman let them go. At least, she meant to, but:

"Officers?"

They stopped to look back at her.

"I—I hope I don't sound like the neighborhood gossip. But Bobby is such a nice little fellow . . ."

"Yes?" Jonas changed his mind: Maybe this old lady did have something for them.

She frowned. "He nearly died once. Did you know that?"

⬛⬛⬛⬛

Dr. Nicholas Sand knew precisely what time it was: nine months and fourteen days into the first year of his residency. And forty-five minutes into his tour of duty. UCLA Emergency. Every day an education. Anything could come rolling in the door and usually did. But, even for this grab bag of the healing arts, today was special.

If the music used to be Bacharach or Neil Diamond, today it was "Top Forty" hard rock. People calling from all sides. Simultaneously. Demandingly. Continuously. Endlessly. Walk in, punch in and watch out. The first forty-five minutes were chaos.

Burn victim: three-year-old girl who turned a skillet of bacon fat over; the drippings went down her chest. An amateur carpenter who power-sawed a digit and a half away with the bookends. Two old codgers who squared off for a John Wayne–Victor McLaglen punchout in the Senior Citizens' Center that ended only when one antiquarian lost his false teeth and the other accidentally stepped on them. A nun on a nature walk who sustained a splinter under her thumbnail; her four sister nuns insisted on being present during the extraction. Plus the usual assortment of skateboarders with twisted ankles that did not turn out to be broken, gasping twice-a-week tennis players who might be genuine coronary victims and the bloody remnants of the nearby freeways and byways.

Nick Sand's personal favorite of those initial forty-five minutes was a housewife with a cracked pelvis. She had been sitting quietly at the kitchen table in her second-floor apartment reading "Dear Abby," unsuspecting that directly below her neighbor was cooking corned beef and cabbage —in a pressure cooker. A clogged old pressure cooker that did not release any pressure; the apparatus efficiently compressed all the steam until the cooker exploded—propelling the lid, followed by the corned beef, through the ceiling into the apartment above. Knocking the woman off her chair and onto her pelvis.

Nurses had come running while Dr. Sand was treating

this victim. Attracted by a braying noise that turned out to be laughter. The doctor's. He couldn't help it; her sad story had been aimed at his heart but had hit his funny bone.

And now, as life calmed down a little, there were these two cops. Asking about a case that had taken place months and months ago.

"You gotta be kidding," he told them. But when he found the file, Dr. Sand was surprised that he did remember. Distinctly.

"Happens every day," Sand explained. "Nobody's looking. Kid gets into the medicine cabinet, pops off a couple of loose caps. Starts gobbling up the pretty colored pills."

"Pretty colored pills," Jonas repeated.

They were at the reception desk. Forms were being distributed, filled out, handed back. Agitated people waited on benches. Wheelchairs pushed by purposefully. And from down the hall somewhere a woman's voice could be heard cursing in Spanish. Closer by, in one of the many cubicles, someone was moaning; not unpleasantly, a Crosby-style croon of pain. A bell dinging melodically on the floor was ignored by the nurses rushing from one place to another like waitresses in a jammed lunch-hour restaurant.

Brenner watched Sand: a blond, baby-faced kid in soiled white medical coat, corduroy pants and scuffed thick-soled Thom Mc An shoes. Talking about life and death, pretending it was routine.

"Anything special about this one?"

"Pumped Bobby's stomach. We were in plenty of time." Sand's fingers worried the platinum mustache that was growing in slowly and unevenly. It made him look a little older. "Only thing special was the mother."

"How's that?" Brenner said.

"She was at the hairdresser when the kid did it. I remember, we located her there, called her—told her the kid was going to be okay. She said terrific, she'd be right over. As soon as she finished under the dryer." Sand closed the file. "Sweet, huh?"

▰▰▰

It was a problem for Claire. Selecting the proper clothes always was. When she was a little girl the Catholic school solved it for her. Everyone dressed the same: blue skirt, white blouse, knee-length blue stockings. Momma picked her shoes.

Momma was the one who first told her the secret. "You are what you look like, honey." Claire always remembered. Whatever you wanted to do, whoever you wanted to be—clothes were the way.

The airline understood that. They had spent a lot of money having the right uniform designed for the stewardesses. More thought went into how the stews looked than the pilots. After all, who saw the pilots? But the stews! There was the spacewoman outfit worn in the terminal, with the cape. Once on board, the cape was removed, but the short skirt and severe jacket remained—with the clever pucker ruffles that made every girl look like a pair of 38Ds was lurking under the brass-buttoned tunic. The perfect outfit for handing out magazines, demonstrating oxygen masks. Then, off with the tunic, revealing the misty white tapered blouses, for serving the drinks. Finally, the aprons and flat mom's-in-the-kitchen shoes for delivering the meals. Perfect. When the landing wheels came down, the high heels, tunic and cape came on again—a touch of unattainable glamour flaunted before tourist and first class.

She reached into the bedroom closet for a pants suit. The two little lights, she noticed, were still glowing on the telephone.

After she married Harold, that's when the problem became hers. She was required to wear a different kind of uniform: Mrs. Successful Businessman. But there was no one to dictate dress code or issue the clothes. She had to pick for herself. And Harold didn't want to know details. If she didn't look beautiful, he complained. If she did, he never said anything. But when other people complimented her, Harold took the credit. "I pay the bills, don't I?" he said when she mentioned it once; she never mentioned it again. Lately, though, he had begun questioning bills, limiting her spending.

Claire gazed at herself in the mirror. Wrong. She took off the pants suit, dropped it on the bed with the other discards.

She had a good eye and she used it. Claire knew she had no sense of style and she mistrusted her own taste totally. So she used her eye. If she needed tennis clothes, she studied what other women at the club wore and bought accordingly. Cocktail ensembles, beach clothes, lunching outfits, party gowns, all were researched. She subscribed to the better fashion magazines, patrolled the better stores appraising the new merchandise and who was buying what. Now she had built a solid, varied wardrobe. Whatever the occasion, she was prepared. Except . . . except . . .

Claire saw that her hands were shaking. How long had they been doing that? And the lights, damn them, like two unblinking, tiny ferret eyes, gleaming on the nightstand. Watching her. Seeing her confusion and uncertainty. The stack of clothes that had grown higher and higher on the bed, and still she hadn't found the answer.

Clothes for every occasion, except . . .

How do you dress on the day your son disappears?

■▀■▀■

"Mort, listen to me." Harold Montrose sighed into the phone. He liked the effect. "It's a rip-off, Mortie. The store is making a schmuck out of you. Yeah, I'm sure. I checked, a *lab*, fucking experts. I'm telling you. Scientific evidence! Look, you want to pay 'em go ahead, but I'm not reimbursing anybody. Not one fucking centavo. The store is just trying to bail out. Understand? There's nothing wrong with my plastic and nothing wrong with your seat covers."

Montrose leaned back into the gold cushions of the couch and let his eyes wander up to the pattern on the ceiling. Rippling lines and forms. The sun's rays refracting off his pool outside, doing a dance across the top of the living room. Mort Drucker would come around. After all, Mort had inherited his father's best qualities. Gutless but greedy.

Drucker had bought $9,000 worth of plastic from Montrose and manufactured car seat covers. Now most of the shipment had been returned by the chain of automotive supply stores that placed the order. The store buyer claimed the plastic was defective: All the zippers were tearing loose.

The chain of stores was one of Drucker's biggest customers, so he was all set to take back the seat covers and eat the loss. Sharing the disaster with Montrose, of course. Putz! It took Montrose twenty seconds to figure out what had happened. The seat covers just weren't moving: He'd warned Drucker that the buyer had picked a turd color. But Mort, the mastermind, said give the customer what he wants. Now those shit-colored covers were sitting on the store shelves and the buyer didn't want to take the rap. So he took a pliers to the seat covers, pulled out all the zippers and pronounced the merchandise defective. And Mort was going to eat it?

"I'll tell you something, Mortie, my friend," Montrose sang into the telephone. "I don't think we've got a loss: I think you've got a lawsuit. Against that cunt at the store.

You call him up and tell him an independent lab found plier marks on the zippers, yeah, you tell him that, look, can you hold on a minute?"

It was time to pay a little attention—just a little—to Lujack. Montrose had him dangling on the other phone. He enjoyed talking to Lujack. How could you feel any other way about someone who was out to screw you—when you knew you were screwing him?

Montrose pushed down on the lighted button. "Harry? Hey, I'm sorry, fella. Just an incredible day, you know?" Montrose asked Lujack to hang on again. He pressed the hold button before Lujack could protest. And Montrose smiled. Lujack would hold.

Nobody else in town would do business with Lujack. His method was well known. Order everything on thirty-day payment, then delay payments several months, place new orders, get way ahead. Son-of-a-bitch wanted to operate his business with your capital. Twice before, when he'd siphoned enough money out for himself, Lujack had gone Chapter Eleven, declared bankruptcy, kissed off all the bills owing.

Montrose was tickled to do business with him. He let Lujack maneuver his usual game. And Montrose played his part. He begged after past due bills, whined his gratitude when Lujack finally paid March in July and simultaneously doubled the order for August.

Because what Lujack didn't know was that even with his drag-ass pay system, Montrose was winning—by trimming ten feet of plastic off each new roll shipped to Lujack. Ten feet a roll, every roll, for over a year now. Everybody in town pitied Montrose for being involved with a bastard like Lujack, but Montrose kept a private count: He was ahead thousands. Right now. "Harry, still there? Be just one more minute, babe."

This mess with Bobby getting lost had disturbed the

day's schedule, but now he was catching up on calls. It was like being in the office, juggling two phones at once. Actually, without Sandra, that idiot secretary, he was doing better. Handling the calls himself, right here at home. No question, the business was all him, wherever he was. And it followed him . . .

He had left the office at eleven thirty this morning. A customer was out from New York and Montrose was showing him the sights. "Disneyland," he had promised the customer. "For lunch."

They drove to Bel Air and the customer admired the way the trees were always green and the grass was there all year round. Not like New York, where the cold killed everything that the muggers missed. The customer laughed, so Montrose laughed, too.

The house on Stone Canyon had a circular driveway and was set back as the better houses were. Lunch was buffet style, catered by Nate & Al's deli. And the first course was Jackie and Lynn, the two delicious young hostesses. The customer picked Jackie, a tiny honey-blonde with a pug nose and firm silicone-enhanced breasts; they were off in the back bedroom getting his horn tuned. Montrose was in the walnut-paneled den with the nap of the nubby couch fabric pleasurably irritating his bare buttocks as Lynn, the redhead, crouched naked between his legs; he was in her mouth when the phone rang.

Lynn withdrew her wet lips and fondled him handily as she whispered "Hello?" into the phone. Then she passed the phone up to Montrose and went back to her life's work.

Sandra. The dumb bitch!

How she knew he was here, but she did—and maybe it was time to think of hiring another secretary. One who didn't know that much about his business and just did what she was told. He gave her hell on the phone, all the while feeling Lynn's delight flowing up his loins and that's how he was when Sandra managed to interrupt long enough to tell him that Claire had called and Bobby was missing.

"Harry? How's it going, kid?"

Montrose had finished the call to Mort Drucker, but now he had Chicago on one line and was still dangling Lujack on the other.

Claire stood in the doorway and saw that the two lines continued to be tied up, the two little lights on the phone glowing. His and Hers. And Harold was hogging both, shouting into the mouthpiece, switching back and forth, business as usual, in that loud kidding-insulting way he used on the customers.

She came closer to him. He was slouching on the sofa, his suit jacket folded neatly beside him, necktie fixed exactly in place, gold cuff-linked sleeves not rolled up. She tried to catch his eye and he waved her off, pointing at the phone, indicating that he was busy, talking.

Claire fluttered her hand. He glanced at her again. And frowned, half-turned his face away from the distraction.

"Do you—mind?" she asked softly.

He didn't look at her.

"Do you—mind," she said again, louder. He looked at her this time, but went on with his conversation and Claire was amazed to find her hand slapping at Harold's face, now the other hand, too, hitting him for the first time in their married life. Slapping and pummeling him with a light rain of blows that struck his cheeks and forehead and chest. The back of her left hand flailed against the side of his nose and the diamond engagement ring drew blood. A tiny red diamond bubbling, gleaming on his skin.

The look of amazement on Harold's face was replaced

with rage. He made a growling sound, dropped the phone and slammed his big hand hard across her breasts. Claire tumbled over backward onto the floor. The skirt of the cream-colored suit she had put on hiked up so that her stockinged thighs were visible.

She lay there on the gold carpet, breathing heavily up at Montrose. He glared down at her, rubbing his face with his palm, erasing her ridiculous flea-power assault. Gingerly, Montrose touched his nose, streaked the dot of blood and licked his fingers.

"What the hell's with you?" he demanded.

"Do you mind?" she repeated and the words sounded strangely formal and meaningless to her, too. "You're—tying up the phones."

"I'm trying to do a little business. You know, earn some money so we can pay *our* bills?"

"But you're . . ." she blinked. "If somebody wants to call us, you're . . ."

"Like who? You expecting a call?"

"Maybe. About Bobby. If somebody . . ." She stopped.

"Oh. Yeah. Well, I guess I ought to keep the listed line open."

"Harold. Do you know?"

"Do I know what?"

She took a deep breath. "Anything. About Bobby. Do you know about . . . ?"

Now he was really mad. The nerve of the bitch. Even suggesting. His own son!

"Do you?" he asked.

She flinched and groped for words. And then the doorbell chimed.

The mobile TV unit was parked in the driveway behind the gold Cadillac. Chuck Weston, KNXT's man in the field, pressed the bell and heard the chime sound again. The door was opened and there stood the lady of the house.

A well-tailored suit, lacy white high-collared blouse . . . ashen-faced, eyes misting, hands wringing a tissue. Portrait of a distraught mother. Beautiful!

Weston solemnly introduced himself and was pleased to see the flicker of recognition. She knew him from the nightly newscasts.

"If we could just talk to you on camera for a few moments, Mrs. Montrose," he said in his warm, deeply modulated voice. "About what you're going through . . ."

Behind him at the station wagon with the KNXT decal, Claire saw the cameraman hoisting the shoulder rig into place. Claire glanced back over her shoulder. Harold was on the phone again. But only one of the little lights was glowing. She nodded to Weston and went outside to the driveway, closing the front door behind her.

There was a clown waiting for them at the corner of Olympic Boulevard and Roxbury Drive. Jonas was driving and when the car stopped for the light, Brenner looked through the side window. The face of the clown was pressed close against the glass. He was wearing an orange fright wig and a bulbous red nose in the center of his painted-white face. Black mascara tears were drawn on his cheeks and the Emmett Kelly sad expression outlined his mouth. But he was smiling at Brenner.

The clown rapped on the window and Brenner rolled it down.

Probably handing out balloons left over from a kid's birthday in Roxbury Park. But instead he silently offered Brenner a pamphlet. The car radio crackled a radio call. The clown snapped to attention and brought his hand up to his brow in a palms-out British Army salute. As he stepped back, Brenner noticed the clown was wearing faded jeans and a T-shirt with the big yellow "Smile" face.

Short hair, mid-twenties, with the happy-fevered eyes of a zealot. Brenner waved to him as Jonas put the car in gear again.

"Panhandler?" Jonas asked.

"Jesus freak." Brenner scanned the pamphlet. It was done in comic-book cartoon fashion. "The Adventures of Don Quixote." A circle in the upper corner of the page contained the smaller words: Donation Suggested.

" 'He lived in a world of fantasy, where all were mad but he,' " Brenner read aloud.

" 'Be a clown, be a clown,' " Jonas sang the old song badly. "What else?"

"Commercial comes at the end: 'For the foolishness of God is wiser than men. And this world's wisdom is foolishness to Him.' "

"Is that right."

Brenner shrugged. "It's Scripture."

They rode along the fringe of Beverly Hills and Jonas continued the story he had been telling:

". . . so Connie is mad, she and the kids were looking forward to doing something with the day off, but what am I going to do? This real estate guy called and he can throw a lot of work my way."

Jonas was skilled at remodeling houses and augmented his cop's salary with jobs on the side.

"I go out to this big place at the beach. The lady answers the door. A really heavy-looking chick. And she says, 'Oh, you're the cop who's a carpenter.' I walk in and there's this dog. A monster, and he's got my arm, sleeve and all, just holding it in his teeth—growling, you know?"

Jonas was baring his teeth in a snarl to demonstrate and clutching his own sleeve with clawlike fingers while driving one-handed.

"But the chick, it's like she doesn't notice. She just starts walking. 'Right this way,' she says." Jonas did a seductive Mae West imitation. "And the dog brings me along like he's the butler—leading me by the arm. Every step of the way, I'm watching that dog and I'm saying to myself: 'Bite, you monster! *Bite*—and I own this place.' "

Brenner laughed and Jonas felt rewarded for the effort he had put into the story. Lately, a good belly laugh out of Brenner was a rare thing.

"Hey, we're in luck," Jonas said. There was a parking space waiting for them in front of the office building.

■▪▪▪

Shielded by translucent panels that covered the ceiling, rows of fluorescent tubes beamed their cold light down on rows of desks at which young secretaries clattered out triplicate forms on electric typewriters. There were windows in the air-conditioned insurance company office, but they were of gray-tinted, glareproof glass that made it seem perpetually cloudy outside.

The receptionist guided them to the door they were seeking: MR. MORRISSEY. The name plate was hand-painted, implying permanence, but it was mounted in a slide-on track on the door. It could easily be replaced by another name.

Kenneth Morrissey stood behind his neatly kept desk. "Sit down, gentlemen, sit down."

Brenner and Jonas took the only two chairs, wedged in between the front of the desk and a small metal bookcase. There had been an attempt made to create executive suite elegance, French Impressionist prints on the walls, interspersed with framed "Outstanding Insurance Underwriter —Southwest Division" plaques. But the office was too small to bring it off. There wasn't room for a couch, because the file cabinets occupied that space and there was a coatrack, not a closet. Mr. Morrissey was a very junior executive.

"Now, I understand this has to do with car insurance?"

"Well, with a car." Brenner showed his identification to Morrissey. "This is Detective Jonas. We're on an investigation. Had a report that a car with a license-plate number similar to yours was seen in an area adjoining Beverly Hills early this morning . . ."

Like clockwork. Morrissey stared at them. He had known he could count on it. From the moment the newspaper headline caught his attention, he'd known they'd come. But, he hoped that for once he'd be wrong. Big joke. It took them even less time than usual.

Morrissey sucked in a chestful of air and got up, moving to the door, closing it so the people outside couldn't hear.

He turned to face them.

"You know, you guys ought to get together and come up with a new story. That one's a little tired." Morrissey went behind the desk again. He looked smaller—and suddenly very tired. But he sat very straight.

"Nobody saw my car anywhere this morning. You just got my name out of your files. *Then* you looked up my license plate so you could come in here and make conversation. What you want to know is where I was, right?"

"You're a registered sex offender," Jonas said flatly. His lip curled slightly, revealing his distaste.

Morrissey had been talking to Brenner, now he shifted to Jonas. "Does that mean every time anybody pats a kid on the head anywhere within fifty miles, you guys come knocking on my door?"

Jonas gazed at him coldly.

"That was years ago," Morrissey said. "I was a kid, just a mixed-up—look, I was punished, paid my debt to society, I was treated—years and years of therapy. I've got a good job here." Couldn't they understand? "I'm not the same guy anymore."

■ 60 ■

Morrissey waited for . . . something. A flicker. He thought he saw that much in Brenner's eyes, but it was Jonas who spoke, implacably:

"About the car . . . ?"

There was something about these "reformed" freaks that ticked off Jonas. Maybe it was having kids of his own at home. Or just that . . . you could tell at a glance. Jonas was convinced of that. Even if the file hadn't fed them the information, Jonas knew he could spot an asshole pervert like Morrissey from three blocks away.

"My car," Morrissey answered wearily, "was in the garage being serviced. It's still there. The 76 station down on the corner. You can check. I was in San Francisco on business, came back on the noon flight. Want to see my ticket?"

Without waiting for a response, Morrissey leaned forward and delved into the open attaché case on the corner of his desk. He found the stub of an airline ticket and held it out. Brenner took it, glanced at the ticket, then back at Morrissey.

If you didn't know, you'd never guess, Brenner thought. He looks just like anybody else. Brenner put the ticket stub on the desk and stood up.

"Sorry to have troubled you, Mr. Morrissey."

Jonas rose, following Brenner toward the door.

"Sure, sure," Morrissey accepted their departure. "It's just . . ."

Something in his tone stopped Brenner at the door.

"When does it end?" Morrissey asked.

Brenner considered it for a moment. "I don't know, buddy," he finally told Morrissey. "But if you had our job, where would you start looking?"

"Zip," Ramirez said. "Big zero—so far."

There were maps on the walls. The City of Los Angeles. Their particular division. And now an enlarged map with a red circle drawn around the location of the Montrose house.

Ramirez looked around his office in that building without windows. The furniture used to be old and battered wood, now it was new, nicked metal. Different rooms, but the same. Different faces—the ones he knew best were almost all gone now—but the job was always the same.

They were in rolled-up shirtsleeves, plastic I.D. cards hanging from their breast pockets, holsters clipped to their belts, styrofoam coffee cups in their hands. Cigarette smoke curled in the air above them. Nobody had a dynamite answer, they all knew that, but Ramirez patrolled the room in search of one.

Playing coach, he thought. Locker-room time. Chart some strategy, stoke up the troops. "Okay, what've we got?"

"The ex-maid," Elgort said. "Doreen Mason."

"Split," Ramirez said. "Left town. Maybe south—Mexico." He jabbed the air with his finger. "We've got lines out."

"She still sounds like the best bet." Brenner was standing near the file cabinet, examining a newly arrived carton full of papers.

Ramirez moved through them restlessly, walking around Jonas' chair and avoiding Hyatt's outstretched legs. Spit and polish, can you believe it? Ramirez shook his head. Here six years and Hyatt's still wearing goddamn Wyoming cowboy boots.

"Scuba crew looked all over the reservoir," Ramirez said. "Uniform boys have been through everybody's backyard and swimming pool. There are guys beating the bushes on the hillside, helicopter checked the woods further up." He quivered the fingers of his outstretched hands at them insistently. "Come on, come on—what else we got?"

"Sex offenders in residence in the area," Brenner said.

"How many?" Elgort asked in that funny, raspy voice of his.

"How many you want?"

"Dozens?" Hyatt was hopeful.

Brenner rippled through the carton of papers. "You got hundreds."

Jonas sighed and looked at the floor.

"Go figure," Elgort said. "It looks like such a quiet part of town."

It got a laugh. Elgort usually did, but this time Ramirez stepped on it.

"We check 'em all," he said. "What else?"

"Mommy and daddy don't come up smelling too good," Jonas offered.

"They're coming in tomorrow," Ramirez agreed. "We're gonna run 'em through the polygraph. See if the machine thinks they're straight."

Hyatt snorted. The machine. The magic machine. Knows all, tells all—detector of lies, finder of truth. Bullshit. "Maybe we can ask the machine where the kid is," Hyatt suggested laconically.

Ramirez was a steamroller. "I'm asking you guys." He had come full circle, back to the position of command, behind the desk. "I'm adding extra crews to work this. Fill 'em in on where you are before you go off tonight. Nobody takes days off this week—till we get on top of it. Okay?" Ramirez looked around for objections. Comments. There were none. "Okay!"

Brenner drove down Overland Avenue past the May Company on Pico Boulevard. Big Business now: a major department store, surrounded by satellite shops and a two-screen movie theater. Optimum use of valuable real estate.

For years that corner had been Kiddyland. A dozen or so creaking rides. Merry-go-round, toy cars that ran in a circle, boats that did the same in a murky moat ("Don't put your fingers in the water, Mike!"), a baby ferris wheel and a midget locomotive that tooted its whistle and pulled a mini-train of barred animal cages, circling the amusement area.

The ponies!

Brenner remembered the ponies. Moth-eaten, sway-backed creatures, gallumphing along like sleepwalkers, following the deeply worn ruts in the riding ring. Twice around like marathon dancers nearing collapse, then suddenly shifting without provocation into high gear, a spirited near-jog for the last quarter-turn that led back to the stalls. A thrill finish for the kids.

All gone now. The rides were probably mashed into junk metal long since. But where did the ponies go to?

Brenner's car crossed the railroad tracks at Exposition Boulevard and made a right turn into the short street that flowed into Selby Avenue.

It was still a nice street. These small houses were G.I. tract, built in 1945. They cost $14,000 then. Ten years ago, you could buy one for $20,000. Now they were worth at least $40,000 but there were no "For Sale" signs on the trimmed front lawns. People moved in here and stayed.

Brenner pulled into the driveway and parked behind the small station wagon.

He got out and unlocked the trunk. There was a large gift-wrapped package inside. Brenner carried it up the path to the front door.

Old habits asserted themselves. Brenner automatically reached for the knob and opened the door. He was about to enter when he caught himself. Close call! Brenner carefully shut the door and rang the bell. He only had to wait a moment. Footsteps and then Phyllis was there.

First, she was surprised. Then she smiled.

He had been after her those last few years to let her auburn hair grow longer and wear it fuller around her heart-shaped face. Now she was doing it. Her smile wasn't really lopsided, it just seemed like that because of the dimple in her left cheek. He used to tease her about it.

"Hi—just passing by?"

"Sort of . . ."

She pointed at the package he was holding. "Beware of men bearing gifts."

"Yeah, well, that's only supposed to be Greeks." He shifted his weight on the doorstep. "It's for Mike. Is the coast clear?"

"Sure, come on in. He's down the street someplace playing."

In the hallway, Brenner paused at a closet door. "Hide it in there?"

"Good as any," Phyllis said.

Brenner knelt to secrete the package deep in the closet, behind rubber boots, umbrellas, the old folding chairs.

"I've got a feeling this means you're not coming to his party," she said behind him.

He swiveled his head to gaze up at her. "You always were a terrific guesser." Brenner stood up. "Never find it in there."

"Unless it rains," she shrugged.

Phyllis was wearing jeans. Not many gals looked that good in pants. And a pretty flower-pattern blouse, his old "What's Cooking?" barbecue apron on top.

"I got a bad one going down," he explained. "Little kid disappeared."

Her brow furrowed. "The one on the news?"

"I guess so." Then: "I feel real lousy about the party."

■ 65 ■

"Duty calls," she said lightly and closed the closet door. "Like a drink?"

Before he could answer, she moved off through the dining room area toward the kitchen. He didn't follow, but called after her:

"Hey, you're probably right in the middle of . . ."

He heard her laugh, while clattering pot lids. "Oh, come on, stay a minute, have a drink. You can make me one."

Brenner advanced deeper into the house he once lived in.

"There's some white wine in the refrigerator," she said. He found the bottle, a tall one, half-empty. The cork came out easily and he got two of the good goblets down off the second shelf.

"He all excited?" Brenner asked.

"You only get to be nine once." Her back was to him at the stove and she was stirring tomato sauce with the wooden spoon. "Hey, I didn't tell you. He got a citation."

"That good or bad?"

"Good. For citizenship." Brenner brought the drinks over and she took one of the goblets. "The number one citizen in the fourth grade. For this quarter. Your son!" She laughed. "Some honor, huh?"

Brenner smiled. "Just don't let it go to his head."

He held out his wine glass. She touched hers to it and said, "Clink!"

"Clink," he repeated. "To—good citizenship."

He laughed and so did Phyllis. Brenner sipped his wine, she just held her glass. And, abruptly, conversation completely dried up between them. They both realized it and Phyllis took a quick sip, put her glass down and herself in motion to cover the awkwardness they felt.

"Know who sold their house?" She was bringing the milk carton out of the refrigerator, putting it on the table which was set for two. "The Fausts. Remember them?

Down the street, they moved in right after we did. He got transferred to Virginia, they . . ."

She stopped as they heard the front door slamming. Brenner turned expectantly toward the kitchen entrance.

"*Mom* . . .?" The boy's voice sounded excited. Now he came into the kitchen. "Is dad here?" And Mike Brenner stopped in the doorway as he saw his father. He grinned.

Brenner felt terrific.

"Hey, big fella." Brenner held out his arms, hoping that the boy would come running and jump on him. But he didn't. Mike approached slowly, still beaming happily.

"Hi—saw your car." Mike shook his hand, one of those clasp-handed grips the black kids had started and everybody was doing now. "You eating dinner with us?"

"No," Brenner said quickly. "Just stopped off to leave you a surprise—*big* surprise. For tomorrow."

It was a thirty-buck jet car outfit, orange plastic ramps, miniature electrically charged Formula Ones and a plug-in generator to juice the toys for their travels around the track. Brenner knew the boy would like it.

"Your dad has to work tomorrow," Phyllis mentioned from the stove. She did it nicely, delivering the bad news for him. Brenner appreciated it.

"But I'll be out on the weekend. Sunday." He glanced at Phyllis and she nodded. "We'll have a special day. You know, an extra celebration. Do something terrific, I don't know what yet, but it'll be like having two birthdays in the same week, okay?"

The boy bobbed his head. "Sure—yeah."

The helmet of long wavy brown hair, that little face. Like looking into the mirror, Mike resembled him that much. The same easy wrinkle-eyed smile but the glimmers of pain still show through, Brenner thought. He's too young to do a good job concealing it, but he'll learn.

Brenner tousled Mike's hair and bent to kiss him on top

of the head. Mike ducked and leaned against Brenner's side.

"All right," Brenner said, his arms around the boy, rocking together for a moment. "All right."

They walked out of the house together and went toward his car. Phyllis stayed inside.

"Hear you've been doing good in school," Brenner said.

"Guess so," Mike said. Another step and another, then: "Some of the guys are mean."

Brenner looked down at him. He wasn't the tallest nine-year-old around. But Brenner knew better than to make more of it than the kid did—and it didn't seem like a big thing.

"Tell 'em your old man's a cop," he said.

Mike peered up at him. Brenner knew he was thinking something, but he couldn't read it. Mike opened the driver's door for him. Brenner didn't get in. He touched the boy's shoulder.

"Better get inside. Your mom's got dinner."

"Okay."

Mike backed off a few feet as Brenner slammed the door and turned on the motor. He looked out at Mike through the open window.

"Sunday, okay?"

Brenner smiled. Mike waved and watched as Brenner rolled out of the driveway. In the street, Brenner gestured for Mike to go in the house and the boy nodded.

The car moved off but Brenner glanced in the rear-view mirror just before he made the turn at the corner. Mike was still standing in the driveway looking after him.

The shimmering September sun still was in the process of squatting down on the horizon of the ocean beyond Santa Monica, but the "No Vacancy" sign was already lit on the front of the motel on Ocean Avenue as Brenner drove into the courtyard.

The parking slot right before his door was available. He turned off the ignition and hefted the bag of groceries off the adjoining seat.

He was fitting the motel key into the lock when he heard the voice behind him:

"Hold on there!"

Mr. Atkins was advancing on him with a pleased expression. He was carrying a gray cardboard box tied with string. "Good news," he proclaimed. "Your shirts—back a day early."

Brenner took the laundry box from the elderly motel proprietor. Mr. Atkins was dressed as always, baggy pants, frayed white shirt and shiny black tie encased in a roomy mustard-color cardigan buttoned completely over his sprawling middle. A small man with thick rimless glasses, thinning hair, prissy manner, he looked like a retired grade-school math teacher. Actually, for twenty-two years he had been the clerk behind the five-dollar window at Del Mar race track.

Same difference, Brenner thought. Five and five make ten. "How much do I owe you?"

"The missus put it on your bill. Just like usual."

Brenner was ready to go into his room, but Mr. Atkins had some more news.

"Hear about the liquor store?" He lowered his voice to keep the grim tidings away from the ears of Mrs. Atkins in the office. "Over on Colorado. Couple of no-goods with a gun. Terrible . . ."

Mr. Atkins' lips were pursed tight, his eyes all-knowing slits.

"No, I didn't hear," Brenner said.

"That's why the missus and me—we enjoy having you

with us," Mr. Atkins glowed. "Kind of gives us a sense of security."

"Sure," Brenner said. "Well—the groceries."

" 'Night," Mr. Atkins called after him.

There was a wall-size mirror in the wash basin alcove at one end of the room. The small refrigerator was below the vanity counter, and Brenner finished unloading. He didn't keep much, just cookies, apples, some cheese, a pint container of milk to go with the coffee. The coffee maker was part of the motel wall. Light housekeeping. He closed the refrigerator door.

He had left a mess in the morning, tangled bedsheets and cigarette-filled ashtrays. But the good fairies had come and restored—what? Beauty? No, simplicity. There wasn't one extra piece of furnishing or decor in the room. Goldilocks must have been the interior decorator. Not too much, not too little, just right. And Brenner had supplied a matching spirit: There was nothing here of himself. No photograph, no memento. If I didn't know better, he thought, I wouldn't even know I live here. He smiled.

There—that's a little bit of me.

He unclipped the holster with the .38 and put it on the nightstand. Then his badge beside it. Be it ever so humble . . .

Brenner draped his jacket over the desk chair and sat down on the bed. As he pulled off his tie and started unbuttoning his shirt, he wondered what Mike was doing. Still a few minutes of daylight left, maybe he was out skateboarding. The kid was like a ballet dancer on that damn board. Brenner tried to focus the picture in his mind. He used to see Mike at play all the time, but never really look at him. Not really. Now it was like a home movie going by in a blur, and he tried to freeze the frame and see it clearly.

Brenner got up and went to the telephone on the desk. He dialed and waited.

"Monty? Ed Brenner. Anything doing on the Montrose kid?" There wasn't. "Yeah. I just wanted to check. Right . . ."

He hung up the phone and tossed his shirt on the bed where it landed on top of the carton of fresh shirts.

Brenner turned on the TV set as he passed en route to the wash basin. He splashed the cool running water on his face and then began to soap his hands.

Behind him, the TV picture burned into sharpness. An evening news show was in progress, but in pantomime: the sound volume was very low. The anchorman, a woman with an intelligent face and a windblown hairstyle, appeared properly grim in keeping with the worldwide disasters she was describing. On the scrim beyond her head, still pictures and film clips gave clues to what she was saying. A scrawny pop-eyed terrorist being dragged off by burly European police. One of the network's correspondents standing before a field of Middle East oil derricks. Red lava pouring from a South Sea volcano—a spectacular night-time aerial fireworks vision. Meanwhile, back home, the lady continued her somber Cassandra's recitation, confiding eyes staring directly into the camera . . .

Brenner turned off the water tap and began toweling his face dry. He observed the face in the mirror. What do you look so tired about? And then his attention went to the reflection of the TV set.

Bobby Montrose was on TV. The same fuzzy smiling photo Brenner had been given earlier.

He went to the TV set and made it louder. Bobby's face vanished and the newslady reappeared at her desk.

". . . as police continued their search for the missing

four-year-old boy," she intoned. "This was what the scene was like at the Montrose house earlier today."

Now Claire was here. Her face filled the screen and was larger than Brenner's, watching her. Superimposed across her chest in white letters were the words: MOTHER OF MISSING BOY. Lipstick, Brenner observed, eye-liner and mascara—demure, expensive clothes. She was standing in front of the house. Neighbors in the background were watching sympathetically while positioning themselves in hopes of making it onto the tube. A microphone was being held in front of Claire's mouth. Were there tears forming in her eyes? The voice was shaky, hands fluttering as usual. She seemed confused.

"I don't know why—or how," Claire said. "It's so— All I want is my baby back. That's all I want."

And she was gone.

The newslady turned to the next page of her script. "On the Southland sports scene today, there were winners and losers. And Don is here to tell you all about it . . ."

Brenner pushed the button turning off the TV set and the color picture disintegrated into a rainbow fireball that went black. He lifted the towel to finish drying his face; through the terry cloth he rubbed his eyes, pressing them until he saw red and gold starbursts under the lids. It was something he had not done in years. Often, as a child while lying in bed waiting for sleep, he had viewed the kaleidoscopic light show inside his head. It was still the same.

For an instant when Brenner took the towel away from his face the flashing strobelike patterns continued to dance before his eyes. As he scrutinized the TV screen, the patterns seemed to be superimposed, and he tried to recall the face of Bobby Montrose, there only moments ago. But the image would not return; the dazzling lights faded and he saw the TV screen was blank and gray.

7

The boy was asleep as the car approached the outskirts of Bakersfield. His eyes parted and from his vantage point high in the back of the car he could see through both the windshield and the side window: There were oil derricks and pumps visible on all sides. Just like back home, the boy thought.

Home. It was here, really. In this car.

They had started with two cars, this one hitched to another by a towbar. His father had heard that cars were going for a lot in California, so the plan was to sell the other car there for a profit. But the second car had bad tires and developed front-end problems by Wichita, so they got rid of it there at a loss and heaped all their belongings into this one. The back seat of the Dodge was stacked, stuffed and piled, but a little room had been left for visibility and for the boy to lie on top and sleep.

His father took No-Doz and coffee and they made it to California from Oklahoma in two and a half days and nights.

"Hey you, Ed," Sam Brenner had called at first light as they came riding across the endless flat emptiness that he had fallen asleep on last night. "Ve're here . . ."

Even before he heard his father's deep German-accented voice, Ed Brenner was awake. The acrid sulfur fumes from the flaring match, followed by the cigarette smoke and his father's familiar coughing had ended his night.

Ed Brenner wiped the sleep from his eyes and watched the oil fields go by and it felt good, up here in this snug place, surrounded by everything they owned, close to his father for once. He was seven years old . . .

The flame pushed aside the darkness for an instant. Zippo. Always a light, never a miss. Ed Brenner, thirty-one years old, inhaled on the Marlboro. The smoke tasted foul, but it filled his chest. He sat up in the Santa Monica motel bed. Sleep was gone, but he didn't turn on the lamp.

Lately, it had become a pattern: feeling tired, almost exhausted, dozing off early, falling into a deep fitful sleep. Then, waking suddenly—totally. Sticky with sweat and thinking of—nothing.

Or was it nothing?

There were people who made a living out of interpreting dreams. Yeah. But there were other guys who told fortunes by reading the bumps on your head, so who's to say what anything means?

During a humid hot spell as a kid, Brenner complained to his father he couldn't sleep. His father asked him if he was thinking, reviewing in his mind what happened that day?

Brenner admitted he was.

"Dot's vot's keeping you up," Sam Brenner said. And he whispered a secret in the boy's ear.

"Votever you're trying to figure out ven you're going to

sleep, you von't. You'll just keep going around and around, but you'll never decide nothing." He smiled at Ed. "So vhy vaste your time? Go to sleep. Don't think about things so much."

It was the only piece of fatherly advice Sam Brenner had ever given his son. And it didn't work. Brenner smiled now in the motel, sucked more smoke into his lungs and flipped the switch above the nightstand that activated the TV set across the room.

John Garfield joined Brenner in the night. Blind, the poor son-of-a-bitch. Eleanor Parker was trying to console him. "I don't want your pity," he told her. Treat 'em rough, babe.

It was *Pride of the Marines*. A favorite. John Garfield alive again on Channel 4. That walk—the little guy shouldering forward, taking those too-big strides; and the voice, "I'm gonna be champ, Ma, champ! I'm gonna be *somebody!*"

They said he died making it with some chick, and all the guys at Merle's poolroom in Bakersfield elbowed Brenner and one another and said, "If you gotta go, that's the way. Tall in the saddle!"

Moist, soft lips. On television, Eleanor Parker was taking John Garfield's shit and smiling. Lips kind of quavering, but then smiling. Forgiving him. He didn't mean to hurt her, she knew that. He didn't have to say it—she understood. People were always dumping on Eleanor Parker: Cagney, Kirk Douglas, Dennis Morgan, even Ronald Reagan. She took it and came back for more; but for John Garfield there was a special tenderness. She saw things in him that no one else did . . .

He was a rigger in the oil fields and looked like it: the Li'l Abner shoes and coarse-fabric workclothes faded by a hundred unsuccessful washings. She was a secretary in the front office: soft and clean, starchy and pert. It was an accident that they met.

Correction.

It's an accident that anybody ever meets. But his job didn't include running paperwork to the office, except this one day. So they met. And then again in the canned soup aisle at the A&P a few days later. When he remembered her and she didn't remember him. So he reminded her. And she smiled.

Soft, moist lips—inside the fogged windows of his car at the drive-in movie. Brenner's hand reaching up under Phyllis' sweater, his mouth on hers, feeling the tension in her lips and when he touched her she was wet and there was a hungering that matched his own and . . .

Bullshit.

Not how it was at all. For Gable and Myrna Loy maybe. Paul Newman and Joanne Woodward. Not for them. He had dirty fingernails and horny hands and she was a scared kid far from home who wanted to talk to somebody. He wanted to get laid. She never had been.

It was intimidation at first glance for him: She simultaneously outclassed and attracted him. So he bluffed and succeeded. This was a nice girl, but maybe you scored the same way as with the other kind.

They all liked to talk. All he had to do was be quiet and wait long enough. He offered sympathetic conversation and when he made his move she spread her legs in gratitude. She made him feel strong: he made her feel safe. Illusions on both sides: the basis for an enduring relationship.

And so they were married. The smart-ass roustabout from Bakersfield and the lonely pretty office worker from L.A. They were in love and it would last forever.

■ ■ ■

Phyllis was homesick and pregnant. So what could he do? Brenner and a buddy came down to L.A. to take the civil service tests. Work for the post office, or the city, maybe the firemen, a road construction gang. Something steady. Trying for the cops was the other guy's idea. They both took the exam. Brenner passed, his buddy didn't.

Mike was born the month after Brenner graduated from the Academy. Phyllis liked being back in L.A. but she didn't like his being a cop. They both understood that it was just going to be temporary, until something better came along and some of the bills were paid off.

"Vait, vait!"

There was a commercial on TV. Some asshole doing Sid Caesar as the German Professor. The broken top hat, sad tuxedo with the baggy britches that looked like he'd pissed his pants and didn't even know it. Selling underarm deodorant. W. C. Fields imitators hustling beer, Jean Harlow lookalikes hawking douche sprays, Chaplin's Tramp transformed into a cigarette. Immortality, American Style.

The guy doing the Great Caesar wasn't bad—maybe it's him, who knows? Funny accents, always good for a laugh.

Eleven fucking days in a row . . .

When Sid Caesar was at his peak, all the kids in junior high school would "do" him. "Herr Professor!" Then Brenner's father came to see the principal about "a disciplinary problem with Edward," and Harold, that scrawny prick monitor in the office, heard Sam Brenner talking. And in the schoolyard after lunch he "did" Sam Brenner and everybody fell down laughing. So Ed Brenner told Harold to shut his ass and because he was bigger Harold did. But it caught on and pretty soon Ed Brenner was "Herr Professor" and everybody was laughing and doing it and . . .

Eleven days in a row.

One bastard bigger than the next. Or did it just seem like that? Fighting a different guy after school until there wasn't anybody left making fun. He lost most of the fights, but the laughing stopped. Nobody was going to mock the way his father talked. To them it was a joke, but to him it was . . . it was . . .

He hated the way his father sounded.

It was different. And it made him ashamed. Why the hell couldn't he talk like the other fathers? Why did it have to be like . . .

"Tell me about her, Papa."

"A vaitress. Dot's vot she vas, your mama—a vaitress in a restaurant."

But what color was her hair and how did she move and talk and what was her face like when she looked at me?

"Appendixitis she got and dot vas dot."

Ignorant fuck. Appendi*citis!* Nobody dies from appendicitis in the twentieth century—but his mother, the Tulsa waitress, did.

End of story. Sam Brenner wasn't big on talking. Hard worker. Hard drinker. Muscles in his arms as thick as your thigh, a chest out to here, when he'd spank his son, watch out.

Vatch out! *Watch* out! The sky is falling, Chicken Little.

A clump of steel fell from up high somewhere on the drill rigging and landed on Sam Brenner's head. Bad luck. Nobody's fault. Company pays hospitalization, of course, but . . .

He was like a balloon that the air had gone out of and his lips moved but he didn't say anything. Just lay there in that big white hospital bed. For three weeks, Ed Brenner went to see his father. Physically, Sam seemed to have shrunk. Brenner was never sure that his father knew him, but the eyes would stare at him and the lips would work. He wants to talk to me, at last he wants to tell me! And

Ed Brenner would put his ear close to his father's mouth and listen. But he never understood anything Sam Brenner said; it was just gurgling and swallowing and dribbling and straining and nothing that meant anything.

End of story.

In the ground. May his soul rest in peace . . . well, why not? Ed Brenner was fourteen years old.

John Garfield was alone now.

He couldn't see but he knew they were all dead. The others. Only he was left and he could hear the enemy out there. Maybe that was enough—if he could hear them! He was blind but still alive and wherever he heard the sounds he fired the machine gun and the mocking voices in the jungle were silenced, one by one—but there were so many of them, so many.

It was a nightmare. Brenner had lived through it with John Garfield before. Alone in the darkness, surrounded, you became him . . .

"Knock-knock, who's there?"

"Butcher."

"Butcher who?"

"Butcher back against the wall, 'cause here I come—balls and all!"

Fall down laughing. Street corner shit. Knock-knock jokes. The things we once laughed at . . .

Ganzer. In the middle of the night. Out there right now, manning the Property Window, carefully itemizing the droppings found in the pockets of scumbags. "One beer opener, one matchbook, thirty-seven cents in currency . . ."

You were the best of 'em all, Ganzer!

"Ready?"

Brenner nodded. On opposite sides of the apartment

house doorway. Ganzer drawing back one big foot and slamming into the lock. Plainclothes, guns drawn, racing into the apartment before the assholes can flush the shit down the toilet and—surprise!

No assholes.

Mr. and Mrs. America.

Sitting at the kitchen table, eating spaghetti, looking up at them like they're from Mars. Wide-eyed, simon pure, supersquare solid citizens.

The Wrong Apartment!

It comes to both of them in the same blinding flash! We've kicked in the door on the wrong fucking apartment!

But what to do?

Ganzer's greatness manifests itself.

He just keeps going, flying past ma and pa at the dinner table, pulling Brenner with him. Yelling back as they disappear out the back:

"That'll teach you to mess with the FBI!"

Let the irate phone complaints fall where they may: Ganzer and Brenner in a night alley a block away. Choking, cackling, gasping . . . clutching at each other to keep from falling down . . . laughing . . .

. . . firing the machine gun that slices the jungle with light from tracer bullets that John Garfield can't see . . . but the bullets can find the enemy . . .

In another alley.

He is me and I am he. Partners, that's what we are. Me and Ganzer. I feel what he feels.

Scared.

Burglary call. No moon. No streetlight. Black inky darkness. And there's somebody out there behind the house. You go that way, partner. I'll go down the alley.

Lousy neighborhood. What's to steal around here anyway? Why not go to Beverly Hills? Breaking-and-entering for fun *and* profit!

There's somebody.

Coming toward me.

I can't see him. Must be my partner. I'll whisper it, let him know I'm here in the darkness . . . so he doesn't shoot my ass. "Partner?"

He's still coming. He hears me! "That you, partner?"

Why doesn't he answer? So dark, but . . . it's him! Got to be him . . . can't be the burglar! That turkey would be fleeing, high-tailing the other way. Sure. They always go away from you, never come toward you, never, but suppose . . .

"Partner, is that . . . ?"

Screaming. Like something dying. The noise, so loud, so close. *Shrieking!* It's him! The man in the darkness of the alley. My partner. But *not* my partner! Flame. And then the noise. Yeah. Seeing and *then* hearing. Impossible, but . . . like a jackhammer smashing into my side!

I'm whirling, don't fall, God damn it! And that scumbag is running toward me and I clutch the .38 in both hands and fire.

Hit him, yes, good! I hit him!

He's ten feet away and I'm shooting and he's shooting and he's still yelling and I'm hitting him, I know I am, squeezing off round after round. He's firing wild! But I'm hitting him, so please God, why won't he go down?

He's down.

I'm reloading and my fingers are shaking, I dropped a fucking cartridge, where is it? On the ground, forget it, get another one from the belt, *quick*! He's getting up, in the darkness, *he'll kill me*! I'm firing again, like in the shooting gallery. Bull's-eye but the duck won't stay down. He's shooting at me again, he'll hit me, we're so close! Lousy .38 police issue slugs, toy bullets, no stopping power, we need .45s, I need . . . *where's my partner?*

Somebody else.

Over there . . . yes . . . shooting.

Not at me. At him. At that fucking werewolf bastard! Crossfire! Maybe my partner's got the silver bullet! No, I do, it's me, I hit him again and look at the way he's falling, *I got him!*

It's . . . over.

He's on the ground. Not moving.

The voice comes from the darkness.

"Partner, you okay?" I shine my light. And check out the fallen burglar. And walk toward Ganzer, who cannot answer.

Ganzer is leaning against the wooden alley fence, clutching his side where the first bullet struck. A clean wound, the doctors would find, through and through.

And the burglar.

Still breathing. Later count would show that he was hit nine times. But no vital organs were damaged. The burglar would live another six hours and die at the hospital from loss of blood.

I ease Ganzer onto the packed-dirt alley.

"It's all right, Marty." God. He's shaking all over. "It's all right . . ." Don't let him die. "You're okay!"

He is me and I am he. Partners. I feel what he feels. Hurt him and you hurt me.

The flag waved and the anthem played. Brenner didn't rise out of respect. Sleep had returned at last. Merciful sleep that lasted until morning through the hum and glow of the TV test pattern.

A sleep without dreams . . .

Montrose picked up the crumpled sports section from yesterday's L.A. *Times* and turned pages without looking at them. He and Claire were on the second floor of police headquarters in a small alcove that had the feeling of a dentist's waiting room. Outside the open doorway, uniformed cops moved about their business.

Time is money, Montrose added up. This horseshit is costing me money. He vented his anger on Claire.

"You're stupid, you know that?"

"Harold . . ."

"You believe everything people tell you. Just because they tell you it's routine . . ."

"Then why didn't you say something? The lieutenant told us both."

He pretended to read the newspaper. She persisted:

"If you don't want to—your lawyer said we don't have to . . ."

"I know what my goddamn lawyer said. Son-of-a-bitch

computes conversation by the quarter hour, that piece of worthless advice cost me twenty dollars."

She stood up, smoothed her skirt. "Then let's go."

"No. It's all right." He didn't move. "We're here and we've got nothing to hide, right?"

Ramirez had explained it to them. In a case like this, certain procedures had evolved over the years. One of them was to question the parents on the polygraph machine.

"The lie detector?" Montrose had bristled at the suggestion.

"Strictly routine," Ramirez finessed. "We're going to be talking to a lot of other people, taking up a lot of their time and ours. So just to be sure there's no confusion on the basic details . . ."

What could Montrose say except, "Yes, of course." Typical. Your son disappears, you call the police and what do they do? Where do they look for an answer?

"Mr. Montrose? This way, please." The uniformed cop was standing in the doorway.

Montrose rose and tossed the newspaper down on his chair. Claire gave him a wavering smile that he supposed she meant to be encouraging.

He followed the cop off down the corridor.

I'm not here, Montrose calmed himself. I'm at my doctor's office, yes, in one of his tiny white rooms. For my yearly checkup. Sure. Same look to it all, not so strange. The technician wearing a white medical coat; instead of one of those X-ray exposure-quota badges, he has a police I.D. card clipped to his pocket. The machine —sort of like the EKG apparatus.

The technician's name was Krasny. He was a police sergeant, specially trained for his task. He hung Montrose's tailored jacket on a hanger behind the closed door of the small room that had a wall-size mirror, two comfortable chairs and the polygraph machine.

Krasny seated Montrose so that he was facing away from the machine—away from view of the roll of graph paper and the red marking arms that would chart the interview. He directed Montrose to roll up his sleeves and wired up the connecting sensors from Montrose's arms and chest to the polygraph. Then, with an on-off flip of the switch, he tested the results.

"All set. Now just relax, sir. Close your eyes and please keep them closed. I'm going to ask you a number of questions that can all be answered yes or no."

"Sounds fair." The machine was on.

"Your name is Harold Montrose?"

"Yes."

"You live in Los Angeles?"

"Yes."

"Have we ever met?"

"What?"

"Calibrating the machine. Yes or no, please."

"No."

"Thank you. You have one child?"

"Yes."

"Is his name Robert?"

"Bobby. Yes."

The graph paper was an unending road traveled by drunken red lines that climbed hills and dales without encountering any mountains yet. Krasny entered marking posts along the way.

"Is Bobby at home?"

"No."

"Do you know where Bobby is?"

"No."

"You last saw Bobby when leaving home yesterday for your place of business?"

"Yes." Getting tense. Relax!

"You are in the plastics business?"

"Yes." Easy . . . easy . . .

"Has Bobby ever been absent from home for extended periods of time before?"

"No." Moving away, he thought. No problem. Ask me anything.

"Did you recently employ as housemaid a woman named Doreen Mason?"

"Yes, I certainly did."

"Just yes or no."

Now it was Claire's turn.

She hated this room—the machine—and this man who hardly looked at her. Men always did, but he was into his wires and switches. She was a schoolgirl again and the teacher didn't like her but he was calling on her and no matter how hard she had studied she knew the teacher would ask a question she hadn't thought of . . . and she could smile and be cute and make excuses, but it wouldn't do any good because no one was looking. Except the machine. It could see inside of her and she felt empty.

". . . and Bobby was gone?"

"Yes."

"Do you know a reason anyone might have had to take him away?"

"No." Ask me if I love Bobby, ask me that! Because I do!

"He was wearing blue pajamas?"

"Yes."

"Any other articles of clothing missing?"

"No. I don't think so."

Ramirez was on the other side of the one-way mirror. On the outside looking in. She's nervous. Too nervous?

How can you tell? Yes or no answers only. She's entitled to natural anxiety related to the boy's disappearing, plus confusion in unfamiliar surroundings, fear of that fucking box! Everybody's scared of it. What kind of world would it be if we all told each other only the truth every minute of every day? Yeah. What kind of world . . .

"You want generalities or specifics?"

Ramirez walked briskly down the corridor with Krasny. "Whatever you got."

"Jumpy. Both of them," Krasny said.

"More than usual?"

"I think so."

"But don't ask you to swear to it?"

Krasny grinned. "To who? My hocus-pocus box isn't admissible anywhere, right?"

"Okay. Be specific."

"Only one flat-out lie."

Ramirez stopped. "Montrose lied? About what?"

"Not him. Her."

"Tell me."

"When I asked her if she is married to Harold Montrose. She said yes."

"And . . . ?"

"Machine registered tilt."

"That was a throwaway, filler question. Why would she . . .?"

"I couldn't figure it either. So after the session I asked her. And she told me." Krasny bent his head to take a sip of water from the fountain near the elevators.

"She's Catholic," Krasny said. "This is a second marriage. Had a church wedding when she was a kid, but it only lasted a year or so . . ."

"Legally." Ramirez understood.

Krasny nodded. "State of California says they're married, but she thinks she's a sinner."

"Funny," Ramirez said. "She doesn't look Catholic."

The squad room was growing old quickly. Several years of three shifts a day, seven days a week, had worn the shine off the rows of metal desks and chairs, the crammed pastel filing cabinets. The new squad room looked much like the old squad room by now. Patient men on telephones, victims wringing handkerchiefs and repeating details of their outrage to shirtsleeved two-finger typists. Coffee stains on desk blotters, overflowing ashtrays and an air of resignation: it's all happened before and it will all happen again. But professionals know how to deal with it.

Ramirez sat down on the corner of the desk. He picked a Marlboro out of the pack lying there and Brenner supplied a light. Jonas was on the phone.

"So?" Brenner asked.

"They just left." Jonas hung up the phone and Ramirez included him. "Polygraph. Official results."

"Yeah?"

"Maybe you guys don't like 'em, but the machine says they're straight."

Jonas sighed. "Okay."

"But you guys are in luck." Ramirez tossed a sheet of paper on the desk. "San Diego cops turned up a goodie. Doreen Mason."

"Finally." Brenner picked up the paper. "Tijuana?"

"T.J. cops are holding her for us. A little illegal favor," Ramirez said, "to make up for an illegal favor or two we've done for them. Have a nice trip. And let me hear from you . . ."

■ ■ ■

South of La Jolla the highway found the sea again. Brenner slouched in the sunlit passenger seat and watched the Pacific waves rolling in along deserted shores.

Jonas was driving one-handed, while working the radio dial in search of a music station to replace the one they had lost in their travels. Now he discovered a blast of tinny brass and rattling maracas backing a plaintive Spanish voice.

"Want to get in the mood?" Jonas smiled.

"Too soon." Brenner reached out to punch a button on the radio. Diana Ross' velvety coolness filled the car:

". . . Hey, wasn't it yesterday
We used to laugh at the wind behind us?
Didn't we run away
And hope that time wouldn't find us,
Didn't we take each other
To a place where no one's ever been . . ."

There was a large stately house that had become a small lovely hotel in La Jolla and the second-floor rear suite faced the ocean. Even with the windows closed the beat of the waves pounding on the rocks below could be heard. He and Phyllis had created their own rhythm in that room one summer weekend too long ago.

They had a little boy, back in Los Angeles with a baby-sitter. But for those few days they were honeymooners again celebrating their delight in each other. Walking along sunset beaches and dining in candlelit sea grottos.

". . . touch me in the morning,
Then just walk away.
We don't have tomorrow,
But we had yesterday-ay-hey . . ."

Mission Bay was coming up now. All I have to do, Brenner thought, is sit here and watch entire sections of my life flash by: On your right, ladies and gentlemen, the turnoff to Sea World, home of Numu the killer whale! Now passing Vacation Village, the only motel in Southern California with its own cuckoo's nest . . . a watchtower high above the Bay, reached by ascending an outdoor spiral staircase. Mike was five, maybe six—Brenner would follow him up and down those steps like a mountain goat until they both couldn't walk.

Now downtown San Diego, the highway cut through the center of town. Airport on the seaside, San Diego Zoo up in the hills. Always best to go there in the morning, before it gets too hot. Phyllis and Brenner making faces at the monkeys . . . making Mike laugh. God, how the kid used to laugh, like he couldn't stop.

"Why'd you turn off the radio?"

Brenner shrugged. "Give it a rest."

At the border crossing there were lines of vehicles from several states. Sightseeing families in station wagons, holidaying couples in convertibles, groups of T-shirted young guys in sedans, all being briskly passed through into Mexico. The area looked like two matching sets of bridge tollgates, but instead of a bridge between them there was an empty paved no man's land joining the two countries.

Jonas parked in the auto lot on the American side. They locked their holsters and .38s inside the trunk of the car and then walked into Mexico. Taxicabs were waiting to carry those too cautious to drive into Tijuana.

The mustachioed taxi driver grinned like a Chesire cat after they gave him the address. He was a small man perched on an air pillow that barely brought him up high enough to peer over the wheel that he clutched and swiveled through traffic, honking to let the world know he was coming.

"Say, you mens is cops?"

"Yeah," Brenner said.

"I know when I see you." He honked and cut in front of a bus. "You comin' here to make troubles for peoples, right?"

"Where'd you learn to talk English?" Jonas said.

"I talk *American*! Three years I live in Brownsville, Texas. Till they catch my ass an' send it back. Fuckinshit, Uncle Sam!"

They drove past the outskirts of town where entire families lived and died in cardboard crates, drove into the tourist part of town.

The driver let them out in front of the Tijuana police station. Brenner paid him in dollars and got a receipt. Jonas nudged Brenner: There was a dusty, dented green VW camper with California plates parked across the street. A skinny, gangly, long-muscled black man in his fifties was leaning against the VW; he straightened up and grinned at them. One of his front teeth was missing, his head was shaved and he was wearing a striped tank shirt, crumpled white bell bottoms that were too short for him, and huaraches; he gave them a small wave of greeting.

They didn't know him, but they waved back and went inside to talk to Doreen Mason.

She was massive, a big woman who had gone to fat but still carried herself with imposing dignity. About fifty-five —maybe older, Brenner guessed—with arms like a dock walloper. A fierce scowl pinched her strong features, but the ebony skin of her face was soft and unlined.

"You the ones?"

She glared at them and the holding cage suddenly wasn't

big enough. Jonas had his back to the barred door. Brenner was at the wall next to the rust-stained sink, watching Doreen Mason sit erect as a Tahitian queen on the tacky cot. The walls were scarred with graffiti: same old words, but written in Spanish, Brenner thought.

"You the ones," she repeated, "makin' me this grief? Me and Junior botherin' nobody out there! Camped on Rosarito Beach and they come and bust us for nothin'."

Jonas gauged her. One big mama! If she was coming your way on a dark street, good idea to go the other. But capable of kidnapping or . . . ?

"We just want to ask you some questions," Brenner said.

"Look here! Got to rattle bars to go to the toilet! And I been sittin' here since last night, Junior waitin' for me outside, me locked away in this bird cage. So you ask what you want." She took a breath and her eyes narrowed knowingly. "It's him, ain't it?"

"Who?" Jonas said.

"That creep! He put you on me, didn't he? Montrose. Mister Harold Lowlife Montrose."

A glance flashed between Brenner and Jonas, but Brenner's voice was casual:

"Why would he do that?"

"Because he—hey, we playin' games or somethin'? *You* tell *me*—what you want?"

"Mr. Montrose fired you last week."

She focused her contempt on Jonas. "I quit. Work for a man with a bad mouth like he got—stayed too long already, would've quit before 'cept for . . ."

Doreen stopped abruptly.

"For what?" Brenner prompted.

"It's more than that, ain't it?" she said slowly, the thought forming as she spoke it. "More than just he say I stealin' from him, pumpin' up the grocery bills. Say he call the police."

Doreen looked at them both, waiting, but they didn't say anything.

"But you—you wouldn't go runnin' all over everywhere for just that. I been too mad to figure it but you wouldn't . . ."

"You see a lot of kids down here at Rosarito Beach?" Jonas said. If she's faking, she's good.

She sat there. Tight-lipped, irritable.

"When's the last time you saw Bobby Montrose?" Brenner said.

"Bobby?" Her expression was changing: the hostility mixing with fear or . . . "They done somethin' to Bobby?"

"When's the last . . ." Brenner started to repeat, but Doreen interrupted him impatiently.

"When I packed up and left. A week ago. What's wrong with Bobby?"

"Where were you two days ago?" Jonas said.

"Right here." Her head was whipping back and forth between them, her eyes wider now, searching their faces. "Tell me about Bobby."

"We're going to check what you say," Brenner told her.

There was anger now, but not like before. Dread was part of it. "Check all you want. Talk to the people down to the beach. I been right here for five days. Now you tell me . . ."

"He's gone," Jonas said flatly.

It knocked the wind out of her. "What you mean—gone?"

Brenner's eyes never left her face. "We don't know. He's disappeared. Playing in the street. Then—gone."

"And you thought maybe—I . . ." She stared at them.

"You went. Then he did," Jonas said.

"Get the hell outta here!" She rose from the cot and towered over Brenner. "Go do your checkin' and askin' and pokin'—just get the hell outta here!"

Jonas shifted his weight onto the balls of his feet. Doreen was inches away from going for Brenner, but she moved away from him, rage contorting her face.

"You figured I could've hurt that little boy! Or maybe stole him away!"

When she turned back, the danger was over for them. But not for her.

"Well, I'll tell you. I thought of it. Takin' him from them. I thought of it sometimes. And I wish I had the nerve to do it. Leavin' him with those people. Alone with them. Bobby's the reason I stayed there long as I did."

She wasn't going to cry. There was too much hate and sadness.

"You see them," Doreen Mason said, "his 'mom' and his 'dad,' you tell 'em—I didn't do it. But I wish to God I had."

The night street in Tijuana was festive and crowded with tourists flowing from one open-fronted store to the next in search of bargains and finding almost identical merchandise in every stall. Serapes, sombreros, piñatas, puppets, hand-carved ashtrays and hand-woven wicker furniture.

Doreen Mason and Junior were reunited on the sands of Rosarito Beach. Her story had checked out. Brenner and Jonas had stayed for dinner and now strolled with the tide of pedestrians.

In the old days, the hustlers and promoters were as thick as flies and even harder to fend off: "Hey, meester, you like some fun? What kind fun you like?" Now, if you continued moving, it was enough to keep most of them off your lapel. But two gringos by themselves on the street at night attracted offers.

"For you, hombre, for you." The old man looked like a refugee from a Diego Rivera mural; he was dangling a gold chain with a figurine ornament in front of Brenner's face. "For you girl friend, she like it, you girl friend."

"For Christ's sake," Brenner smiled.

He showed Jonas the gold chain. The figurine wasn't an abstract shape, as it appeared from a distance. On close inspection, it was a tiny gold-plated penis and testicles.

"Talk about Goldfinger," Jonas said.

"You like?" The old man's laugh was a cackle. "Very reasonable. You got girl friend?"

"Let her get her own." Brenner gave the chain back.

Up ahead, people were blocking the pavement. Brenner and Jonas reached them and started out into the street to get around. And then they saw the center of attention.

The crowd was gathered in a half circle, giving a lot of open room on the wide sidewalk to a powerful young Mexican who was standing stripped to the waist on the curb with his back to the slow-moving, noisy traffic.

His heavy black hair and strong features clearly reflected back country Indian ancestry. In one hand, the young man had a twelve-inch transparent glass ginger ale bottle with colorless liquid. In the other hand, which he kept extended at full arm's length, he held a stick of wood with a flaming rag knotted around the end: a homemade torch.

Now the young man put the bottle to his lips. He filled his mouth and cheeks with the liquid, but did not swallow. Drawing air in through flaring nostrils, his chest billowed. Then he brought the torch closer . . . holding it out before his face.

All at once, he began to spray the flammable liquid out of his mouth at the torch: a ten-foot jet of flame leaped across the sidewalk. The pedestrians in the line of fire shrank back. A blaze of colors showered shards of red-blue-yellow light across the mesmerized faces.

The wonder was that the fire-eater was not consumed by his own creature. The flame dragon coiled and pranced in the air, constantly threatening to turn on his master. The young Mexican maintained his dominance by spewing more fuel as the fiery beast tried to back its way into his lips. Suddenly, the young man lowered the torch and the monster vanished.

He bowed, his body almost doubling in half, making obeisance to the awesome presence. Applause rippled through the crowd and a waiting friend took a jingling basket to the watchers, collecting coins and bills, the price of wonder.

Brenner couldn't take his eyes off the fire-eater.

Now he straightened from his bow, thrust hands up over his head with the torch held high. Excess liquid trickled down his jaw and the rivulets combined with sweat and rolled across his bare chest, following the ridges and contours of the powerful pectoral muscles and down his washboard-flat stomach. He smiled; it was a statement of his triumph.

"Schmuck's gonna barbecue his tonsils," Jonas said.

Brenner ignored Jonas. The young man was going to perform his miraculous feat again.

The torch was ready. And the cheeks of the Indian were round and firm, bursting with poison. Now! The evil Genie emerged from his lips! A brilliant cascade of heat, light and pain vomiting into the night, a soul on fire with everything foul inside the man flooding out to be purged, cleansed, cauterized—all wounds seared and closed, purifying by destroying, incinerating to make him whole again.

"You couldn't pay me enough," Jonas said as he stared. "Why does he do it?"

Brenner knew the answer. "Maybe it feels good when he stops."

"I could have died . . ."

The blonde one with the heavy cleavage had brought a

Silva Thin to her ruby red lips. Jonas started to offer a light and then saw she had the cigarette ass-backward, filter tip out toward the match. And that sparked the reminiscence:

". . . I was waiting for a bus once and there's this gorgeous guy waiting, too. He was picking up on me right away with big brown warm eyes and I knew it but I didn't want to let on. So real cool like Faye Dunaway I reach in my bag, take out a cigarette, put it in my mouth, very sophisticated, and I light up. I take a peek at him—he's hysterical. Hooting and laughing! 'Cause I don't have a cigarette in my mouth—it's a Tampax. On fire! I could've died."

They all broke up, Jonas appreciatively pounding the table in the small booth. Brenner and he were wedged in with the blonde one, who let it all hang out and did all the talking for herself and her friend, the thin raven-tressed one in the knit dress.

The cocktail lounge was across the street from the Jai Alai Palace. Prices were bad, even for Tijuana, but the drinks were fine. They had started out at adjoining tables and graduated easily and comfortably to the booth. The ladies were from Seattle, they said. Interior decorators, they said. Department store salesgirls more likely.

"And what do you do down there in Los Angeles?" the Blonde asked Jonas.

"Movies. Make movies," Jonas said.

"You're kidding."

"Really. I produce pictures. He's my assistant." Brenner wasn't helping much, just letting Jonas run with it.

"You hear that, Helen?" she demanded of her friend, the Raven, who nodded and grinned. She was either very quiet or very high. But she had excellent legs; a body that's more angular than thin, Brenner decided, with the kind of sharp bones that could stick you if you're not careful.

"Imagine! Hollywood producers." The Blonde blew smoke in Jonas' direction. "How about discovering us? You got a part in one of your pictures for us?"

"Nothing in my feature films, honey," Jonas said. "But I think there's something big coming up for you in my shorts."

The Blonde didn't get it, but the Raven burst into giggles. Then the Blonde reproached Jonas, slapping him playfully on the wrist. "That's—terrible!"

"Do we know any of the pictures you made?" The Raven could speak.

"You see *The Sting?*"

"You made . . . !" The Blonde was bouncing up and down on the booth cushion.

"Mas Margaritas, por favor!" Jonas signaled the waiter.

"What's Robert Redford like?" the Raven asked Brenner.

"A sweetheart."

"Go on," Jonas said, "tell 'em the truth."

"You tell 'em," Brenner said.

"Tell us." The Blonde couldn't wait to hear.

"A problem. Bob's a big problem."

"How?"

"His hair."

"Beautiful," the Blonde said.

"Not his own," Jonas confided.

"No!"

Jonas shrugged. "It's kind of a trade secret, but—we lose a lot of time in makeup each morning with Redford. I'm not saying he isn't worth it, but—would you believe? *Hours* to get him looking the way you know him."

The ladies were shaken. "Exactly how much—I mean how little . . . ?"

"Less than I have." Jonas patted his own sparse pate. "Look, I've told him, 'Bobby, why be self-conscious? Bald can be beautiful.' But he . . ."

"*Bald?*" The Raven quivered her tresses.

Jonas leaned across the table and both girls brought their faces close to his in order to share the secret.

"Just between us?" Jonas said. "A childhood illness. Not one hair of his own—on his entire body."

"Not even . . . ?" the Blonde began.

"The eyebrows?" the Raven said.

"False." Jonas nodded authoritatively.

"Wow," the Blonde sighed. "The poor man. I mean, you think of him, that beautiful hair and teeth . . ."

Jonas shifted his eyes evasively, and she detected it.

"The teeth . . . ?" she asked.

"Here are those drinks," Jonas welcomed the new round. "Now we need a toast."

"That poor man!" the Blonde lamented.

The Raven turned to Brenner. "You're the quiet one?"

"We take turns."

"What's your sign?"

"Aquarius."

"I thought so."

"Yeah." Did they ever say anything else? "It's my time."

"Are you into astrology?"

"No. I'm into other things."

"Such as?" she challenged.

Brenner started another Marlboro. "Bondage. I'm into . . ."

"Bondage?"

"You know. Tying people up, having them tie me up. Like that." He waited for her reaction; it came slowly: interest.

"Which way do you like it better?"

"Well," Brenner reflected, "mostly I like doing the tying

—but no rough stuff, you know? I only use silk ropes and . . ."

The Blonde had stopped licking the salt off the rim of her Margarita glass to stare at Brenner.

"You're either full of shit or . . ."

"Let him talk," the Raven insisted.

Jonas yawned and tilted his head back against the car headrest. His long legs were drawn up, knees planted on the dashboard.

"If you hadn't started with that kinky stuff," he mildly accused. "We were goin' great."

Brenner kept the car going down the near-empty highway at a steady seventy miles an hour. A road sign identified the inky blackness they were passing as Camp Pendleton, the Marine base.

"Gotta sound 'em out. One way to separate the interior decorators from the schoolteachers." Brenner smiled. "They sure did take off fast."

"It's guys like you who give Hollywood a bad name," Jonas said. "I mean, we were all set . . ."

"Hell, you get nervous just drinking the water down there."

"Gotta take a chance sometimes." Jonas yawned again. "Know what? I think you used to be after cunt more when you were married."

"Pressure's off me now," Brenner said.

They drove in silence with the dashboard lights dimly illuminating their faces. Brenner saw that Jonas was awake, half-closed eyes fixed dully on the highway ahead.

"Suppose Connie found out?"

Jonas grinned. "You mean something happened—and she knew it? She'd cut my balls off. Hang 'em on a chain, just like that old fart was showing us. You weren't much in the mood tonight, were you, Ed?"

"Guess not."

"So we'll get home a little earlier. What the hell?"

By the time they passed San Juan Capistrano, Jonas was snoring softly, slack jaw resting on his chest. Brenner played the radio low. The "Extra Music" station broadcasting from Tijuana. Few commercials, hardly any talk, instrumental tunes only, no identification of the records. Just music. But incomplete snatches of partially remembered lyrics sang in his head. A collage of thoughts that blended with the cone of light revealing the unchanging highway before him; the car was on a treadmill, marking time, until the right road sign would appear and allow them to get off.

". . . I hear laughter in the rain wider than a mile crossing you in style one day by day along the Nile watch the sunrise on a tropic isle and then it couldn't happen again she'll be rising by the time after time I tell myself that I'm Puff the magic dragon lived by the sea . . ."

And the face of the boy crystalized in his mind. Zigzagging through the street traffic tonight, before the bar, they had suddenly been confronted by a feisty nine-year-old boy with a cigarette butt clamped jauntily in his teeth, begging for loose change. Brenner gave him a buck but something jogged his memory. Now he remembered what: Four years ago, after visiting the San Diego Zoo, coming to Tijuana for the afternoon with Phyllis and Mike. Another day, another beggar. Also a kid, a couple years older than Mike, but no bigger in size than him.

"What's wrong, son?"

"Does that guy have to do that?"

"Guess he does."

"Can't you help him?"

Brenner assured Mike the boy-beggar was all right, probably made a lot of money that way, what can you say to a kid? They had continued down the street, Phyllis and he trying to distract Mike. But Mike kept looking back at the boy.

Kids see things we don't, Brenner thought. The face of the boy from long ago was clear to him again now—as clear as the face tonight. Except it was the same face and he knew that wasn't possible.

■.▪.▪.▪.

Once Santa Monica was a thriving resort community, the Atlantic City of the West, a city separate and apart from Los Angeles, reached by railway cars that traveled through fields and groves to the ocean.

It was in those luxuriant, ambitious, sunny days that the adjoining area of Venice, California, was developed and attempted to emulate its namesake. Moorish domes and rococo archways came into being to shelter grocery stores, butcher shops, post offices and restaurants. And a house on the canal was the best of it: Actual gondolas were on the waters then, children frolicked there, women with parasols paused on the footbridges to smile.

Now the waters were bilious. Venice had run down with the years. Some said it was because the Gulf Stream had shifted, cooling the ocean and the weather; but perhaps Venice had simply outlived its time. Even the recent nearby coming of sumptuous, swinging Marina del Rey had failed to restore the style of living along the canal.

Elton Smiley peered out through the curtain of his bedroom window. His sagging wood frame house overlooked the canal in Venice. From where he stood, clad only in his one-piece underwear, the shimmering outline of the moon was on the black waters like a beacon of truth.

Smiley was a squat, gnomelike man of sixty with a prominent jaw accentuated by a bulldog overbite. His eyes were his best feature: hazel with brown flecks—direct and all-seeing. He stared off into the darkness and did not turn when he heard the creaking of bedsprings as his wife, Grace, became aware of his absence.

"Elton . . . ?"

He didn't answer. She knew where he was and why he couldn't sleep.

"You've got to tell them," she said from across the room.

He continued gazing intently off at the black, still waters.

❦

Rank has its privileges. Ramirez put his size elevens up on the desk. After all, it was his desk. The grunt detectives shared space with other shifts. But this was his place. He had come to work thirteen and a half hours ago. Now he was about ready to pack it in for the day.

A good day. Busy. The troops finally got lucky and brought down "The Gentleman Rapist." He had been working one narrow sector of town for several weeks. In fact, nailed the same girl five times. The last midnight he grabbed her in the parking area of her apartment building, she had pleaded:

"Please don't hurt me . . ."

"Have I ever hurt you before, Marie?" he asked.

And today a former victim, shopping in a supermarket, made him: one of the checkers. Been standing right there all along. Like he was waiting for somebody to put the hat on him.

The day's most colorful beef had come from a kennel off Ohio Avenue. Burglary. They trained guard dogs, the Dobermans programed to tear out your throat and liver. Department stores used them at night, used-car lots after closing. Somebody had broken into the kennel and stolen all the dogs; actually, just let them all run loose. Dozens of antisocial, snarling canines reported snapping at the mailman, small kids, old ladies and anything else that moved. It was a mess. Investigating Officer's Suggested Motive: "Guess one of the breaking-and-entering assholes got mad. They know who those guard dogs are supposed to guard against."

And the "R.T.D. Ripper" had been run to ground. Moose-size kid who got on the Wilshire bus yesterday and raised hell. Terrorized the senior citizens aboard, demanding money, breaking windows and finally setting fire to an old man's hair before crashing out. Ramirez was particularly pleased with the apprehending of this sixteen-year-old mini-Ripper. Because it was Ramirez' suggestion:

"Cover the bus. Maybe he'll get on again."

And sure enough. Same time, same place. Continuation School kid. Troublemaker with fourteen previous raps, currently on probation. Big enough to squash you if he sat on you, mean enough to want to sit on you—but still a kid who only knew one way to get home from school.

The process involved in the solution of this case illustrated one of Ramirez' basic approaches to police work. He called it "The Technique of Digging for Apples." Everyone knows, of course, that apples grow on trees. Except maybe the poor slob who's got the job of finding them. So he's out there in the field, digging away. Finding one now and then, usually rotten, but still looking, gradually moving closer, toward the tree, until finally he gets lucky enough to look up and—there it is. Apples.

Ramirez figured that was a good approach: If you expected you'd have to do the job the hard way, you could never be disappointed. And all surprises were pleasant ones.

He reached for his hat on top of the filing cabinet and flicked off a piece of lint. In the days when "The Hats" were riding, Ramirez was young, big and cocky enough to think that it was all simple: that great galloping squad of giants would descend on a situation and, no matter how hinky, it was the situation that would yield, not them.

His reputation as a member of the legendary "Hat Squad" had been useful over the years. But Ramirez had long since pierced his own legend: It wasn't that we were bigger and better, but that we thought we were. That was the secret.

As he rose in rank, Ramirez had imbued this kind of camaraderie and confidence in the men who came to serve under him. The Department ran on paperwork, time cards. Ramirez didn't give a damn who walked in a little late in the morning, but by God, nobody left at night until it was wrapped up.

Try to meddle with the workings of his division and Ramirez was known to slam the phone down on captains, commanders and deputy chiefs and walk out in the middle of the afternoon. Taking the entire squad of detectives with him. To the nearest bar, where Ramirez would buy for everybody and sit in stony silence until he felt he had punished the administrative assholes sufficiently. Ramirez was completely for the cop in the street, because he had never for an instant stopped being one himself.

When he worked, everybody worked. And when he played . . .

It was part of the folklore of the squad room: that Christmas party when Ramirez threw open the lockup and transformed the sole occupant, a car thief, into bartender for the evening. Sundry ladies joined in the merriment. And the bartender got lucky: he hit on the girl of his dreams, a file clerk from Ad-Narc. He mixed an Old Fashioned that melted her heart. She didn't know the bartender was a semiofficial guest. And when it came time to tell her, the car thief threw himself on Ramirez' mercy.

Just let him see the lady home and he'd be right back. An oath, the promise of a man in love.

Ramirez did more than grant the favor. In the yuletide spirit, he gave the car thief the keys to the car. A police car. All would undoubtedly have gone well, but the file clerk was carried away by passion on San Vicente Boulevard. She kissed the driver and grabbed his crotch; he responded by driving into a lamppost. The cop car was totaled, the lamppost drooped across the boulevard like a wisteria bush, but the lovers emerged unscathed. And word of the mishap rapidly reached Ramirez' ears.

Immediately, a rescue team was dispatched. Police cars and tow trucks arrived. The file clerk was sworn to secrecy and seen to her door, her Lothario whisked back to the slammer whence he had officially never left; two uniformed officers rode in with the wreck and filed a triplicate report of a highly imaginative, unsuccessful high-speed chase in pursuit of suspected car thieves that ended not with a bang but a crunch. Merry Christmas!

Ramirez turned off the lights in his office as he went out. He waved at the night-watch dicks as he passed through the squad room and strode flatfooted down the corridor.

The good old days. For him, they were now. Because he had enough time in grade and maintained a solid crime clearance record and a crusty, cantankerous manner he was given a fairly free hand to run his own operation as he saw fit.

Take the Montrose case. Another guy in his spot might just go through the motions. Play the wait-and-see game. Most cases either solved themselves or were forgotten. But not around here. That lead into Tijuana had sounded promising, but the phone call from Brenner and Jonas tied it off; they would have to look somewhere else. Okay. He had the manpower, he could afford to spend the company hours necessary to follow it wherever it went. Some things were worth it, and when there was a kid involved . . .

"What do y'say, Ben?"

Ganzer, in uniform, was relaxing in the doorway near the Booking cage. Ramirez stopped in the corridor.

"How's it going?"

"Bundle of thrills," Ganzer said. "No telling who's gonna come through those doors. Or what treasures their pockets will contain. A wino an hour ago was packing a can of Sterno. Dude last Tuesday had a deck of playing cards made out of porno pictures. I can hardly wait to come on duty each night. Want some coffee?"

He held up his coffee mug.

Ramirez looked at it and shook his head. "Full up, Marty. Thanks." He could smell the steaming brew, heavily laced. Viennese coffee and Irish whiskey, an unbeatable blend.

"What's the magic number?" Ramirez asked.

"One hundred and twenty-three," Ganzer said without hesitation. It was a countdown of days remaining to retirement.

"You can do that standing on your head."

"Just watch me." Ganzer lifted the coffee mug, grinning, and took a big swallow.

The noise preceded them:

"Bitch!"

"Haul ass, freak!"

"Stop your shoving!"

Now they appeared in the corridor: an unlikely-looking trio. There were two longish-haired men in windbreakers, sports shirts and khaki pants. Saidiner was dark, burly, rough; Rooney was platinum blond, boyishly slim. Between the two vice officers was an older man, wearing a denim jacket and matching jeans, dark glasses and a farmer's yellow straw hat. He had flared, elongated white sideburns and he was very unhappy.

"You know what you can do!" he venomously suggested to Saidiner, who smirked.

"Want to show us? Again?"

"And what have we here?" Ganzer asked.

"Fruit of the loom," Rooney said.

"The queen tried to nibble on Rooney's joint in the men's room of the Burger King," Saidiner said.

Ganzer went behind the mesh wiring. He put a brand-new plastic bag on the counter.

"Naughty-naughty," Ganzer said to the aging homosexual.

"Animals! Entrapping people! Why aren't you out solving crimes?"

"Empty your pockets of all personal belongings," Ganzer droned. "We can start with the shades."

The man took off the dark glasses and put them on the counter. He blinked at the icy glare of the fluorescent lighting. His eyes were tired and frightened.

"One pair of sunglasses," Ganzer noted on the form.

Ramirez watched: a good street cop being used as a checkroom attendant. He waved at Ganzer, who nodded as Ramirez moved off.

"Stay loose, Ben," Ganzer called after him.

Ramirez came out into the night, adjusted the hat on his head until the brim was at the proper angle. He found his car in the parking lot.

There was a hot meal waiting for him. He knew that. Evelyn hadn't said anything about it when he phoned just before leaving the office, as was their habit, to let her know he was on his way. No questions as to why he was so late. Just a friendly "Hurry home."

They had been married thirty-one years and he still

looked forward to the smile that would greet him. Together, they had grown old—well, older anyway. The marriage was good. She was there when he needed her, anticipating his moods, worrying only about the small dangers: Did he take the umbrella on a rainy day? Don't forget to stop for lunch! Mothering him. Maybe it was because they never had children of their own. But he had to admit—though never to her—that he enjoyed it.

Ramirez drove carefully down the dark street, away from the building without windows, heading for home.

The pale blue-green water sparkled crystal clear. Sunlight played off the surface of the swimming pool as if a handful of glittering diamonds had been tossed into the air.

Bobby Montrose, wearing a red swim suit, stood in the water up to his knees. He smiled and waved.

"He likes the water," a voice said from the darkness.

They were in the Roll Call Room, but the lights were out. The only sound was the 16-mm projector running the reel of home movies on the screen that had been pulled down from the top of the blackboard.

"There she is—mother of the year."

Brenner turned to see who had spoken. Elgort. He was slumped down in shirtsleeves, curls of smoke from his cigarette undulating up past the white glare of the projector lamp, spiraling toward the ceiling. Brenner looked back at the screen.

Claire Montrose was stretched out on a chaise longue beside the pool. She wore a skimpy bikini and she wore it well. The wavering hand-held amateur camera zoomed closer on Claire and an unheard voice called to her; she looked up through oversized dark glasses from a magazine in her lap and gave a half-hearted don't-bother-me wave and a forced smile, then went back to her reading.

"A sixty-dollar bathing suit that never got wet," Hyatt said.

Now the camera was back on the pool. The tile was immaculate and the water inviting—there was Bobby again.

His hair was shorter, he looked younger and he was still on a step at the shallow end, by himself, playing with an inflated duck. The film jumped and suddenly Harold Montrose appeared—posturing, taking off his beachrobe, striking a Strong Man pose, flexing his muscles and laughing at his own antics.

"Mr. Universe," Jonas said.

"The All-American Asshole," Elgort agreed.

The film jumped again and now Montrose was in the water, up to his chest, waving and gesturing. The camera panned to the side of the pool where Bobby, hair still dry, was being implored to leap into the water—into the waiting arms of his father.

"Pool looked a helluva lot better then," Jonas said.

"When were these taken?" Brenner asked.

"Eight, nine months ago," Hyatt said.

"That was just after they put the pool in," Elgort added.

Bobby had gathered courage and now he plunged; Harold Montrose caught his son and dunked him under the water. The boy came up giggling with pleasure and his father held him—laughing, playing with him.

"How old was Bobby then?" Hyatt said. "Three and a half?"

"These are the last movies they have of him," Elgort said.

Jonas, sitting beside Brenner just in front of the projector, gazed at the screen.

Bobby was climbing out of the water now, running along the decking of the pool to his mother, still on the lounge, smoking and reading the magazine. Claire wrinkled her nose as Bobby dripped on her, but smiled genuinely and wrapped him up in a big beach towel. She rubbed him and laughed and adjusted the towel on his head so that he looked like a little Arab.

"Guess there was a time when they did pay more attention to the kid," Jonas said.

Brenner, watching the screen, shook his head.

"Guess again."

On the screen, the camera was moving off Claire and Bobby in a fairly smooth panning motion—back to a picturesque view of the pool. Empty at first, then a jump to Claire, with every hair in place, standing on the diving board posing. Suddenly she was gone, the diving board deserted—the pool like a resort postcard. The camera explored the pool lingeringly from end to end and then zoomed in on the inflated duck floating alone. The film was running out now, sprocket holes starting to show . . .

Brenner rose irritably and turned. Part of the picture beam ran across the front of his white shirt.

"Don't you see it, guys? It's not the kid they're taking movies of—it's the pool. Taking pictures of their new toy. Before they lost interest in that, too."

At the very last, Bobby reappeared for an instant, flashing across Brenner's shirt. Bobby was sitting poolside, kicking his feet, waving at the camera.

■▪▪■▪

Through the years, the birthday cakes had grown increasingly complex. When Mike was three years old, there had been the Disney cake: Mickey Mouse, Donald Duck and all the gang romping amid the candles. Successive years saw Batman and Robin chasing The Penguin and assorted other villains through the "Happy Birthday" message; a baseball game with nine little fielders and Hank Aaron at bat on a diamond made of icing; and, of course, a Spaceshot replete with rockets and Apollo astronauts who walked on the moonlike surface of the cake.

Phyllis and Ed Brenner used to joke about it when they went to buy the cake each year: Anybody could get his face on a magazine cover, but when you made the birthday cakes—that's famous!

This year the cake was a simple one. Big and white, but no elaborate motif. Mike had declared "That stuff is babyish" and Phyllis respected his request: frosting, "Happy Birthday, Mike!" and nine candles, plus one for good luck. That was it.

The kids were noisy and Phyllis was glad for the abundance of sounds and the demands of the occasion: stringing the bunting and balloons, pouring the Kool-Aid, mopping up the spills, serving the hot dogs and potato chips, ice cream and cake. The frantic activity kept her from dwelling on the fact that this was the first birthday party for Mike since they had stopped being a family.

A couple of the other mothers stayed for coffee and they helped guide the party. It followed the pattern Phyllis and Ed had evolved together. Start them off in the yard, playing games: "Simple Simon," "Red Light, Green Light," relay matches—games to burn off some of that boundless energy a dozen small boys possess. Then serve the food, bring on the cake, make a wish and blow out the candles. Everybody out of the kitchen into the family room, sit on the floor and tear open the presents.

It was the usual yelling, shoving, pleading contest: "Me first!" "Open *my* present now!" "Ohhhh, lemme see!" "That's neat!" "Here, this one, open this one . . ." and

Phyllis collecting the ripped wrappings and prompting: "Read the card, Mike, tell who it's from."

But she didn't prompt when he tore off the paper on the big box. She knew who that one was from; she had taken it from the closet and added it to the pile herself.

The boys chorused approval of all the gifts, but this one got a special reception. An elaborate set of mechanical cars and a color picture showing them in action on the raceway of ramps included inside.

"Hot wheels, wow!" Mike beamed.

This time it was one of the other kids who asked: "Who's it from?"

Mike found the card. "It's from . . . my dad." He looked funny—sort of surprised, almost. Then he smiled his pleasure.

"Isn't that terrific?" Phyllis called to Mike. "Maybe you guys want to set up and play with it now."

The suggestion was a popular one; in a matter of moments, the family room was a web of ramps. Indianapolis speedway on the carpet, in and around the furniture. The kids were enthralled. At first they let Mike control the operation, but pretty soon the cries of "Can I?" "Gimme a chance, huh?" were answered. They were crowding each other, playing with the set of cars, and Phyllis had just returned from the kitchen with a fresh cup of coffee. She looked around for Mike and found him standing silently beside her.

"Nice party?" she asked.

He nodded. Looking off at the kids enjoying his game. One of the zippy little cars shot off the ramp on a turn and hit the wall. The boys cheered.

"Know what I wished? When I blew out the candles? That dad was still living here."

Mike looked up at her. Really looking. He's testing, she thought.

"Now I told the wish. Guess it won't come true," Mike added matter-of-factly.

He went to rejoin the game. Soon he looked as jubilant and carefree as any of the other boys, but Phyllis sipped her coffee and continued to watch.

■▪▪▪▪

"You look gloomy, Brenner."

Ramirez came up to the desk in the squad room as jaunty as if he had won the Sweepstakes. Always up. The guy must go off in a closet by himself to be sad, Brenner thought.

"So you ran your butts off chasing a hot lead that went nowhere." Ramirez perched as usual on the edge of the desk and mooched a Marlboro.

"That's what we did, all right," Jonas said. And then, to start the day off in bang-up fashion, they had checked two more ex-molesters off the list: Jonas' least favorite pastime.

"Time to worry is when we run out of possibilities." Ramirez gestured at his office. "Come on in, I want you to meet somebody."

"This something interesting?" Brenner asked as they walked with Ramirez.

"Maybe. Man says he knows where the boy is . . ."

Elton Smiley stood before the street map on the wall of Ramirez' office. But for the faded forest-green sports jacket, he was wearing his perennial uniform: hiking boots, tan work pants, short-sleeved white shirt with a Western drawstring tie boasting a turquoise stone clasp. His right hand floated over the surface of the map area not far from where the Montrose house was located.

"He's about here," he said and turned to look at them. Brenner was seated closest, Jonas in a chair behind him. Ramirez leaned against the edge of his own desk.

"That's where Bobby is." Smiley's voice was nasal, mid-western, but confident and certain. "That's what the first call said."

Brenner uncapped his pen and pulled a note pad on the desk to him.

"At first," Smiley remembered, "I didn't know what to do—what it meant. So I didn't do anything until the second call came. By then I'd seen the TV news about little Bobby, so I understood and I contacted the lieutenant."

Smiley looked at Ramirez, who nodded encouragingly.

"Calls—from who?" Brenner asked. He had started taking notes.

"That's difficult to say. I've never been able to trace the calls. They just come to me. Sometimes when I'm sleeping, usually when I'm alone, but hardly ever as clearly as this one."

His eyes were fantastic: riveting, bottomless. The ugly little man seemed to grow larger—formidable. Jonas leaned forward tentatively.

"You're talking about—visions?"

Smiley nodded. Now they understood.

"Visions? Yes, I suppose—in the sense that certain people can see things where others cannot."

"And you're one of those people," Brenner said slowly.

"It's a gift. What I do most of the time is, I help people find water. I've had a lot of success where the geologists have failed. They don't think there's anything there. But I come—people listen to me. And I find it."

Brenner looked around. Jonas was leaning his chair back on two legs, eyes half-shut. But Ramirez' expression hadn't changed: polite patience.

"Hey, fellas," Brenner said, "we got water. What we're missing is a kid." He capped his pen and tossed it on top of the pad.

Smiley was busy. He lifted a battered black custom-made case onto the desk. There was a key ring on his belt that extended on a spring wire; he selected a key that unlocked the case and then unfastened the clasps.

Jonas wouldn't look, but Brenner and Ramirez watched as Smiley revealed the purple velvet lining; he lifted the divider and there, like the crown jewels, resting in a fitted recess on a foam-rubber mounting was a thin, well-worn, Y-shaped tree branch. The bark had been sanded away and the wood was pale white.

Elton Smiley touched the dowsing rod. "Sometimes I can find other things," Smiley assured them. "It's my gift."

The sun was a shimmering glare sending down waves of wet heat. On the hillside, the vegetation was brown and burnt, bushes and weeds that had sprung up unnoticed and uncared for—but serving a purpose: roots binding the slopes and inclines of Los Angeles' mountains together, minimizing the destructive force of the rainy season mudslides.

But today the air was still and heavy. And the earth was parched. The sticky-sweet stench of dying plant life filled the throats of Brenner and Jonas as they awaited a miracle.

Elton Smiley stood alone.

His eyes were closed and his hands clasped the divided end of the rod, with the pointer held at chest height, parallel with the ground.

The tip of the stick began to vibrate now, as if responding to the pulls of a force field. This way, that way, then . . .

Smiley's eyes opened very wide. But trancelike, unseeing. He began to move, awkwardly, almost falling forward, following the tug of the divining rod.

Brenner and Jonas exchanged glances and then picked up the shovels they had brought. In the distance behind, houses were visible. They were moving farther away from them, up the hillside into thicker brush. Now they picked up their pace, because Smiley started to run.

He was incredibly swift and sure-footed. The power of the rod led Smiley on—faster and faster—threading his course upward . . . unblinking, unfocused, the whites of his eyes showing, his short legs pumping—onward—ever closer . . .

Behind him, Brenner and Jonas paused to gasp for breath.

"He's a—goddamn—galloping—gazelle!" Brenner said.

Jonas, wheezing, hanging on his shovel, pointed: "Look!"

Elton Smiley was outlined against the sky. He had achieved the crest of the hill above them and stopped. His eyes were tightly closed again, face contorted with the intensity of his concentration. Again, the rod was quivering, dancing in his hands—responding to an invisible force. And then . . .

The divining rod suddenly plunged downward—pointing at the ground.

"Here!" Elton Smiley's eyes popped open. "He's here!"

Brenner and Jonas ran, stumbling, up to where Smiley was poised. And as they reached him they looked down at nothing. Just another piece of packed, arid soil. But Smiley's hands holding the stick were rock-solid, designating this specific spot on earth. His eyes were closed again.

"Dig. *Here!*" he pronounced solemnly.

There was no sign that the ground had been disturbed here recently; no indication of anything buried beneath the surface. Brenner and Jonas looked at each other and—what the hell? Jonas stepped forward with his shovel and gave the first thrust. The ground was so hard, the shovel bounced—barely chipping the soil.

Brenner took off his jacket. They had been through it

with Ramirez: Once a case like this hit the media, it brought out every fucked-up fruitcake who owned a TV set. But Ramirez' policy was to follow all leads—that meant *all*. And in the back of their minds was the memory of the "Boston Strangler" investigation and the clairvoyant who did see things and nobody would listen. So here they were . . .

The hole was waist deep. Brenner and Jonas were both inside of it, still tossing out shovels full of dirt. Smiley was above them maintaining his vigil. A statue, unmoving, scarcely breathing, not perspiring despite the oppressive heat—the dowsing rod fixed, frozen in its bird-dog insistence that this was the place.

Jonas mopped his face with a handkerchief. His hair was stringy and wilted, revealing his baldness. "Nothing here," he called up. "Mr. Smiley, I said there's . . ."

Brenner stopped digging as the divining rod came to life. It began to pulsate again and Smiley's glazed eyes snapped open. The rod took off with Smiley in tow behind it. Brenner and Jonas watched him go.

"I don't believe this," Brenner said.

They climbed up out of the hole and started to pick up their jackets and shovels. It was then they heard:

"Here! Dig here!"

The hillside had become a battleground. Land that had lain fallow and untouched by man now had felt his hand. It was a Vietnam scene: a suspected enemy emplacement after it was clobbered by artillery. The hillside was pockmarked with scattered, patternless craters. Hole after hole after hole . . .

And Elton Smiley marched on, his dowsing rod taking him forward.

A distance behind Smiley, Brenner and Jonas trudged with their shovels. They were sweaty, dirty, their clothes clung to them, the bushes tore at them, but they were too tired to care.

"I knew it . . ." Brenner swatted at a mosquito.

"Knew what?" Jonas said.

"Kid's not here—Bobby's still alive."

"For sure. Bet this son-of-a-bitch can't even find water." Jonas stopped. "Uh-oh . . ."

Up ahead, Smiley had found a brand-new spot. He went into his number again: eyes closed, face scrunched devoutly, giving birth to the discovery—down went the dowsing rod.

"Dig—*here!*" he commanded.

Brenner and Jonas had been leaning heavily on their shovels, watching the ceremony. Now, as Smiley stood transfixed with the pointer aimed at the ground, Brenner tapped him on the shoulder.

There was no response.

Brenner tapped again. Harder.

Now the closed eyes popped open.

"*You* dig." Brenner thrust his shovel at him. "*Here!*"

Smiley looked at Brenner, then at Jonas. Something told him he better . . .

Elton Smiley took the shovel and began to dig.

The car moved slowly, the driver scanning the streets carefully as he cruised the neighborhood. Now the car came around the corner and at once he spotted the small boy sitting alone on the curb in front of the house.

The boy was very still, hands on his knees, watching the car come closer—slowing—stopping beside him.

Brenner rolled the window down.

The boy stood up. He was wearing his going-out clothes: clean jeans without patched knees, polo shirt, and his best sneakers.

"Hi," Mike said tentatively. Brenner looked for even the suggestion of a smile to match his own, but there was only that level, steady gaze.

"All set?" Brenner asked.

"Sure."

"I better tell her we're going."

Brenner pulled the car farther up the driveway and got out. As he went toward the front door, he looked back.

Mike was climbing into the front seat, slamming the passenger door, settling down.

Phyllis came out before he reached the door.

"Thought I heard you," she said. "Right on time."

"That's what I thought." He had come into the area fifteen minutes early and had been idly touring the familiar streets in order to drive up exactly at the appointed hour.

"How long's he been sitting out there?" Brenner asked.

"Couple of hours. I told him not to."

"Why's he do that, Phyl?"

"Gets excited—on the days you're coming."

Brenner shrugged, glancing at the car. "Sure covers it good when I get here."

"Just like his father." She said it with a smile, but it still made a bump in the conversation. Brenner could ask what she meant, or—he let it pass.

"Okay. Well, we'll see you later."

"Have a nice day." She waved and called to her son. " 'Bye, Mike!"

Brenner got back into the car. He turned on the ignition, started to back out slowly. Mike silently watched every movement.

Phyllis was still at the front door. She waved again as the car drove away. For an instant she had thought of telling him about Mike's birthday wish. Actually, she meant to mention it the other night when Ed phoned to find out how the party went. But it didn't seem to work into the talk then, and now she decided to leave it up to Mike: He could tell his father if he wanted to.

He was lying face down in the bilge water when the priest and the blonde girl in the thin winter coat rushed down. He had been savagely beaten by the men. They knelt and turned his face upward. It was bloody, dazed.

"Terry . . . ?"

The eyes fluttered open. And the priest explained it to him: The longshoremen were waiting, they would follow him in and gangster rule would be broken at last on the waterfront.

"You hear that, Terry?"

"What—I have to do?"

"Walk. Can you walk? To the pier . . ."

"And we'll walk in with you!" one of the dock workers called.

Terry struggled and they helped him.

"How're you doin'?" the priest said.

"Am I on my feet?" Terry asked.

"You're on your feet," the priest told him. "Finish what you started."

"Okay—okay. Gimme that hook."

They handed Marlon Brando the cargo hook. Folded his fingers around it—and the hook dangled limply at his side.

"In God's name," the blonde cried out, "what are you tryin' to do to him?"

"You can," the priest urged. "You can . . ."

Marlon Brando stumbled up onto the dock and began to stagger toward the cavernous door leading onto the pier. The fat shipowner's representative in the expensive suit, with the big cigar, was there in the open door. That was the finish line—up there—so far away.

He swayed down the path they had made for him. He was cradling the cargo hook to his chest now, holding himself together with his own hands—one wavering step at a time.

The music was pounding and the audience was silent. Brenner glanced at Mike beside him; the boy seemed totally absorbed. And Brenner looked back at the theater screen.

■ ■ ■

They walked out of the black-and-white darkness of the Hoboken docks into California sunshine and the striking modern architectural design of the County Museum of Art. On the plaza level there were strollers and free-form steel sculpture overlooking a fountain geysering in the center of a moat that half surrounded the building. Someone had tossed a box of Tide into the moat and a layer of soap suds was rapidly spreading on the waters. Lovers walked hand in hand, ignoring the proliferating mess; kids clung to the rails above admiring the foam; and Wilshire Boulevard traffic streamed by thirty yards away, unaware of the bubbles rising festively toward the sky.

Brenner had spotted the retrospective showing of the old movie classic in the paper that morning. Taking Mike to the movies had always been something special for them. Rather than relying on TV, Brenner had sought out revival showings of pictures that he liked as a child. *Gunga Din, The Flame and the Arrow, High Noon.* Once, when Mike was five, he took him to see a picture Brenner had always heard about. *Wings.* Only after they were inside the theater did he discover that the movie was a "silent." But he held Mike in his lap throughout the showing, reading the title cards softly in the boy's ear, and to this day Mike remembered the movie as a "talkie."

Going to the movies had been an event. But since the divorce, even that had changed.

They bought some potato chips in the museum cafeteria and walked across the plaza munching on them. Brenner asked Mike what he thought of *On the Waterfront.*

"It was okay," he said. And then dropped it. Brenner didn't know what he wanted the boy to say, but that wasn't it.

". . . so Tim broke his skateboard, just the back wheel. I had an extra couple wheels, so I told Tim he could have 'em. So he goes, 'Really? Hey, I . . .'"

"Who's this Tim?" Brenner interrupted.

"Tim! You know Tim . . ." Mike looked up at him and then away, realizing. "Oh, yeah. I guess you don't know him."

There were more and more new names cropping up. Links that weren't shared. Tiny inadvertent reminders of separation. Of the gradual process of becoming strangers.

"Well, what about Tim?"

Mike shrugged and chewed another potato chip. "Nothin'. It was, you know, just—he fixed his skateboard. And like that . . ."

Brenner waited. There was no more. "That's good," he said. "Tim sounds like a nice guy."

▪▪▪▪▪

"Look at yourself, Norm."

Jonas did and saw himself reflected in the three-way mirror in the men's department of Bullock's. The sports coat fitted him well.

"I don't want another jacket," he said to Connie. There were three of her in the mirror, too, each one prettier than the other: She was petite but beautifully formed, a perfect little figure that having two daughters had not disturbed. Honey-blonde hair worn short and girlish, a ready smile and a bossy way that he adored. She wasn't much more than half his size and they formed a Mutt and Jeff team that evened out delightfully in bed. And she enjoyed dressing him up.

"You never need clothes until the old ones fall off you." Connie tugged at the back of the coat, smoothing out the folds. "It looks good on you."

The Van Nuys department store was crowded with Saturday afternoon customers. That morning Connie had announced they were going shopping for the girls, but on arrival she had nimbly dropped off Nancy and Joan in the teen department and guided Norm here.

She paid for the sports coat with a store credit card and the salesman punched up the transaction on the electronic computer register that automatically entered all the pertinent information somewhere or other. The console made sounds, flashed digital lights and typed automatically. The salesman was very nonchalant about the whole thing, like the Wizard of Oz behind the curtain, working his mumbo-jumbo machine.

"Sign here please, Mrs. Jonas," the salesman said. Apparently the machine approved of them.

In the teen department, Connie found a seat near the dressing rooms and parked him. Both girls had an armful of possibles. Connie disappeared into the little cubbyholes with them and soon they began to reappear.

Jonas leaned back contentedly in the chair. It was his private fashion show. First Nancy, then Joan, then Nancy again—pretty colors and fabrics, skirts and tops and sweaters and dresses.

They both resembled Connie. Small, nearly tiny. Same fair coloring, light hair, blue eyes. Occasionally Connie would detect a fleeting expression on one of their faces and say, "Just like daddy." That he never saw it. And he was glad.

"My face on a girl?" he would tell Connie. "Bad enough I've got to wear it."

And that was her cue to tell Jonas that he underrated his appearance. "You're a very attractive man." He knew he wasn't—but to her he was and now there were two smaller replicas of Connie and they both would gaze up at him with the same slightly wrinkled brows over the lovely happy faces.

As usual, they had eliminated all the things they had

chosen to try on. Shopping was its own enjoyment. He had found that out long ago with Connie.

They walked together toward the street. Time for a late lunch in the coffee shop and then more shopping. Lately, with the pressure on to find the guy who raped little Vickie Weston, followed immediately by the search for Bobby Montrose, he hadn't seen much of his own family. He knew it bothered Connie. After the Tijuana trip she even said something:

"I know it's important, looking for that poor boy. But your own kids are important, too."

And that was it. No nagging. Just mentioned it once. And that's why today was good.

Jonas caught a glimpse in the glass of the showcase window outside as they passed. Three dainty little porcelain dolls accompanied by a hulking, powerful man—all right, maybe a little overweight—towering protectively over them. It was very nice.

░░░░

Brenner and Mike bought ice cream bars at the Good Humor wagon and looked through the fence at the animals. A dinosaur. That was the only one Brenner knew by name: a thirty-foot-long, fifteen-foot-high super-lizard. The other models he knew by sight. One was like a monster elephant with tusks that wouldn't quit. And some kind of huge bat with razor teeth. They were all in a simulated nature scene, gathering near a watering place.

The prehistoric models had been here in the park before the adjoining museum was built. And once, in an incredible other time, the actual beasts roamed here. Mike and Brenner had just come from the small circular shelter where the last of the LaBrea tarpits were preserved.

Brenner read the signs on the wall aloud, as if to himself, actually trying to capture Mike's interest. And they had looked down at the sump of tar that didn't seem like much by itself but it was still bubbling and cooling the way it had a hundred thousand years ago. The story had been pieced together from fossil remains: swampland; great, indestructible creatures coming for water and after they drank—unable to escape.

"They got stuck?"

"That's what happened, Mike."

The boy nodded. Now, at the fence, he looked up at the reconstructed models.

"Pretty big guys, huh?"

Mike shrugged and went on eating his ice cream. They climbed the steps back up onto the museum plaza and stopped to watch a young guy in white face and white clothes practicing mime. He had attracted a small group of passers-by and was conjuring up a flower plucking and sniffing scene—now he ate the invisible flower. Three little kids sitting on the ground up front giggled.

There was a broken top hat in the center of the play area —for donations.

The mime was pretending to be a mechanical man, walking tick-tock fashion up to members of his audience, staring with blank and eyes into their faces, smile on, smile off, holding out his palm to shake hands, suddenly about-face and tick-tock away—up to Mike.

But Mike wouldn't play. Brenner's smile faded as he saw: Mike was scared. Brenner took his son's hand and led him away, tossing some coins in the hat as they went.

"That guy's—weird," Mike said. "Why's he do that?"

"It's kind of a joke. Like a clown."

"Clowns are funny."

Brenner saw the outdoor phone.

"Hold on a second." He fished out a dime and went

over to the phone. Mike waited close by, working on his ice cream bar, while Brenner dialed. Then, as Brenner started to talk, the boy took the opportunity while Brenner was partially turned, focused on the call, to study his father's face. Abruptly, Brenner hung up and Mike quickly looked away.

"Okay." Brenner rejoined Mike.

"Thought it was your day off."

"It is. Just wanted to check. There's this thing. Kid who got lost."

They started to walk again, licking at their melting ice cream.

"That's what you're working on now?"

"Yeah."

Mike began slow. "In the movies—when Clint Eastwood's a cop. There's always all these guys trying to kill him."

"That's in the movies." Thank you, Dirty Harry, teacher of the young.

"Not for real?" Mike asked.

Brenner darted a glance at the boy. Was this what it was all about? What was the kid really asking? Am I going to come home from school some afternoon and they're going to tell me you're dead? Brenner shook his head casually and took a bite of ice cream.

"Not for real," he said.

"That's good," Mike said.

They were walking up the street away from the museum, away from the park.

"What's the worst thing ever happened to you—as a cop?"

Brenner grinned. "Mike, buddy—I'm eating."

"Sorry, didn't mean to . . ."

"It's okay." He meant it as a gag, but the boy took it as a squelch. Brenner tried to restore the moment.

"Worst thing ever happened to me as a cop? Let me see— Well, one time I was chasing this guy, see, *and*—I got a flat tire on the freeway."

"That's the *worst* thing?" Mike chortled with delight.

"Yeah. So far . . ."

It was the law in the State of California. If a pedestrian stepped off the curb, the cars had to stop. Definitely when the pedestrian was in a marked crosswalk, but even if a person jaywalked or strolled out in the middle of the block. Out-of-state motorists, accustomed to bullfight-arena rules of the road, found it hard to accept. But the logic of the law was unassailable: Dented people could not be pounded out and touched up as quickly as dented fenders.

Brenner was in a hurry, but he stopped at the unmarked corner for the girl. She looked eighteen and was probably sixteen. Long, straight chestnut hair and a long, sensual body. She wore sandals, fitted pants and a tight T-shirt that outlined up-tilted full breasts. Her nipples were showing through the thin fabric under the emblazoned message: "My Body Belongs To Me!" Smaller letters beneath added: "But I share . . ."

The girl sauntered out from one curb to the other. When

she was directly in front of Brenner's car she paused to flash a promising smile at him through the windshield and she held up her hand, thumb out, in the hitchhiker's going-my-way gesture.

Brenner smiled back at her and shook his head slowly. He was turning in two blocks.

Her eyes continued to beam mockingly. But she stuck her tongue out at him. The effect was simultaneously erotic and childlike.

Inside the car, Brenner laughed out loud and appreciatively watched her body as she continued to the sidewalk. He rolled on but in his rear-view mirror he could see her on the corner, thumbing. Not for long. A car was stopping for her and she was opening a door.

Brenner made his turn east.

Ganzer had a booth and a cup of coffee. Brenner slipped in beside him. Ganzer put down the morning newspaper and flicked his cigar ash into the ashtray.

"Any trouble finding the place?"

"Just traffic and I got a slow start. Didn't fall asleep until late and then I went right through the alarm," Brenner said.

"Tell me about it. That's why I work nights now." He signaled for the waitress, who brought menus. The restaurant was new but a typical franchise coffee shop not far from the West L.A. station.

"They all look alike, don't they? These places," Ganzer said. "Even the names. Huff's, Biff's, Mac's, Jack's, Carl's, Bob's, Norm's. Like it's one guy who runs them all— maybe he's got a whole bunch of sons and he names each joint after another one of 'em."

"Yeah," Brenner said. "Whatever happened to Pop's Café, Good Eats Our Specialty?"

"You made up your mind?" The waitress had returned.

"Sure have, honey," Ganzer said. "But we're going to eat here anyway."

Brenner asked for pancakes, Ganzer went for eggs. She poured coffee for Brenner, filled Ganzer's cup again and went off to deliver the order to the cook.

"So how the hell are you?" Ganzer gripped the cigar in the side of his jaw and grinned the way he always did. Brenner pointed at the cigar.

"You know, if a horse ate one of those things, it'd kill him."

"Then he better smoke it instead," Ganzer answered and they both chuckled. It was an old gag between them.

They had been running into each other in the halls and parking lot for weeks and saying they ought to get together. Now they were doing it. Ganzer had just come off duty, Brenner was due on in a half hour.

"Last couple times I saw you," Ganzer said, "you got me worried."

"How's that?"

"Nothing you did, just—I heard you're still crashing in some lousy motel."

"That's right."

"Why don't you get out of there, kid? Find yourself a nice apartment, someplace that's yours."

"Motel room's mine. Number eleven. Want me to show you the key?"

"Nobody likes a smartass. Didn't I teach you that?" He looked at Brenner. "I know where you are, Ed. I been there."

"I'm okay."

Ganzer puffed on the cigar. "Whatever you say."

The waitress brought the food and they began to eat.

"How're your kids?" Brenner asked.

"Terrific. All those years holding the marriage together

for them—my getting divorced was the best thing ever happened. For them, too. Improved my relationship with both boys. Ronnie's finishing law school next June, you know. And Wally, I'm over there and his wife cooks me dinner every week or so. I was scared they'd, you know, take sides or something. But it's cool—I like 'em and I still get respect from them."

"Or you'll kick ass?"

Ganzer smiled. "You know me."

"What're you planning after you pull the pin?"

"Take the car, go up north. Oregon. Throw a hook in the river and stay there till the fish are tired of looking at me."

"And after that?"

"Who knows? The Department pension goes wherever I do. I'm about to be a man of independent means."

▪▪▪▪

Brenner slammed the filing-cabinet drawer shut and carried the folders he had extracted across the bustling, noisy squad room. He sat down at his desk and started to open the top folder.

Jonas was across the way talking to a plainclothesman Brenner vaguely knew; he was dressed like one of the street people and Brenner remembered he was with Administrative-Narcotics Division.

"Ed?" Brenner looked up at Jonas. "You better hear this."

Brenner got up and went over to them.

"You know Lou Himes, don't you?"

"Sure." Brenner nodded hello. "How you doin'?"

"So-so," Himes said. He sounded like he had a cold and he blew his nose in a Kleenex. "Just telling Jonas, there's a thing we've been checking out for a while. Nothing nailed down yet, but you might be interested."

"A narcotics thing?" Brenner said. "We're on . . ."
Jonas interrupted. "Ed, he knows what we're on."

The playroom was red and betrayed the stylized hand of an interior decorator as surely as the gold-and-white living room. There was embossed red flocking on the walls and deep pile scarlet carpeting on the floor. Ripples of light from the pool outside the sliding glass door formed moving lines on the ceiling, which had been painted red.

Beyond a doubt, it was a playroom. An old potbelly stove served as a color TV stand, there was a penny gumball machine on the fireplace mantel, a set of valuable vintage toy trains out of reach on shelving, and a genuine wooden Indian standing stolidly in the corner. Original Coca-Cola and Burma Shave signs adorned the walls. The center of the room was dominated by an expensive antique pool table with ornate pockets and claw feet. There was a huge Tiffany lamp hanging over the table.

"I don't think I understand what you're getting at." Harold Montrose chalked a cue and lined up his shot.

Brenner and Jonas were on the other side of the pool table, watching him.

"We asked you before about business associates," Jonas said. "You know, competitors, enemies . . ."

"And I told you to forget it," Montrose said briskly. "Nothing there."

Montrose made his shot easily. But what was more important, the cue ball ended up where he wanted it. A good player, Montrose knew, always positioned himself for the next shot—and the one after that.

"You mean, in your plastics business," Brenner said.

Montrose tightened his grip on the cue. But he smiled at them. "What other business did you have in mind?"

He moved around the table for his next setup. Jonas

made room for Montrose, who leaned over the table with his back half turned away.

"This is very unusual, Mr. Montrose. Ordinarily, we would never mention this, but because of the importance we all attach to the search for your son . . ."

Jonas was very uncomfortable. Montrose didn't know why, but he assumed it was a sign of weakness.

"Cut the conversation," Montrose said. "Bottom line— let's hear it."

Jonas' face flushed slightly. Montrose saw he had judged wrong: not weakness, but the effort to contain anger. It was the other one who came on now. Flat, quiet, watching for a reaction:

"We have information that you've been trafficking in pills," Brenner said. "Bringing 'em in from South America."

"What sort of pills?" Montrose seemed calm.

"Speed," Brenner said. "Amphetamines."

"I suppose," Montrose began righteously, "you're ready to substantiate what you're . . ."

"Look, buddy!" Brenner's voice rose. "We're asking you—does this have any connection with Bobby's disappearance?"

Somewhere in the house a phone rang—once, twice then stopped.

"Any 'connection'?" Montrose repeated with a harsh chuckle. Shitheel cops making believe they're Popeye Doyle. "Is that supposed to be funny?"

Jonas frowned and sucked in breath to cool his frustration.

"I'm in the plastics business! If you've got proof of anything else . . ."

"Hey!" Brenner was as loud as Montrose. "We're not interested in anything else! We may have blown several

months of another division's investigation by just mention-
it, but we're . . ."

Now Montrose's smile was real. Fuck it, he had them, he
knew it.

"Then you admit you don't have any proof, you just
come in here and . . ."

Before he could complete his injured-citizen declaration,
the door to the kitchen was thrown open.

Claire Montrose rushed into the room.

"Harold!" She was shaking. "The phone—they just
called—Bobby! They've got him!"

Jonas had been bent over the pool table, hands tightly
clenching the rim. Now he straightened in surprise to his
full height and looked at Brenner, who was staring at
Claire.

"Who?" Montrose said in confusion. "Who called?"

"I don't know. They'll—they said they'll phone again.
With instructions." She was gasping out the words. "They
want money—twenty thousand dollars."

Relief flickered across Brenner's face. Jonas saw it and
nodded.

"But Bobby's alive," Claire Montrose told her husband,
trembling joyfully. "He's alive!"

The phone was ringing. In another city, there would have been pedestrians to answer it. But although it was the middle of the day and Wilshire Boulevard traffic honked and screeched in full flow, there was no one on foot to hear the ringing.

It was an outdoor plastic telephone pod near a boarded independent gas station that had gone out of business during the first big energy crunch. A vengeful joker had left the price markings posted: Premium 29.9 Regular 26.9.

The gold Cadillac pulled out of the traffic and into the station, parking at the abandoned pumps. Montrose heard the ringing even before he threw open the car door and ran for the phone. It was hot and dry, the fire season had not found relief in rain yet, and like most Septembers this one had brought the stale-tasting Santa Ana winds. Montrose carried a large brown Von's Supermarket shopping bag that he had stapled shut, according to instructions. Inside the bag, there was twenty thousand dollars in used bills, all fives, tens and twenties.

He was sweating. Not the languid perspiration that came from dozing on a chaise beside a sunlit pool or the delicious sticky-sliding comingling of perfumed and cologned scents that a matinee performance of pumping and biting and sucking and groping produced. This was sweat. Liquid fear staining his armpits, trickling in acrid warm rivulets down his chest and belly, soaking damp spots onto the front of his blue chambray shirt. Montrose hated the sensation and he despised the voice that he prayed would be on the other end of the phone as he fumbled the receiver off the hook.

"Hello? Hello! Are you there?"

"Where the fuck were you? I was going to hang up." The voice was familiar by now. High-pitched and annoying. Giving him orders. Montrose had formed a mental image: a gawky faggot freak—telling him what to do.

"There was traffic, I missed the lights." Montrose loathed the whining sound of himself.

The voice interrupted.

"Hey, daddy. Listen to me! You want your kid to stay alive?"

"Yes. Of course, yes . . ."

"Well, I've got hold of his tiny little pecker right now and I'm gonna rip it off. Yeah! I'm gonna cut Bobby's cute little balls off, you hear me?" Montrose couldn't answer. *"You hear me?"*

"Yes . . ." Choked. Sweat like tears running from his brow down into his eyes. Burning.

"I've got the razor in my hand! I think I'll just carve me a little blue eye right out of his head and flush it down the fucking toilet! You want me to do that? *Do you?"*

"No-o-o-o, I . . ." It took place before Montrose knew what was happening. The bitter lump in his gut rose with surprising, retching swiftness. Montrose began to puke, yellow-green vomit spewing over the phone, splashing his clothes as Montrose clutched his chest and heaved uncontrollably.

"What are you doing, you son-of-a-bitch?" the voice wanted to know. "Montrose, listen to me!"

Montrose swallowed, gulping air and bile, panting with the effort, forcing himself to speak. "Don't, please, don't hurt him."

"You want me to have that money?"

"I do . . . !"

"Then here's the next step. Look over your shoulder." Montrose did that. "You see the bus coming?"

The Rapid Transit bus was a block away.

"Get on it, Montrose, and bring me my money or I'll give your kid back to you in little pieces."

Montrose heard the rest of the instructions, bobbing his head on every word as if to convince his unseen tormentor that he would do exactly as told. Now the click at the other end signaled dismissal. Montrose hung up and ran for the bus. There were no other riders waiting on the corner, so the driver had not opened the front doors. Montrose pounded heavily with his fist. He could not miss this bus and it seemed about to roll on without him.

The doors opened and he climbed aboard, cradling the brown paper bag in his arms like it was a child. He dropped coins in the box and swayed as the bus lurched forward. Montrose walked down the aisle to the rear and found a seat. He had never been on a bus in Los Angeles before. Only the aged, infirm and indigent rode the buses. Filing clerks, cleaning women and college students. Those too poor to own a car or otherwise unable to drive. Maids and muggers. They rode together with drivers who were frightened of everybody. Only Exact Change, the sign up front read. Driver Does Not Carry Change and Cannot Open Cash Box.

Montrose remembered the sound of Bobby's voice.

"Bus." Pride of discovery. Of accomplishment. *"Bus!"* The child had been a very late talker. When he was a little over a year old, they had consulted the pediatrician and despite his assurances that Bobby would talk when he was ready they were considering specialists. Their beautiful golden child was flawed, perhaps retarded, they had become sure of it. Then along on a Sunday drive up to Malibu to visit an important buyer, Bobby had pointed out the window at a passing Greyhound and spoken. The first word uttered by a child is supposed to be "mama" or "dada," but Bobby's was "bus." In honor of a favorite TV cartoon show he had been in the habit of watching, starring a talking bus. After that the boy was a chatterbox, talking and talking; Montrose wished he could hear him now.

The heavyset black woman across the aisle was staring at him. There was no telling how many of them there were. Could she be one? Montrose turned away from her, then saw out of the corner of his eye that she was rising. He stared up: The woman had covered her nose with a handkerchief and she moved to another seat. Montrose realized that what she smelled was him. He took out his white handkerchief and began to rub at the vomit splatter on his clothes; the suit wasn't bad, the shoes were the worst.

He bent over to reach them. The stench was thick in his nostrils—and the rage, a flood of blind all-encompassing anger. Hating the man who was doing this to him and the people on the bus for being witnesses to his humiliation and Claire for allowing it to happen through her negligence and—and—he began to gag again as a wave of revulsion swept over him. He pushed the thought back out of sight, but it re-emerged: He was angry. At Bobby. For all this.

He felt shame at what he was thinking, but the anger was still there.

Montrose balled up the ruined handkerchief and tossed it under the bus seat. He leaned back and looked out the window. They were passing through Beverly Hills now. The voice had eyes, it could see him. But there were other eyes. He couldn't see them, but Montrose knew they were out there somewhere. Following. Watching. They had to be there, they had promised him they would be there.

"From phone booth to phone booth, all over town, now onto a bus?" Jonas was at the wheel of the blue Chevrolet. The top of the bus towered over the roofs of the cars a half block ahead.

"We got a tap dancer, Norm," Brenner said. "Real fancy."

"They waited almost two weeks before they even called. Why so long?"

"Bashful." Brenner shrugged, scrutinizing the passengers getting off the bus at the corner of Linden Drive. A big black broad and two preteen girls wearing parochial school skirts and blouses. Montrose was still on board. "Maybe they wanted to make 'em sweat."

"Well. It sure worked with Montrose." From a distance, they had both seen Montrose get sick in the phone booth. "Soften 'em up so they pay easier, that's probably it." The bus was passing the Beverly Hilton now, heading out of Beverly Hills. "Where you think we're bound for now?"

"Another phone someplace," Brenner said, then added: "Clint Eastwood."

"Yeah." Jonas tossed a grim half salute at the windshield. "Thanks a whole helluva lot, Clint."

"Dirty Harry." He started it all. The elaborate ransom delivery pattern: a string of directions leading from phone booth to phone booth. Supposedly, it guaranteed that no one could possibly be following. Actually, with enough unmarked radio cars and a crossover pattern, there was no problem keeping watch on the bag man. But the dipshits calling the shots didn't know that; this Mickey Mouse stuff made them feel like masterminds.

Not that it had never been done this way before Clint Eastwood drew his .357 Magnum for the first time. But since then, it had become virtually a required procedure for kidnappers. A thousand times in cities across the country—around the world. Who said nobody ever learned anything by going to the movies or watching TV? Assholes with their eyeballs glued to the screen, getting bright ideas, perfecting their techniques.

"He's getting off," Jonas said.

"I see him. Let me out. You circle and I'll talk to you."

Jonas stopped briefly in the No Parking zone in front of the Kirkeby Center. Brenner hopped out and strolled away. The blue Chevrolet continued off into the Westwood Village traffic.

They still called it Westwood Village. But it wasn't a village, not anymore. Brenner could remember a few years ago when there were quiet streets of small shops and the sleepy atmosphere of a college town. Now Westwood was Big Business.

UCLA had grown larger, to multiversity size, but that wasn't what did it. First, Hollywood went to hell and the entertainment center of L.A. tilted west. Hollywood Boulevard was once the main hub from the Pantages Theater at Vine Street to the phony pharaoh-adorned Egyptian Theater and Grauman's Chinese with its forecourt of footprints near Highland Avenue. Now it all belonged to the bizarre, perverse and perverted. Midnight Cowboy wasn't a movie, it was a street show. Flaming fruits, sad-faced stray kids, wet-lipped transvestites, blank-eyed hookers and marauding muggers owned Hollywood Boulevard.

It was a zoo, the happy hunting ground for the vice squad. The civilians moved on to Westwood for their good times.

And Westwood obliged by expanding like a jack-in-the-box. The area now boasted almost anything anyone wanted except parking.

Brenner walked on the west side of the street past an excavation that used to be a parking lot and now promised more progress. Montrose was ahead of him, across the street, zigzagging quickly through the strollers and window-shoppers who clogged the sidewalk.

It was as if the Pied Piper had led the children here: Everybody in Westwood was young—or at least tried to look that way. The clothing was a riot of colors and it seemed like a costume party was about to begin in the neighborhood. There were people dressed as pirates, peasants, elves, hobos, harlots, cowboys, white hunters, Indian princesses, lumberjacks, pimps, Cossacks, farmers, beachcombers and tennis players. A tribe of exhibitionists in search of voyeurs, but nobody seemed to notice and everything was taken for granted. No wonder a man in a stained, sour-smelling Carroll & Co. suit could hurry down these streets without attracting a glance.

Brenner kept Montrose in easy view without ever gazing directly across the street. Separated by the flow of bumper-to-bumper traffic, they both left their curbs and crossed moving north. Jonas passed between them in the Chevrolet, riding the center lane heading south, looking at neither of them. There was another outdoor phone pod on Montrose's side of the street. A barefoot nubile nineteen-year-old with pressed blonde hair, tight dirty-white shorts and bikini halter was talking on the phone. Montrose stopped nearby and waited.

Across the street, in front of the Bank of America, Brenner pretended to examine the rows of newspaper vending machines. There were only two daily metropolitan papers left, but there were ten machines lined up and chained down to protect against vandals. *California Business* weekly. *Rolling Stone.* The free-wheeling *Free Press* with its famous classified ads. And then the special interest publications: for homosexuals, for singles, for thrill-seekers. "Make Me Come!" pleaded the headline on *IMPULSE,* a paper featuring a nude pair of longhairs (He and She) with air-brushed black dots discreetly covering key junctures. "When She Said 'I Want To Eat You' I Felt My Thighs Ease Open. See What Happened Inside." The fold of the paper concealed all other mysteries. "Jackie Onassis Fights Blindness" heralded another headline.

Montrose was still waiting for the phone across the street. Brenner turned away, toward the sound of approaching tambourines.

A band of Hare Krishna followers came around the corner, chanting their endless toneless litany, "Harree-harree-krishna-harree-harree . . ." They also were young, men in their late teens and early twenties with shaved heads and hairy legs showing beneath crumpled saffron-colored caftans. As Brenner gazed from one face to the other, enveloped in the sound of their chanting, all the faces looked the same. Of course, some noses were bigger and some ears jutted out, but the glazed-joyful expression in the eyes transformed the features and merged them into a series of mirror images. They shook their tambourines and danced in a circle in front of the Bank of America.

The robes shone in the sun and glints flashed off the metal on the tambourines and Brenner stole a glance: That curvy little piece across the street was still on the phone. Montrose was prowling up and down the pavement, staring at her—staring. Brenner felt eyes watching him. He turned and saw . . .

The boy.

A miniature version of the others. But his eyes were different. It was still a game for him. Maybe seven or eight years old, with shaved head like the others, in a robe that almost touched the sidewalk. On his feet, he wore a pair of mud-smirched zip-on house slippers with bunny faces.

One of the grown-up followers with the fixed-happy stare had hold of the boy's hand and danced with him. Maybe he was the father. Brenner knew about these kids: There had been some complaints filed, kids kept out of school, kids being brainwashed.

"Harreeeeeee-krishnaaaaah!"

The boy was frolicking and while he danced he never stopped looking straight into Brenner's eyes and the man with him never let go of the boy's hand. Brenner suddenly recalled a day at Knott's Berry Farm: he and Phyllis on a Sunday outing with Mike at the amusement park there. Brenner holding his son's hand as they stood and watched a gypsy organ grinder make music while a monkey on a long chain danced and danced and begged pennies from the bystanders. Mike asked Brenner for money and with a combination of fear and delight put the pennies, one by one, into the twitchy little hand of the monkey. After each coin had been collected, the organ grinder would yank sharply on the chain connected to the collar around the monkey's throat and the monkey would scamper back to drop the money in the tin cup, then doff his little red hat in that funny way that made all the children watching laugh.

"Harreee-eeeee-krishna-a-a-a-ah-harrrr-eeeee . . . !" Brenner jerked his eyes away from the boy. Montrose. Across the street. What the hell was he doing?

Patience wasn't possible, but Montrose had tried to fake it. Shifting from foot to foot, pacing up and down, moving closer to the phone once, attracting the girl's eye, pointing at his watch, smiling. She had smiled back, held up a finger to indicate "in a minute"—minutes ago.

He didn't know what to do. To tear the phone out of her hand and shove her away risked creating a scene. The girl might scream, she looked the type. But the voice was undoubtedly calling him. Now. Getting a busy signal.

She was talking to a girl friend. Sally. Giving advice. Sally was a fine arts major considering a proposition from a physical education major. "Sometimes it's a good thing," the barefoot cunt philosophized, "to date somebody who's beneath you metaphysically."

Now the idea came to him. So simple.

Montrose walked up to the phone and stood there. Annoyed, she turned her back on him, facing the other way. Montrose moved around so he was facing her again. Not smiling, his face only inches away from hers, his body close.

Her pique mixed with puzzlement and when she began to smell the vomit and see his unblinking stare, he knew he had won. She was scared and the endless conversation trailed off. "Sally, I—I better call you back, there's somebody, er-r-r, there's somebody waiting for the phone . . ."

She hung up and fled from Montrose, with only one backward glance to be certain that he wasn't following her. But by then the phone had already rung and Montrose had forgotten about the girl as he frantically apologized—and then listened obediently to the voice.

"He's moving again." Brenner spoke quietly into the small black radio transmitter as he stood in the doorway of a shoe store, his back to the street, watching the reflections in the plate-glass window. "Heading north. Toward Weyburn."

Brenner pocketed the transmitter and strode out onto

the sidewalk. Past Alice's and Old World, brand-new restaurants built to look old-timey. Bookstores, record stores, ski shops, camera stores—people on the pavement with "Legalize Marijuana" petitions—and up ahead, across the traffic, invisible on this street except to Brenner: a father with a bag of money, trying to buy his son back.

"Going onto the UCLA campus," Brenner reported. "Still on Westwood." He looked through the glass street showcase containing handcrafted metal jewelry and saw the young couple. He was bearded, she wore no makeup. They were curiously studying him—and the transmitter. Without a word, Brenner hurried on toward the brick buildings of the university. As he crossed Le Conte Avenue, Brenner paused to let several cars making turns get through onto the road crossing the campus. One of them was a brown Chevrolet. Hyatt was driving and Elgort slouched beside him.

The last time Brenner had been down this street a war was going on. On another autumn day when these kids, who now rushed for classrooms, walked slowly down the center of the road—carrying candles. A parade of the young, marching to protest death and to tell a disinterested government that they opposed continuing the war. They sang songs as they marched in the candlelight procession, and the songs were the same ones that had been sung by the civil rights workers because nobody had written new songs of protest for an undeclared war. Brenner was assigned to keep order at the demonstration and control the violence that was predicted but did not materialize. It was a windy night and many of the candles blew out, but the students tirelessly relit the tiny flames that together pushed back the darkness.

Montrose was at the student recreation center now, looking around—for what? There were three glass-enclosed phone booths and Brenner assumed he was bound for one of them. But instead, Montrose walked past them—past the bicycle racks and the entrance to the student center—and darted across the road toward a grassy area where several students were sprawled with books spread open. Montrose walked beyond them along the sidewalk. As he went by a large open litter barrel, he tossed the bag of money in with the trash and kept on going.

This was the end of the line.

Montrose's part of it was over, he was out of it. The rest was up to Brenner and the others. If anything went wrong now, it was their fault.

The kiosk was near the entrance to the student bookstore. Brenner could see the trash barrel from here: No one was near it. He couldn't stare. So he looked at the kiosk, which was covered with leaflets, ads, messages. *Room Service* with the Marx Bros., Friday at 8:30. Blood Donors Needed. Ralph Nader to Speak. Dermatologist: Remove Unsightly Hair. Fraternity Dance Scheduled. Need Easy Rider—Driving L.A. to Chicago, Leaving Oct. 15. Brenner had to get the others clued in. He walked casually to one of the empty phone booths and closed the door.

From here, he still had an unobstructed view of the pathway leading past the litter barrel. The words on the side of the barrel were large and clear: KEEP YOUR CAMPUS CLEAN. Brenner lifted the receiver and pretended to dial without actually depositing a dime and when he spoke it was intended for the small black transmitter that he had placed inconspicuously on top of the phone directory on the metal counter beneath the coin box.

Brenner described the situation to the radio cars and suggested safe positions for them. In the parking lot across from the grassy area. Up the street, the hedge a block beyond the litter barrel. Along the winding pathway between two adjoining library buildings.

And the tentacles of the stakeout spread out. Brenner

remained in the booth, nodding and occasionally mumbling into the phone to convey the illusion of conversation. He tried to spot the other guys taking up their positions and he thought he caught sight of Hyatt, but then the figure came closer and it wasn't Hyatt. Enough time had gone by so that they were all out there now, a half dozen strong, but Brenner couldn't see any of them and that was the way it should be. Everything according to the book. Pros at work here.

Somebody was coming. Two big lanky blacks loping in a dodging, twisting pattern down the pathway. Tossing something in the air between them. They came closer, God, they were big mothers, both six-four or better— trying hook shots with a crumpled ball of newspaper, blocking the throws, feinting, running with make-believe dribbles, circling the litter barrel as if it was the hoop in their imaginary game of basketball. It was a ballet, they were that good. Two graceful, incredibly coordinated athletes, leaping, crouching, pirouetting, racing sideways and doubling back. Each doing his best to elude and deceive the other. But each instinctively sensing and anticipating the other's ploys, continuously barring a scoring movement. They circled closer to the litter barrel and the player with the "ball" made a sudden breakthrough. Brenner spoke sharply at the transmitter: "Okay! Maybe it's going down . . ." But a final hook shot was tossed for two points; the ball of paper sank into the center of the trash barrel and the two black players left it there, pounding each other on the back as they high-stepped away, laughing with enjoyment at the celebration of their skills.

It was quiet again. A relaxed, almost drowsy air seemed to have descended on the campus. Nobody was rushing. Boys wearing sweaters with letters sewn on them meandered in the sunshine and joked with pretty girls. It was like an old M-G-M college musical. "Hey, kids—I know what! Let's put on a show!" But the show was going on already and Louis B. Mayer would never have made a Technicolor movie whose action centered around a garbage can.

A red-headed beauty in a lavender sunsuit with straps that criss-crossed her gorgeous chest was pedaling an English bicycle down the street. Godiva on her horse never had more to offer. Three full-bearded poli sci majors in jeans and sweatshirts were loudly solving the problems of the world in front of the bookstore. None of them seemed to notice the approach of the sex bomb on wheels, but as her bicycle passed all three heads swiveled in unison to watch the rippling rhythm of her back end as she pumped away.

Brenner smiled and thought of "The Ganzer Test." There are those who look and those who don't. It was a profound observation that grew out of another stakeout long ago on Fairfax Avenue—"Kosher Canyon"—a shopping street bisecting one of the oldest Jewish sections in town. It was a place teeming with life, interlarded with delicious smells. Sauerkraut sold from the barrel and pickles aging in salty-sour brine. Seven-layer whipped-cream cakes and fruit-encrusted Danish and chocolate-covered custard-stuffed eclairs rich enough to transmit calories through the thick glass of the refrigerated showcases and onto the waistlines of passers-by who just dared to look.

Old men with flowing gray beards, dressed all in black from frock coats to flat-topped wide-brimmed hats, argued with one another in dialects from half a dozen Eastern European countries. Little pudgy-cuddly old ladies, pulling wire grocery baskets, crowded the open-air fruit stands to squeeze the oranges and tomatoes.

It was one of the few streets in the city where people walked and even stood around and talked. So the man in the loose-fitting checkered sports jacket, open-collared cream-colored shirt, charcoal-gray slacks and $75 Italian loafers was inconspicuous as he slouched against the magazine racks of the well-stocked quarter-block-long newsstand. He had been there for over half an hour, nonchalantly leafing the tits and beaver six-color foldouts. Chewing gum. Waiting. Brenner and Ganzer, in a car parked in front of a fresh-fish market, knew what he was waiting for—but not who.

Chick Simon was the name of the gum-chewer—about thirty-five, with bad skin that still festered with an adolescent's eruptions. But he wasn't as paunchy as he seemed: There was a plastic bag tied around his waist underneath the silk shirt and it contained $30,000 in uncut happy powder. A snitch had tipped Ad-Narc three days before in a bar near the San Pedro docks. Teams of plainclothesmen had been following the shipment ever since and delivery certainly was only moments away. Brenner and Ganzer would hold back until the buyer arrived and the sale went down. Then they would bust Chick Simon and his distributor, and a series of additional arrests would be triggered across the city. This was to be the culmination of several months of intensive, delicate, risky work.

And that was when Brenner had seen the little fat guy.

He was in his fifties and had the face of a happy fool. Partially bald with what was left mowed short in a porcupine crewcut. He hadn't shaved recently, so the stubble on top of his head seemed to continue on across his cheeks and chin and throat. The smile was borrowed from a jack-o'-lantern: extrawide, but with prominent gaps where teeth presumably as yellowed as those left were missing. The total impression he projected was a soiled, faded grayish-brown: eyes, hair, skin, clothes. Baggy clothes discolored by years of careless wear. On other boulevards, the man would have been thought of as a bum. On Fairfax Avenue, he was a *schlepper*.

But a happy schlepper. With a wondrous secret.

Brenner blinked as the little guy strolled closer. He had a funny way of walking, maybe because the sole on one of his cracked unlaced brown shoes was loose and flapping on the pavement as he strutted, pelvis thrown forward on every other step.

"Marty," Brenner nudged, "hey, Marty. You see what I see?"

Ganzer's head was against the backrest and his eyes were closed. They had been on duty for twenty-seven hours. Without moving his head, Ganzer opened his eyes. "The buyer?" he asked.

"No. That guy coming—don't you see?"

Irritably, Ganzer sat up. He was behind the wheel of the unmarked car and he peered through the windshield. Just another burned-out freak. "What the hell am I looking at?" he grumbled. "Give me a clue."

"You're still sleeping," Brenner grinned.

A blubbery, cigar-chomping fishmonger, wearing a stained gamy-smelling apron, had emerged from the fish market carrying a bucket of salt water, scales, gills and slop. He splashed the contents of the bucket into the gutter, but then his head whipped around to stare after the little schlepper who had just passed him. The fishmonger's mouth fell open as he gaped like a guppy and his cigar dropped into the gutter and fizzled out.

"*He* sees it," Brenner said. And then Ganzer did, too.

"It's hanging out," Ganzer said. "He's got one of 'em hanging out! Bastard's fly is wide open and . . ."

"Look again," Brenner advised.

The fat little guy with the big happy grin did indeed have one enormous testicle showing. But his zipper was properly zipped.

"He's cut a hole in his pants," Ganzer noticed. "What the fuck's he think he's doing?"

"Look at that shit-eating smile," Brenner observed. "He knows just what he's doing."

"Marching down the street with his balls hanging out!" Ganzer was outraged.

"One," Brenner corrected. "Just one."

"Okay. Just one. But it's big enough to toss through a hoop. Let's go get him." Ganzer reached for the door handle, but Brenner caught his shoulder.

"You don't want to do that."

Ganzer sat frozen for a moment, then nodded. "Guess I don't. We jump out after our friend the Fairfax Flasher . . ."

"And," Brenner finished it, "Chick Simon's liable to stop reading his magazine. He takes off and we blow a lot of everybody's time and effort."

"Here he comes back again!" **The little man** had done an about-face and was returning.

"Like a dog with a fire plug. He must like this corner."

"And we just sit here and watch him?" Ganzer lit a cigar.

"What else can we do?"

"Yeah, what else," Ganzer agreed. Then, a hint of a smile appeared. "Never a cop around when you need one, is there?"

Brenner laughed, then poked his elbow into Ganzer's side. "Jesus, he really is hung. I mean, if that thing was any bigger, he'd trip over it."

The little man strutted back up the sidewalk. His exposed private part was quasi-camouflaged. The wrinkled, gray-brown texture of the sac blended nicely with the faded fabric of his trousers. Of course, there was only one area down there with hair on it and that was the giveaway. But not to everyone. Most people were too busy to notice. Unseeing, they swarmed past the little man, oblivious to the jewel he was so proudly displaying.

A lacquered Beverly Hills matron, forty-five going on twenty-one, hurried past the little man, coming toward the car. She wore knee-high calf contoured boots, a riding skirt and, from the waist up, she was totally a creature of Giorgio's Boutique: Italian print blouse, oversize sunglasses perched on the crown of her head, and strands of glittering white-gold chains dangling down her ample Maidenform-architectured chest. Her face was expertly made up and totally composed, until she had gone two paces beyond the little man. Then everything fell apart as the retroactive thunderbolt hit her. The large paper bag she carried, stuffed with rye bread, salt bagels and sundry other noshables, took on a life of its own: It left her hands and flew upward. She grabbed for it, fumbling the bag higher in the air, almost letting it crash to the sidewalk before she subdued the grocery bag and clutched it to her bosom as she stood and gawked at the back of the little man.

"Smile, honey," Ganzer moaned to Brenner. "You're on Candid Camera."

Brenner slouched lower in his seat, holding his sides. "She doesn't know whether to shit—or salute . . ."

On the pavement, the woman abruptly decided. The little man was about halfway down the block when he executed another smart about-face and swung back in their direction. This clearly was becoming his patrolling zone. The matron ran a frantic hand through her sprayed coiffure, messing up her hair, as she yanked down her dark glasses and fled before the happy fool's advance.

The little man now had a technique. The toothsome smile was part of it, but eye contact was even more important. People generally avert their eyes if they find other people looking at them. But the schlepper picked his victims and locked eyeballs. In looking away, their gazes seemed invariably to skid downward to the target area.

"Girls," Brenner said. "Those two coming right at him . . ."

They were teeny-boppers from Fairfax High, dressed in the uniform of the day: tie-dyed T-shirts and jeans that had been soaked and allowed to form-fit dry while being worn. They clip-clopped along in wooden Dr. Scholl's shoes, chattering to each other and blowing huge pink bubblegum bubbles. Now they were into the little man's strike zone.

He grinned and stared.

They spotted his treasure.

Brenner and Ganzer could pinpoint the exact instant: It was when the taller schoolgirl's bubble blew out of proportion—and popped. Pink gooey shrapnel splattered over her face and in her long chestnut hair. Her girl friend started to laugh hysterically at both her friend's hair and the little man's free show. The teener with the bubblegum hair began to laugh, too, picking weblike strands from her cheek as she pointed at the little man's crotch. He blew kisses to them both and continued his stroll down the avenue. And in the car, Brenner and Ganzer were now laughing so hard that they were muffling their noise by stuffing handkerchiefs in their mouths.

The nine-year-old Yeshiva *bucher* was next. He was a miniature mittel-European prototype of the elders who trod these streets. Minus a beard, but with long *payiss*, wearing a white shirt, black suit and embroidered *yarmulka*. He bounced a tennis ball, aiming at the cracks in the sidewalk, skipping along—until he saw the Flasher. The boy's eyes riveted. The tennis ball dribbled out of his hands and rolled down the sidewalk. And the little smiling man, in a graceful swoop, bent down and scooped it up. He looked at the boy, the boy looked back—and then the little schlepper tossed the ball back to the boy, who caught it on one bounce, turned and ran off.

At the newsstand, Chick Simon peered up from his centerfold. Brenner and Ganzer thought he was dialing in on the little man, but his attention went beyond: There was a young woman approaching—as if stepping out of Chick's Hefner-inspired fantasies. She had a small sparrow-like face and a dynamite body. Black satin miniskirt, rainbow-colored wedgies, a black confetti shawl that failed to cover the extra-wide knit beige top through which her thin chest and wide full breasts were bared.

This was to be the ultimate confrontation. Chick Simon stared at the puckered roseate nipples peeking out between the sweater weave. The girl felt his gaze and easily ignored him but her look gravitated unerringly to the little man, advancing on her like a beaming cherub with his love offering. Her reaction was dramatic and unexpected: As her orbs transmitted the startling information to her brain, the girl's hands went reflexively up, palms open, to cover her breasts.

Instantly, the little man responded. Both his hands went down to hide his exposed part, imitating her. It was like an old Harpo Marx–Lucy Ball routine. He mirrored her moves. She opened her mouth wide in shock. He opened his mouth and stuck his tongue out lasciviously. She brought her left hand up to cover her mouth and he did the same. But that still kept his home base covered, while her left tit was now unprotected: The little man evened the score by separating his fingers, tantalizingly, so that she could see as much of him as he could of her. Horrified, the girl moved her hand back for full concealment and he took his hands away for full disclosure.

Chick Simon was laughing so hard that he was banging against the racks, knocking the magazines loose, and he was still cackling as the green car slid up to the curb with one man up front: a face that Brenner and Ganzer recognized. A well-known narcotics dealer. Shaking with mirth, Chick staggered forward to the car and yanked the door open. There was a closed black attaché case on the seat, but business was forgotten for the moment as Chick began to giggle the story to the mystified dealer, who also began to laugh now, for the little man was pursuing the girl, Harpo-fashion, in circles in front of the newsstand, honking his own horn. The two heroin merchants were in hysterics when a pair of laughing policemen descended on them:

"You——you're—under arrest," Ganzer chortled.

"Yeah—both—arrest," Brenner sputtered.

And behind them, a small crowd had formed, the spectators attracted by the screams of the girl clutching her breasts and the little man holding his crotch. By now, it was hard to tell as they ran back and forth up and down the pavement precisely who was chasing who. The girl in her attempts at flight dropped her black featherlike shawl and the little man without losing stride picked it up and tossed it around his shoulders while the shrieking pursuit continued—until Brenner intervened and tried to collar the little schlepper. But he kept running, not trying to get away, just waving the shawl in the air, not wanting it to be over, going back and forth, back and forth . . .

Back and forth . . .

"Here he comes again," Brenner spoke softly into the small black transmitter on the counter in the phone booth. Male Caucasian, about twenty-four, dark hair, approximately five feet eleven inches tall, no visible marks or scars. Nothing to distinguish him from the dozens of other students on the UCLA campus, except this was the fourth time in less than ten minutes that he had passed the litter barrel containing the ransom money.

"Get ready," Brenner broadcast softly. "This could be it."

The guy was heading for the barrel, moving right up to it. "He's stopping," Brenner said. "He's—wait, he's throwing something in, looks like an empty cigarette pack. False alarm, guys, he's taking off, he's—hold on, he's back-pedaling. Maybe he forgot a little something."

The young man had turned toward the litter barrel again, but now he bent over to tie his shoelace. And while he did, he covertly glanced around. Brenner pretended to be talking into his phone, but out of the corner of his eye he watched. Guy didn't look like a kidnapper, but what does a kidnapper look like these days?

"He's up and—he's leaving," Brenner told the others. "Hey, no, it's looking better and better. This time for real, he's goin' for it. I'll give you the word, guys, then swoop. He's at the garbage barrel, the fuckin' shit-picker is dipping his hand in for the goodies. Go! Go for the asshole—*NO! Wait*. He's—he's taking out a newspaper. Just a newspaper. And he's splitting again—there he goes—looks like that's all he wanted. He's—he's walking away. Everybody hold positions."

There was a bench a distance away from the trash barrel. The young man sat down and began to read the paper. "I really think he's reading the fucking paper," Brenner announced.

Slowly, the second hand twitched around and around the face of Brenner's watch. Now there was no one near the little barrel. An empty path and the newspaper reader on his bench.

"He's up," Brenner transmitted. "Must've finished 'Dear Abby' and 'Dennis the Menace' and—here he goes, looks like he's leaving us and— No, just looks like that—he's coming back to where it is. Rolling up the paper, hitting himself on the leg while he walks, looking around a little and—he's there. Get set. He's throwing away the paper. Into the barrel. Neatness counts, no litterbugs here. He's still at the honey pot, he's—look at that! He's taking a teeny peek inside. Likes what he sees—there go both hands, he's going for it—he's— *Hold positions. He came up empty. He's walking away with nothing.* Son-of-a-bitch is playing games with us, fucking cat-and-mouse, Hey! Bingo! The shit-picker's back at the barrel. *GO! Everybody GO!!* Suspect has the stapled bag with the ransom money in his hands now. Heading north on the path. *Get him!*"

Brenner plunged out of the phone booth and began to dash across the street, dodging a car, heading for the path. Bounding over a hedge like he was running the low hurdles, Jonas reached the path first and drew his .38 as he raced after the suspect.

The young man heard the steps behind him. He glanced back and took off across the grass. It was like a football game and he clutched the paper bag to his side as if it was pigskin rather than gold. The danger, he felt, was back of him, but while he was busy glancing over his shoulder at the progress being made by Jonas and Brenner, Elgort materialized. Coming up in front of him, from between two buildings. The young man veered sharply away from Elgort—and suddenly found himself racing directly at Hyatt, who seemed to have grown right out of the ground. Again, the young man demonstrated agility by switching his field quickly, zigzagging to avoid and outrun Hyatt, who was coming for him. He could get away from this idiot in the cowboy boots and then it was wide open—if he could reach the car. Leave them all behind—wide open . . .

Hyatt knew the scumbag was his once he tried to duck Elgort and took those first fancy steps in his direction. You're mine, asshole. Now he sees me. Try to get away. Go on. *Try!* Nice—good moves. I can tackle him—here he comes. Easy tackle, hit him hard, fast and low—bring him down . . . Hyatt could see it clearly: like an instant replay of a moment that had yet to happen. Hyatt positioned himself—and—he let the turd go by.

When Hyatt had played outside linebacker for Montana State, he had made a thousand runs like this—ten thousand! But he deliberately let the cocksucker slip by. The man was passing Hyatt now—ahead of him—just where Hyatt wanted him.

Perfectly timed, balanced exactly right, Hyatt kicked hard at the side of the suspect's leg. The hard-leather tip of his cowboy boot connected with the flesh of the suspect's calf and then hit bone. Hard. The suspect went down, skittering across the grass, and the paper bag with twenty thousand dollars in it went flying through the air.

Let Elgort worry about the money. Hyatt moved in, praying the bastard was okay. Look at him on the grass, crawling, his fucking foot aching him, but the adrenaline pumping, that old survival instinct, get up and maybe you can still make it. Yeah. Come on up. Come on up!

The man on the grass tried to rise but when he put weight on his kicked leg it buckled. He caught himself as the red-haired one in the boots with a gun in his hand reached him. He started to raise his empty hands. The fear he had tried to outrun had overtaken him now.

Hyatt could see it was all over, the man was helpless— no threat to anyone. That was the message coming from those scared, pleading eyes. Hyatt, whose long-awaited first child, a daughter, was now three months old, read the message. He had to move very quickly before the man's hand were fully raised. But he made it. A beautiful shot. This time his pointed boot tip plunged deep through soft tissue, mashing the motherfucker's balls and grinding into his scrotum. The scream was high-pitched and as loud as the sirens on top of the squad cars that were pulling up.

The man was bunched in a fetal ball of agony on the grass. Hyatt put a foot in his armpit and pulled up an arm, slapping a steel cuff around the wrist, swiftly linking it to the other wrist. Then Elgort was there with the money. And Jonas, red in the face, sweat-streaked from the run, with Brenner right behind him. There were more cars— black-and-whites—uniformed guys. "It's all over, no problem, move back, please." Dealing with the instant crowd that had appeared. Other students capable of anger at the sight of one of their own being rousted. "Look at the red-headed son-of a bitch," a Candice Bergen lookalike pointed, "he'll pull that poor guy's arms right out of their sockets!"

Hyatt was lifting the suspect by the cuffs, yanking his arms straight back as he raised him up. Immediately, Jonas and Brenner had the man by the armpits and were propelling him, feet dragging, tears of pain staining his face, toward the open rear doors of the nearest marked car.

"Easy, folks, police business—all over—it's all over!" The reassuring drone of the officers guarding the withdrawal overlapped with the urgent demands that Brenner and Jonas whispered in the suspect's ears:

"Where's Bobby, asshole?"

"Where's the kid, you fuck?"

The suspect shook his head wildly and the tears splashed on his shirt. "Don't hurt me—please, God—don't kill me . . ."

"Tell us where he is, shitface." They tossed him in back and slammed the doors. But the sense of hostile irritation was rapidly dissipating, the tension broken, because it was clear to all the arresting officers that this terrified suspect was going to tell them everything he knew. It was all under control again. A smooth operation had gone down and they knew it and were pleased. It would be several hours before the good feeling eroded.

Two dried-out slices of white bread bracketed paper-thin strips of turkey that looked like salted cardboard. Ramirez carefully plucked out the tired layer of lettuce, dumped it in the wastebasket and started wolfing the sandwich that had been placed on his desk hours before. He chewed hard, biting off each mouthful and each word:

"A vulture!"

Ramirez rose from behind the desk, waving the sandwich.

"That's what we got." Ramirez began to pace. "A piece of walking-talking scum. With a fast-money scheme to pick up some ransom loot. That creep has copped out to everything—*except* kidnapping!"

They were flaked-out around his office. The fluorescent lights were on, but what did that mean in this damn place? Ramirez checked the clock on his desk. 1:47. Incredible. The suspect had been arrested at 3:10 that afternoon. Ten and a half hours later and all he had left was a sour taste in his belly. He swallowed the last mouthfuls of cold coffee left in a styrofoam cup. The sour taste remained.

Jonas was closest to the desk, his long legs stretched out, his head down and eyes closed. He was awake but wished he wasn't. Elgort had tilted a chair precariously back against the wall and crossed his legs; one foot was twitching, but he was unaware of it.

"Maybe we're not asking him right," Elgort suggested. His voice was raspy. He had spent the last three hours questioning the suspect.

"Yeah," Hyatt said. He stood up, crumpling a sandwich wrapper and tossing it at the wastebasket next to Ramirez' desk. He missed. "Let me try him again."

"Be my guest," Ramirez said. He stopped at the big wall map. L.A. And a red spot where a kid used to live. Used to live. "Go try, but we been running relays on him all afternoon and now half the night. He's wiped out, so are we—and we better face it. We got us an extortionist, but he doesn't have any more on where the kid really is than we do."

"But can I try him again?" Hyatt persisted.

"Why not?" Ramirez said.

Hyatt hoisted his pants with his elbows, Cagney-style, tightened his belt and started for the door.

"Hey," Ramirez added. "You go with him."

He pointed at Brenner; no sense sending Hyatt in alone, not after how he handled himself this afternoon. There was a value to having Hyatt go back into the interrogation room, Ramirez recognized, but better to have someone along that had it under control. Like Brenner.

It was the mustache. Not really a mustache, just downy never-shaved dark hair on his upper lip. But from a distance, with the intense dark shiny eyes, it made him look older.

Now his lip was funny. Swollen, split. Giving a monster-like distorted caste to his upper face. A boy monster. He was, they had learned, seventeen years old. If you went by the calendar.

". . . and you understand these rights?" Brenner waited for him to answer.

"Yeah."

"And you understand this conversation is being taped on this machine. And that it can be used in evidence?"

"Sure. Why not?"

"Okay. What's your name?"

"You know my fuckin' name, man. What's your name?" He leaned forward at the table, squinting at the plastic I.D. badge. "I have the honor of bein' hassled by Edward Brenner and"—he turned—"George Hyatt." He had memorized Hyatt's name earlier.

Hyatt leaned against the wall of the interrogation room, shirtsleeved arms folded, watching.

"Clarence, would you like to tell us about . . . ?"

A big grin creased Clarence's face. Too big. The split in his lip stretched and the scab cracked slightly. A dot of blood appeared.

"I don' have to tell you shit, man." Clarence had been terrified when they'd brought him in here. First, the cap-ture—the pain. He was almost getting on top of it all when they arrived at headquarters. But getting out of the car, hustling down the hallway, he had fallen. Been tripped. Hands still cuffed behind him, he pitched forward onto his face. Banged open his lip, and when he looked up it was the cowboy. Red-headed fuckin' pisser standing there then like he's standin' here now—but now Clarence wasn't scared any more.

"Been tellin' you the same shit all day, man. I did not do nothin' to that kid. It was all like a joke, y'know?"

"When did you get the idea, Clarence?" Brenner asked.

"Last week, couple weeks ago—I don' remember."

"Who'd you rap with about it?"

"Nobody, man. Just thought it up and—after a while I done it. Looked in the phone book, y'know? And there he was. Harold Montrose. Just like it showed on the TV."

"So?"

"So I figured, what the hell? All I got to lose is a dime. So I called him. Her and him. The both of them. They were so-o-o scared, man, it was nothin' at all to tell 'em what to do. I mean, I could have told 'em anythin' and they'd do it."

"Did you like that?"

"You like bein' a cop? I mean, you are The Man. You tell everybody. That's okay." Clarence winked. It added an imbalance to his swollen features.

"Why'd you do it?"

"For the money!" Clarence was incredulous: How could his motive be misunderstood?

"Did it bother you, putting Bobby's parents through all that?"

"What's that to me? *Man, I needed that money!*"

"For what?"

"For . . ." he faltered, trying to think of a particular thing. "I just needed it. Look, what's goin' on with that Bobby kid, that's not my scene. But what's the difference if I get somethin' out of it? Big Daddy, you see that fuckin' car he drives? Gold, man, *gold*! I figured he wouldn' miss twenty big ones and I could sure use it."

Hyatt shifted his weight and instantly Clarence's gaze locked on him. Hyatt smiled, pleased at the reaction. Clarence licked away the burble of blood on his lip and reminded himself that this prick had done his worst and that was it.

"You work in a parking lot." Brenner looked at the file. Past. Present. Names, dates, places. Clarence's package: It had grown larger in the last ten hours. "Where's that— right in Westwood?"

"Yeah. This medical building. I handle their cases, all of 'em. Dr. Lincoln Continental. Dr. Rolls-Royce. Dr. Mercedes-Benz." Clarence laughed and tipped his chair back. "When I was a kid I used to work another parkin' lot. I mean, *work*. Rip off stuff from the cars when nobody was lookin' . . ."

"Hubcaps and like that?"

"C'mon." He was scornful. "Go for the big locked jobs. With the goodies. Use a hanger, stick it in between the metal and the window on the door, open the lock. Pop! Good-bye tape deck, stereo speakers, cameras in the glove compartment, whatever."

Brenner tapped the file. "That's all in here."

"Well, what's not in there," Clarence flashed anger, "is how in the parkin' lot I'm workin' at now that kind of shit *never* happens. Not when I'm on the scene, lookin' out for 'em all. No dents or scratches, nobody gets ripped off, not when I'm there."

"We have to listen to this shit?" Hyatt said. Clarence turned on him, flaring:

"Man, you don't have to listen to me, you don't have to fuckin' look in my direction, nothin'! But you can't touch me now that they took pictures. So fuck off!"

Hyatt straightened to his full height and when he stared at Clarence through narrow slits, Brenner thought he looked like an Indian. A red-headed Indian. On the warpath. But Hyatt had it in check.

"We got your ass, scumbag," Hyatt said.

Clarence shrugged and smiled. Nobody was hurt. And he was seventeen. He knew the rules.

Brenner watched him. The file told everything and nothing. Dozens of arrests, detentions, probations, petty crimes and wrist-slapping punishments. Years of brushes with the institution known as The Law. Scary at first, until you get hip. If you're a kid you can do anything and walk away from it. It's how the game is played. Two kids walk into a junior high school yard and blow away another kid. The one who pulled the trigger gets two years in juvie camp, his partner is placed in a foster home near Fresno three weeks after the funeral. Juvenile justice. Clarence is seventeen, Brenner thought, so he's in under the wire.

"That's what I hated, man," Clarence was telling them. "I do all that good for 'em, watch out for their wheels, protectin' them, y'know? And nobody ever said thanks. They never even looked at me."

Now they'll look at you, Brenner thought. For one brief minute, they'll look at you. He turned off the tape recorder.

A long smear of blood streaked the off-white shiny-slick floor across from the Property Window. It was there when Ganzer came on duty at midnight. Zagor told Ganzer all about the excitement during their brief changing of the guard ritual: Zagor gathering up his crossword-puzzle books and the dictionary he cheated with while Ganzer unpacked his Donald Duck lunch pail and took out the two Thermoses of coffee.

"Thing of beauty," Zagor enthused. "Good as having a front-row seat at the Ice Follies. The turkey went right on his face and skidded down the hall like he was a hockey puck. Until he hit the wall."

"Off-the-wall stuff," Ganzer agreed. "Best kind."

As the evening inched on, the corridor outside the Property Window became very quiet. It was a particularly slow night. And, without being told, Ganzer began to sense that something had gone wrong upstairs. Occasionally a pair of dicks would hurry in, returning from a field assignment, checking out the background on the kid they were holding. But the difference between progress and mounting frustration was clear. Ganzer knew. He had been looking at cops' faces for thirty years. Minus a few weeks.

Brenner went by with Hyatt, and Ganzer called to him. But they were in a rush. On their way to the interrogation room. "Busy, Marty," Brenner yelled. "See you later, huh?" Window on the world. Sit here and watch it all go by.

Ganzer drained the last swallow of coffee in his mug and poured some more. Steaming. Up to the brim.

Maybe not knowing was better. Ignorance might not be bliss, but what was it they used to say when we were kids? What you don't know can't hurt you. When Ganzer looked in the mirror these days, a tired old fart stared back at him and he found himself wondering where had it all gone to? Join the Department young, retire young, live and laugh at the world. That was the idea, thirty years ago. Harry Truman was President, the "War to End All Wars" was over—again, and cops were people citizens smiled at in the street. Pat O'Brien. Dick Tracy. "Top o' the morning to ya, officer!"

The coffee mug was empty again. Ganzer refilled it.

Through the grillwork of the Property Window he could see the red smear on the floor. In the old days, a rookie with a mop would have been through by this time in the night, washing away all the sins and blemishes of the day. Cleansing. Disinfecting. But not any more. Someone had decided that was an improper use of Academy-trained personnel. Now a civilian janitorial service had the contract. Of course, department budgets had been trimmed recently and the clean-up man only came twice a week. So the red smear was here to stay. For a while.

Ganzer gazed at it and the smear changed shapes. Like a Rorschach test. Tell me what you see? Well, doctor, I see a red sailboat at sunset heading for the horizon. Ver-r-y interesting! What do you see now? Butterflies, doctor, beautiful white butterflies—that got squashed. Aha, even more interr-r-esting! What it is, doctor, is blood! Some poor sick freak left a little something of himself on the floor, doctor, and everybody's going to walk on it until the guy with the mop comes on Thursday. And they only pay that untrained son-of-a-bitch minimum wage, so he'll probably miss the spot and anyone who wants to can keep on looking at it and trying to make something out of it.

Empty. The mug was empty.

There was more coffee. But when Ganzer uncorked the second Thermos, the steamy aroma told him that the Viennese mix was incomplete. Delicious, but low octane. Unlaced. He had forgotten to add the final ingredient. Brandy. Donald Duck had come out to play with only one barrel loaded. And tonight was definitely going to be a double-barreled night.

He could wait for his dinner break. Or he could take care of the oversight now. Ganzer phoned upstairs and asked for a relief man. They were just sitting around up there anyway. Price. Karl Price, the black kid, came down. He worked the breath meter: Blow in my machine and I'll tell you how high you're flying. But the drunk drivers were running slow tonight, so Price was glad to cover for Ganzer. Nice guy. Time was when a black cop was a novelty and guys worried: When the crunch comes, is he going to react like a brother officer or a soul brother? That locker room argument was settled long ago to everybody's satisfaction. Now the same argument raged about women riding the squad cars. Is she going to behave like

■ 171 ■

a cop or a broad? Ganzer was all for trying it out. Who knows? Maybe if some of the gals find out what it's like in the street, they'll spread the word. Tell the others. So somebody's wife can understand.

Ganzer ambled down the hall, toting the Donald Duck lunch pail. He went into the john and swayed at the urinal. We aim to please, will you please aim? He chuckled and headed out, down another corridor. He peeked around a corner and pulled back out of sight. He leaned against the wall and lit a cigar. Peekaboo! He chuckled again, remembering. First week he was breaking Eddie Brenner in they had answered a call. The man was in his bathrobe. Middle of the morning. Dried lather still on one side of his face. A dazed-scared look in his eyes:

". . . I was shaving. I'm late for the office already. And I get the feeling there's somebody looking over my shoulder. Right there in the bathroom. I turn around and nobody's there. I'm all alone. Door is closed. So I go back to shaving, but I feel it again. I turn around real quick and I catch a glimpse of something disappearing."

"Where?" Brenner was taking the notes.

"Down the toilet. But I go look. And there's nothing there. A ripple in the water, but nothing."

"So?"

"So I try to finish shaving. And I feel it again. This time I don't turn. I just move over a little and peek in the mirror."

"What did you see?"

"A fucking monster! Like a giant snake! Playing peekaboo with me in the toilet. I look and he sees I'm looking and he hides."

It sounded crazy.

It wasn't.

Two hours later, with the help of four zoo attendants and a plumber, Brenner and Ganzer had snared the Loch

Ness Monster lurking in the plumbing. An eleven-foot boa constrictor. Kid down the block had flushed his pet down the john months ago. The pet thrived—and went visiting the neighbors.

"Imagine what might've happened," Brenner suggested in the squad car later, "if the guy had been shitting instead of shaving."

Ganzer was driving. He almost hit a telephone pole. The new guy was going to be all right.

All right. There was a side door, locked from the inside, that led directly to the parking lot. Ganzer pushed it open and was careful to leave it unlatched for his return.

Technically, he was breaking the rules. Leaving the building without signing out, except during mealtime. But it was just across the street and up to the corner. If there was anything to do, Price would do it. Big fucking deal. Check turkeys in, collect the leavings from their mangy pockets. Any kid could handle it if he could stay awake. One key ring, one condom, one nailclipper—one shitty job for a cop who used to be . . .

What?

Used to be an A-Number-One cop. That's what! There was a time when that was a big deal to Ganzer.

Another black face flashed—and then another . . .

Fingers. Ebony black, but the pads and palm were pink. Gnarled. Straining. Gripping the chipped wooden chair she was sitting in. With both her hands. She wasn't a big woman and she didn't look all that strong, but she was determined. She wasn't going with them. No way! But they weren't leaving without her. Ganzer looked over at his partner. Henry Walker. Black face, beads of sweat matching his own. They had been in the same class at the Academy. Now, two years later, they were riding together, both experienced officers. But the two of them, together, couldn't pry this little black lady loose and get her out of her Adams Boulevard walk-up apartment. They couldn't even get her out of that damn chair.

She was charged with child abuse. Beating up on her baby. The family next door had heard the crying and made the call. When they got there, the lady admitted she'd done it and said she was sorry. She wanted to let it go at that. They couldn't. They tried to make the bust. She kept holding on to the chair. Jaw clenched, eyes pleading. All three of them sweating a brick.

It was getting ridiculous.

One by one, Ganzer was prying her fingers loose. Two, three, four and . . . Now the whole hand suddenly came free. Bringing with it a butcher knife that she had been concealing under the seat of the chair.

Her hand went high and Walker grabbed for it. She nicked him and then the dance began. A tango for three with the gleaming razor-sharp blade the prize. It sliced the air, the point tearing their clothes, scratching them. Two guys who each weighed nearly two hundred and they were rocketing off the walls with her, tumbling over furniture, round-and-round we go, and she weighs maybe a hundred and five with her hat on so why can't we wrap her up? Walker! God damn it, choke her out!

And he did.

The knife clattered to the floor.

They cuffed her.

And that's when the trouble began.

When they brought the woman out of the building, there was a crowd waiting. All black. What they saw was clearly a case of police brutality. A black mother crying pitifully for her child. She was smeared with blood. Their blood.

They were only about thirty feet away from the police car. They almost didn't make it. The crowd pummeled and cursed them. Tore at the two terrified cops who pushed their prisoner forward, shoving aside the clawing hands that tried to take her away from them. And the look on Walker's face was one that Ganzer never forgot. For Walker was the focal point of their fury. A honky cop hassling a sister, they could dig. But a black cop doing one of his own! The insults and threats had an intensity, a scorching heat that Ganzer had never experienced.

It was like a nightmare. Going toward the car but never getting there, struggling and slipping and pushing and—we're not gonna make it. We're not—we're there! Somehow. At the car. They slammed the doors. Gunned the motor and got the hell out of there. Rocks crashing at the rear window. But gone—safe. Alive! We made it, Henry!

They booked her. A day later, she was out. The case never made it to court. Child abuse hadn't become fashionable yet in the D.A.'s office.

Ganzer tried to talk to Walker about it. Tried to turn the whole thing into a laugh. But Walker wasn't laughing.

"Marty, it's a bunch of shit," Walker said. "It's not worth it. Just not worth it."

And a week after that, Walker was gone. Resigned from the force. Just gave it all up. For what? Went into the insurance business. Ganzer ran into him recently. Fat and fifty, rich and happy as hell. Running his own office, vacations in Hawaii with his family. Dumb son-of-a-bitch, gave up being a cop for that? When he could have hung on like Ganzer and put in another twenty-eight years and retired so he could spend all his time holding on to a fishing line and hovering around his kids who smiled patiently but made him feel like he bored the shit out of them and thinking about a loving wife who checked out of his life at the twenty-six–year mark. Talk about breaking the rules! The game was almost over then. None of them knew what it was like. None of them.

Marty Ganzer clutched his Donald Duck lunch pail and

scurried across the dark night street into the liquor store on the corner.

❖❖❖❖

"So this night I'm telling you about," Herman Yousha tossed over his shoulder, "I pick up this guy outside a bowling alley in Culver City. And he gives me an address in Downey."

In the back seat of the taxi, Herman's passenger was looking out the window and watching the building tops along the freeway blur past. The man was a captive audience.

"So I go out East Whittier and I'm doing forty miles an hour, because I know that then you can make all the lights. And I'm talking to him like I'm talking to you, mister, and you know what happens?"

Herman paused for the passenger's response. The disinterested man was slow on picking up his cue, but then he did. "What happened?"

"What happens is, I look in the back seat"—Herman did just that to illustrate the action—"and the door is open and he's not there, the guy from the bowling alley. He got out. Jumped out when I'm going forty miles an hour down Whittier. So he won't have to pay two dollars and forty cents on the meter."

The point that Herman Yousha was trying to impress on his passenger was the cheapness of some people. Herman was attempting to make the best of a bad situation. He had been trapped at the airport with this fare going to G-4, which is Beverly Hills. All the cabbies hated G-4. Once you were there, you were in a land of short hauls and the worst tippers in town. Herman's subtlety was wasted. When he cut over on Wilshire from the freeway and dropped off his airport passenger at the Beverly Hilton, there was eight-twenty on the meter and the lousy cheap-skate gave Herman a fifty-cent tip.

Herman Yousha was not universally admired by his colleagues. Because it was suspected that he was a "guz-zler." The accusation had nothing to do with his drinking habits. Herman Yousha was strictly a Diet Pepsi man on duty and occasionally took a glass of thick sweet red wine before holiday meals. When the other cabbies whispered behind his back that "The old bastard's definitely a guzzler," they were referring to Herman's appetite in sipping from the cup of life that they mutually shared.

The rules were clear. In Los Angeles, unlike New York or Chicago, taxicabs were not permitted to cruise. There were taxi ranks in front of various major hotels and at the airports. Riders could be picked up there, but a newly arrived cab had to take a place in line for fares. In addi-tion, there was a central gathering point in each sector of the city where radio dispatchers received the telephone inquiries that were the principal source of pickup calls. A cab driver was expected to be at one of those places, wait-ing his turn to be assigned a call. Unless, of course, he was already out on a call. And that was the loophole that allowed the guzzler to thrive.

When a new call came in, it made obvious good sense for the dispatcher before sending a cab from central to find out if there were cabs already in the requested area. The dispatcher would broadcast the new address, and any cabs out there having just completed a run would radio back their positions. The nearest driver would get the call —without returning to wait at the end of a line for his next fare.

The guzzler would lie. Answer a call even if he wasn't anywhere in the vicinity. Radio in a phony position calcu-lated to win the call. And then tear across town to get there.

It was a risky game. A cabbie could be fired if he was caught guzzling. But in the fast-moving confusion of the streets, it was difficult to prove. So a nervy, nimble guy could book a lot of juicy runs he might not otherwise get. Herman Yousha usually was the high booker rolling out of his taxi garage each week.

He had been pushing a hack for fourteen years, since the hardware store off Crenshaw went bankrupt because the neighborhood changed and those people didn't know why they had to come in and buy something during the day when they could come in and steal it for nothing at night.

On this night, Herman Yousha was making up for lost time. He had been home in bed for three days with the flu. Now he was up and around but his wife, Lillian, was floored by the bug. It was going around. Even their Siamese cat, Ming Su, wasn't feeling too well. Lillian said it was because Herman fed the cat too many scraps from the table, but if you couldn't spoil your family a little bit, then what the hell?

". . . and police authorities refused to comment on reports that an arrest had been made in the two-and-a-half-week-old child disappearance, although witnesses on the UCLA campus . . ."

Herman Yousha didn't want to listen to other people's troubles; he turned the dial of the little pocket transistor until he found some nice lively music. It was going to be a long night. Herman wanted to stay wide awake and concentrate on business.

Speed was important now. He had to get out of G-4 before the rest of the evening got crapped up. Herman was pulling onto Santa Monica Boulevard across from Century City when he heard the call. A "pink" fare at Bundy off Olympic. "Pink" meant an airport run. It could be a whole new night for whoever got back out there. No telling where the next guy getting off a plane had to go. No short hauls and please, God, no more G-4! Herman Yousha radioed his position, describing an intersection five miles away from where he was but only seven blocks from Olympic and Bundy. The dispatcher assigned the run to Herman and he shifted into high, burning rubber down Santa Monica Boulevard. He had miles to cover in minutes in order to get honest.

Herman rolled out of Beverly Hills and into West Los Angeles. As he approached the corner of Butler Avenue, the light went yellow and a block ahead the next light was turning red. It was taking too long to reach the fare, he might make out better on the side streets. Herman signaled left in mid-intersection and simultaneously tugged the wheel. He made it onto Butler going south before the light went red. Marvelous reflexes—not bad at all for a man of his years, he congratulated himself. I'm an old cocker but I drive better than all these kids today put together! He passed the liquor store on the corner and shifted into high again.

As he picked up speed and raced down the dark still street, a shape appeared. Emerging from between two parked cars. Herman didn't see the man until the bumper hit him and the man flew up through the beam of headlights—into the air—like in a movie cartoon, up, up, UP! And then down—straight down.

Herman Yousha screeched his brakes and jumped the curb before he stopped, knocking over garbage cans lined up for collection the next day. He didn't see Marty Ganzer land on his head in the street. The Donald Duck lunch pail that sailed high with him had already crashed into the gutter and split open. The bottle of brandy had fallen out and shattered and the amber liquid was now spreading and staining the gutter.

When the fire started, it was assumed that the cause was a careless night driver tossing a cigarette butt out the window on the last curve on Coldwater Canyon, just south of Mulholland Drive.

It was an area in which the Beverly Hills houses had ended and the less expensive homes on the Valley side had not begun. A few cantilevered dwellings clung to the mountainside along the road, dangling out over the parched expanse of open brush. In the days after the fire was finally brought under control, a special arson squad would try to determine the specific source of the blaze. But whether the answer was a firebug, a thoughtless citizen or simply spontaneous combustion igniting the foliage, the result was the same. It was the price of basking in Paradise and each year the only suspense was where it would happen and at what cost. The fires always came during the long wait for the rains.

The clanging, keening units raced from the Valley

station and from Beverly Hills and from West Los Angeles. Sixteen fire trucks in all—with more in reserve. The logistics involved were similar to a military campaign. The enemy had struck in the area off Coldwater and the prevailing winds were spreading the advance away from the structures in Coldwater but the next canyon was not that far. With more houses. A perimeter had to be established. But all the defensive forces could not be committed on this one front. A rapid shift of the breeze—worse yet, an increase in the velocity of the dreaded winds—and the enemy might open new beachheads anywhere. So forces had to be held in reserve.

During the great Bel Air fire of 1961, flaming shingles were lifted from the roofs of blazing homes and carried by gusts of wind, hopscotching miles, skipping over canyons and the freeway to touch down like a random finger of destruction turning other communities into fire season infernos. The cost that year was in the millions. Refugees had fled before the merciless invader, taking with them only what they had on their backs and what could be hastily carried away. Which portions of your life can be transported on such short notice? Think fast! What can you lift—and what's really important? Family pictures or family heirlooms? One TV set or the kid's favorite dolls? What do you leave behind? What's truly irreplaceable and can it fit into the back seat of a station wagon?

Afterward, there was only rubble and smoldering beams. Occasionally, a brick chimney left standing: chimneys and swimming pools, they had survived. Swimming pools, thick with soot, the aquamarine waters discolored and obscured. In the land of the heated pool, the thermostat had gone crazy: Some desperate residents had tossed sets of antique dining silver into their pools for safekeeping from the flames; the heat in some pools rose high enough from the fire to melt the silver.

The scars seemed permanent. But if some never forgot, there were many others who did: Within a few years, all the houses that burned were rebuilt. New structures rising on the traces of the old. Different people living there, different, and the same. All knowing that next year, and in all the years to follow, there would always be a fire season in Los Angeles. But betting that their time had not come and hoping that it wouldn't happen to them. They tried not to think about it during the other months of the year. And now that it had come, those closest woke in the night to the sound of fire engines and looked out their windows at the red glow in the black sky and turned on TV sets or radio news reports. And for those near enough to feel the warmth of the unreasoning, still-uncontrolled monster roaring and ranting in their world, there was fear. Husbands pulled on pants and climbed to the roofs and began to douse the tops of their homes with hoses—sprinkling holy water on their shingles to guard against the evil.

From the sky came the borate bombers: small planes dropping missiles of fire-dousing liquid. On the ground, firemen, like infantry sloggers, dug ditches, drew lines, scorched fire breaks designed to stop or at least channel the advance of the enemy. There was a war going on, but most of the sleeping people in the city remained unaware. And in their bedroom, on the flatland below, Harold and Claire Montrose slumbered fitfully, no part of the battle being fought a few miles from their door.

■▞▞▞■

Through the thin drapes, Brenner could see daylight beginning to streak the sky outside the hospital. It had come down to the two of them: Brenner and Ramirez. Other guys had been and gone. They stayed. Watching a TV set with the sound turned off in the high-ceilinged empty waiting room. Chester Morris, leading with his chin as always. *Boston Blackie.* Ramirez yawned. It had been a long time since either of them had spoken.

Brenner had watched the dawn appear in another room like this. Nine years before. Mike was born at 7:05 in the morning. Phyllis was in labor over eleven hours. But they allowed Brenner to stay with her most of that time and he got to see her within a half hour after the birth. The actual delivery went easy. Phyllis was tired, but laughing, making jokes when he saw her. "Bet you thought I'd never get it done." Brenner laughed and hid his hands behind him. They were shaking.

Not now. He looked at his hands. Rock steady.

It went down smoothly. The ambulance was there within five minutes and they got Ganzer out of the gutter and into UCLA Emergency fast. They wheeled him up into surgery and a nurse came out to tell them they were lucky, the guy operating was one of the best in the country. And they waited. Most of the cops who waited were still there when the doctor came out two hours later to tell them that Ganzer was resting easy. Still on the critical list. In Intensive Care. Everything being watched. Tests being run, results won't be available for a while. Got to run—another operation scheduled.

The doctor left and one by one the cops left. But not Brenner and Ramirez.

They weren't expecting good news. Hoping was something else. But it felt like a death watch. Brenner was scared. Like the other time he had been in a room like this, scared and powerless, putting his faith in other men. The other time they had his wife—and his son. This time . . .

Why weren't his hands shaking?

There was someone coming. In the doorway beyond

Boston Blackie, the surgeon went by with another guy dressed in hospital operating-room greens. The anesthetist. The surgeon had a cup of coffee in his hand and the two of them were talking and walking away down the corridor when Ramirez caught up to them:

"Excuse me, Doctor." They stopped and turned. For a second, Ramirez could see that the surgeon didn't even remember him. Then:

"Oh, yes, Lieutenant . . ."

"I wondered, you know, if there was any more on Ganzer. You said the tests . . . ?"

"Ganzer? Right. The tests. Well, he's still in Intensive Care. I looked in on him a few moments ago. Doing as well as can be expected. The vital signs are still strong."

"But the tests." Brenner had come up beside Ramirez.

"Rather discouraging, I'm afraid."

"What do you mean?" It always came down to this, Ramirez thought. Asking questions. Waiting for answers. But it was usually easier because it was somebody else's pain you were asking about.

"Well, you must realize that with a cranial injury of the severity sustained by Mr. Ganzer that—er-r-r, brain damage was almost a certainty."

They had been thinking it. But now the man who knows was saying it.

"How bad?" Ramirez asked.

"Quite extensive, I'm afraid. But as I say, the vital signs are all still very strong."

"But what does that mean?" Brenner heard himself. Loud. Too loud. The two doctors were looking at him funny. The way Brenner would look at a witness—saying to himself, keep an eye on this one.

"It means," the surgeon said slowly, "that with the facilities and care available at this hospital, Mr. Ganzer is still alive and doing as well as can be expected."

"That's good, Doctor, but . . ." Before Ramirez could finish, Brenner interrupted.

"It's bullshit, Ben! Didn't you hear him? He said brain damage."

"I said . . ." The surgeon was playing school teacher, explaining the alphabet to first graders.

"I heard you. You said his vital signs are strong," Brenner repeated, "and his fucking mind is gone!"

"Take it easy, Ed." Ramirez was touching his arm. Brenner shook him off and kept his attention riveted on the surgeon.

"His mind's dead but his body is still alive," Brenner challenged. "That what you're telling us?"

The surgeon met Brenner's challenge evenly. "In layman's terms, that's fairly accurate."

The fight's over, Brenner thought. I win. But what? Got the asshole to talk straight stuff. Ain't I terrific? He didn't want me to know, but now I do.

Brenner turned away.

Ramirez gazed at him, but Brenner seemed calm again. Under control. They'd been very close, him and Ganzer. Ramirez was the one who first paired them up, years ago. Figured Brenner could learn a lot from Ganzer. It worked out. You take one sharp older cop and put him with a promising young cop. Simple arithmetic. One plus one. Ramirez heard the doctor talking to him:

"I'm very sorry, Lieutenant. We'll continue to provide the very best care to Mr. Ganzer for no matter how long . . ."

"Yeah, fine," Ramirez interrupted. "Thanks, Doctor."

The two men in hospital greens moved off. Ramirez waited for Brenner, who was leaning against the wall. After a moment, they went back into the waiting room and sat down again. "Boston Blackie" was chasing the bad guy over the rooftop of a warehouse.

"Want some breakfast?" Ramirez asked.

"Sure. Why not?" Brenner said. "Got to take a leak first."

Ramirez remained watching the TV set without sound while Brenner walked down the hall to the Men's Room. The hospital smell was in here, too. Ammonia probably. The only good germ is a dead germ. Brenner soaped his hands in the wash basin and then washed the lather away with warm water. He dried his hands with a paper towel. Rock solid. Ganzer's a vegetable and look at these hands. I got the heart of a surgeon—like that asshole out in the corridor. He crumpled the paper towel and threw it on the immaculate floor of the spotless hospital bathroom.

Brenner came out of the men's room and saw the door marked Intensive Care. A young intern was emerging from the locked room and hurrying away without waiting for the door to click shut behind him. Time froze for an instant: Brenner was watching the door slowly closing—watching—and then it was rapid motion: He was there catching the door and pulling it open. He walked into the forbidden land and it was just another corridor. Small rooms. No one in sight. He walked past one door and then he stopped and backed up.

Ganzer.

Like a horror movie. On a bed. Wires. And machines. And more wires. To his chest and his arms and his legs. An I.V. bottle, his hand taped to a board, glucose dripping into the back of his hand. His head! Look at his head. All bandaged. A helmet of white. A turban—like Sabu, the elephant boy. And wires! Those fucking wires leading nowhere. The Frankenstein monster. When I throw the switch, the monster will live. Not *think*. Or laugh or feel. Not ever again. But nevertheless alive . . . ?

"What are you doing here?"

Brenner turned. There was another punk in a white

jacket. Another medical genius who knew it all and couldn't do shit anymore for Ganzer. Brenner pointed at his friend.

"Why don't you let him go?"

"You don't belong here," the intern said. "This is a restricted area. You'll have to leave."

"Not until you let him go," Brenner said. Still quietly. He wasn't going to yell. Nobody listens to you when you yell.

There were more hospital guys coming now. And the little punk was getting huffy. Didn't the son-of-a-bitch understand English? All that medical horseshit. Latin terms and two-buck words for nickel-and-dime reality. Ganzer's gone. His brains are laying out in the gutter on Butler Avenue. He's not here.

"Let him go!"

Brenner lunged for the machines. He was going to do it if they wouldn't. Pull out the wires. Turn off the machines.

"Who the hell are you, God?" Brenner yelled. *"The man's dead, let him alone. Let him go. Pull the God damn plug!"*

There were people all over Brenner. Grabbing. Restraining. Lifting. Pinning his arms. He didn't want to hurt anybody, didn't they understand? But seeing Ganzer like that. Look at his face. There's nothing there. It's too late.

Ramirez was there now, too, and they were propelling Brenner out of the locked corridor. Slamming him against the wall. The little intern was calling to the nurses, telling them to notify the security detail and then . . .

"Sergeant?" Someone was calling to him. "Sergeant! Do you remember me?"

Brenner focused. Another asshole in a white coat. No. He knew this face. He'll understand.

"You're—you're the doctor. From the emergency clinic

downstairs," Brenner said. "The one who—helped Bobby Montrose."

"That's right," Dr. Sand said. The platinum mustache was growing in better, but the doctor still looked like a kid. Brenner watched Sand's mouth as he spoke. "Are you all right now, Sergeant?"

Brenner nodded.

Dr. Sand turned to Ramirez. "I think you better take your friend home now. There's no point in waiting around. We can call you . . ."

■▪▪▪

On the fireline there was chaos. The steep canyons formed a flue, sucking in the mild breezes that were heated by the flames and blown at increasing velocity down the natural wind tunnel formed by the ridges.

Grimy men poured an endless torrent of water on the fire which so far had claimed one house and caused the evacuation of more than a hundred families of hill dwellers. Most of the time, being a fireman was a cushy job: working forty-eight–hour shifts that consisted of eating, sleeping, playing cards, strumming the guitar, watching TV or tossing a football in the driveway of the fire station. Two days on and five days off. But today, dues were being paid. The gladiators were in the arena and the creature they faced was more terrifying, harsh, unreasoning and unfathomable than the most bloodthirsty beast ever confronted on the sands in ancient Rome.

The conflagration advanced relentlessly, but a line had been drawn. An area of earth had been scorched and cleared. Now the hungry flames were approaching and the fire-fighters frantically dug dirt, widening a natural ditch—and then retreated, sweating, skin stretched taut by the heat, coughing and choking, waiting to see if their efforts to force the roaring dragon to alter course would be successful. It worked. The tidal wave of destruction rolled up to the firebreak and then shifted direction. There were other acres of open brush to feed the endless, searing appetite, and the fire rushed off toward them.

The firemen had secured their first victory, their first step toward containing the blaze. They moved in to douse the residual flare-ups in the desolate no man's land left in the wake of the battle on this front. And it was then that a cry was heard down the fireline, a call that echoed in seconds and brought men running.

A discovery had been made: Digging in the ditch, a fire trooper had found a scorched lump. At first, he thought it was a rock, then the carcass of a small animal trapped by the fire. On closer examination, he saw that it was neither. And that was when he sounded the alarm.

"It's a kid," the soiled, weary fireman pointed with his shovel; the others looked down into the ditch. "Looks like it was a boy."

"What are you going to do?"

Brenner considered the question. They were standing beside his car in the driveway of the house he used to live in.

"I don't know," he told Phyllis. "Take Mike to a movie maybe, or down to the pier."

"You can stay here," she said. "I'm going out for a while anyway. Why don't you? Mike's a little tired, just getting over his cold . . ."

Brenner thought it over. Might be nice. Instead of always going and doing. A day with his son and just do nothing. Relax. Be together. Here. Like it used to be.

"I'll ask Mike," Brenner said. Then he smiled at Phyllis. "Thanks."

The backboard was a little high. Brenner had bolted it into place above the garage door when Mike was only five. In those days, the boy was more into dodgeball at nursery school than basketball in his own backyard. But Brenner used to spend hours shooting baskets, and Mike would sit and watch and start to try and Brenner would show him how. Even though the basket was too high, they learned to make the adjustment.

Brenner dribbled past Mike and shot. "Two points," he said. They were just fooling around, not really keeping score.

The kid was fast. Basketball belonged to the tall guys, but at Mike's age the growth spurts were only starting. So Mike could still make up in speed the couple inches the other guys had on him. Pretty soon, the gap would widen and the giants would freeze him out of the game. Mike wasn't going to be all that tall. You usually don't wind up that much bigger than your father.

"Way to go!" Brenner yelled as Mike faked him out and ran for the basket. Mike shot and the ball hit the backboard, rolled around the rim of the hoop and fell down without going through.

"You should have had that one," Brenner consoled as the boy lunged for the ball. He shot again. This time, Mike sank the ball neatly and smiled at his father.

"You know how you always told me how you practice and practice and all of a sudden you get good?" Mike asked excitedly. "So yesterday I got ten baskets in a row in the schoolyard and all the guys're looking at me and they go, 'Look at him!' 'cause I'm never that good but . . ."

He shrugged and Brenner wagged his head approvingly. Ten in a row yesterday and today the boy couldn't sink one for fifteen minutes when he's playing with his old man. That tells you something, Brenner thought.

"That's the way it goes, Mike."

"Hey," she called to them. "I'm going."

Brenner saw Phyllis coming out the back door. She was dressed different. Going-out clothes. Not flashier than she used to dress. But brighter colors. Phyllis still had almost the same knockout figure that had turned him on when they first met. And now she was wardrobed to call attention to the soft curves of her body. Tastefully. But the kind of clothes he would have objected to if they were still married.

"You look very nice," Brenner said.

"Thank you, sir," she curtsied in the doorway. "Mike, are you getting overheated?" She came down the back steps.

She wasn't alone.

He was tall. Taller than Brenner. Not a bad-looking guy. Good shoulders, bright face, the kind of easy twinkle in the eye that told you he could probably tell a joke real well. Brenner hated him on sight.

"Hi." The asshole was smiling. "I'm Chet Bowers."

"Ed Brenner." And Brenner stepped forward. Smile. Hand out. Let's shake. I got better manners and more cool than you, prick. They stood there awkwardly. Curiously. What else do you say? How ya doin'? Brenner wasn't about to ask and he sure as hell didn't want to know. He's younger than me, maybe a year or two. Or maybe not.

They had both been glancing at each other appraisingly. Now the two men, as if on command, looked away. At Phyllis—and Mike. The two men stood shoulder to shoulder and watched mother and son.

She was blowing down his sweaty neck, fanning Mike with her hand. "You're so sticky," she said. "Now, I don't want you to wear your father out with the basketball."

"Aw-w-w, we're just playing!"

"Well, find another game to play soon," she said, hugging the boy and kissing him on top of his head. "I don't want you missing any school this week. So take it easy."

She looked over at Brenner.

"See you later."

He waved and Chet Bowers moved to join her.

"Nice meeting you," Chet Bowers tossed back.

"Same here, Chet," Brenner answered. "Have a good day." Two points for my side. They were walking away together up the driveway toward the street. She took his arm. A nice-looking couple. Talk about a motherfucker.

The basketball hit him in the gut.

Mike had tossed the ball to him. It was unexpected, but Brenner's hands came up defensively. He bobbled the ball in the air and looked at the boy, who seemed unaware of anything but their game. Mike was waving his hands, covering, blocking, dancing in front of him. Brenner was in control again, he bounced the ball then feinted and shifted, loping past Mike, dribbling and shooting. The ball went perfectly through the basket without touching the sides of the hoop. Talk about a winner!

Now Mike had the ball and it was Brenner's turn to pursue him.

∎∎∎∎

The technique involved was slightly on the gruesome side, but not to the technicians involved. They had long since developed the capacity to compartmentalize, the ability to keep from making irrelevant connections, avoid projecting, relating—or imagining: These were vital attributes in the police lab.

They were using the process evolved originally by the FBI. During the first few years, it was guarded as zealously as the formula for Coca-Cola. Any police department seeking positive identification of burn victims had to deal with Washington. Now the technique was available as a matter of routine in most local police labs. It had proved valuable in deciphering tricky insurance "accidents" that turned out to be homicides. And it was frequently used in the wake of air disasters.

Ramirez always was reminded of the "invisible" writing that everybody did as a kid. Scribble messages in lemon juice; hold the "blank" sheet of paper over the toaster and watch the words appear.

Similarly, the lab technique found something where there was nothing: burn cases so badly charred that even the fingerprints were destroyed. Or were they? The pad of the finger would be stripped off meticulously and paraffin wax, carefully heated, injected under the skin. More times than not, the fingerprint reappeared. Visible again for computer comparison with the ever-increasing files of prints that law-enforcement agencies had available to them: from criminal bookings, national security clearances, motor vehicle licensing bureaus, checking account identification cards, the military services. There were even supermarkets and department stores that kept files as an "extra protection service" for their charge customers.

But when the lab told Ramirez that they had brought out a latent on the right thumb, his next concern was whether all this cleverness had any value. How many little kids had ever been fingerprinted? Not Bobby Montrose. It was a long shot.

The magic computer provided the answer.

Name, rank and serial number. Almost. The boy's name was Harvey Allen Churillo. He was seven years old not four. That's what a fire could do. And the fifth of eight children of Master Sergeant and Mrs. Thomas Churillo, a career soldier recently arrived from a tour of duty in Germany. The children all traveled on civilian passports that required a fingerprint. The family was living in a small rented house off the crest of Coldwater Canyon, not far from the Army Reserve armory in Van Nuys where Sgt. Churillo was assigned. They had been driven from their home by the evacuation. Harvey had been staying the night at a classmate's house and the family supposed he was still there when they cleared out, but the boy had returned and evidently wandered into the path of the fire.

Ramirez leaned back in his chair and shuffled the pieces of paper on his desk that said that one boy he had never heard of before had died and been briefly mistaken for another little boy Ramirez had never met but felt he soon would.

■.■.■.■

The street was shaded with trees, and Brenner could remember some of them when they were saplings. When they first moved into the neighborhood, Brenner and several of the other husbands went on a landscaping kick. Planting trees. Redoing lawns. Working together on the weekends to smooth the soil, spread the smelly fertilizer, toss the seed. The wives took care of the watering. A lot of watering was needed the first few days, but not too much. Frequently, but lightly. Not soaked.

The street was still very pretty.

"You were just a little bit of a kid and I used to push you right down this sidewalk in a carriage," Brenner said as they strolled together.

Mike looked up at him with interest.

"What was I like then?"

Brenner chuckled. "Bald, buddy. You were bald."

"I was *not!*" Mike was smiling.

"Well, you looked bald. Your hair was all white—platinum. Real short and smooth. Like fuzz. That's what I called you. 'Captain Peachfuzz.' "

Mike laughed and Brenner did, too. They walked on along the sidewalk and Brenner took the boy's hand. When he was learning to walk, Mike would clutch hands; not really hands, his whole small hand could barely encompass one of Brenner's fingers. He held fingers. And then later, in crowded places, Disneyland, walking together, the three of them, Mike in the center, holding hands—swinging him between them.

Mike's hand was clasped in his now. Strong little hand. They walked in silence for a few steps, but it was a good silence. Warm. Not like when people didn't have anything to say to one another, but when they were sharing. Happy.

Mike let go. Withdrew his hand.

Brenner looked down at him and Mike indicated a cluster of people up ahead.

"C'mon, Dad. The other guys."

Mike was embarrassed. Babyish stuff. Caught holding hands. The three guys were friends of his. Working on a bicycle that was perched upside down on the sidewalk with the pedal chain off. Mike ran toward them and Brenner sauntered after him.

Chuck Corbin, the father of one of the boys, was pushing a power mower. He turned it off when he saw Brenner and grinned. Chuck was wearing paint-smeared messing-around-the-house clothes and hadn't shaved today. It was Sunday.

"Ed! Long time . . ."

"Yeah," Brenner agreed. "Long time."

Brenner shook hands with his ex-neighbor and wondered if his son had stopped holding hands, too. The boys were about the same age. Just a sign of growing up—when you let go.

"How's business?" Chuck asked.

"Business?" Brenner shrugged. "Can't complain. How you doin'?"

"You're not mad?" Mike said. The boy was concerned. Brenner drew the covers up to Mike's chin.

"Nah. You get tired, you lay down," Brenner said. "That's the smart way. Rest out. Think I never get tired? Everybody gets tired."

"But today's your day. I mean, our day."

"You take a little nap." Brenner drew the curtains shut to close out the late afternoon sun. "Then we'll figure out some other neat stuff to do after."

Mike nodded. "Okay. But just for a little bit."

"Sure," Brenner said. He bent over and kissed Mike lightly on top of his head. "You need something, you just call."

He turned off the lamp and went out. He could see Mike still watching him in the darkness as he closed the door.

The house was all his now. But he was a stranger, walking from room to room, restlessly trying to find a place for himself.

In the kitchen, he stopped for water. As he stood at the sink pouring the glass, Brenner gazed out of the window. An empty yard. A rusty Sears, Roebuck swing set where a child first played outdoors. There was a plant on the windowsill. Some sort of ivy or fern or something. The skinny vine covered with small leaves trailed down onto the counter. Was it new or was it here last time he was in the kitchen? Maybe it had been here for months. Phyllis said he never noticed things around the house unless she made him see them. Suppose this lousy little flowerpot had been there for years? Brenner took another sip of water from the glass and then poured the rest into the flowerpot.

Joke.

Man lost in the desert. Stumbling. Dying of thirst. Staggering. Hoping . . . praying for water. Suddenly, he sees something. Someone. Another man. A little old guy coming toward him. Closer. Carrying a small suitcase. Now the little old guy reaches the man, opens the suitcase and reveals—neckties. A whole suitcase full.

"Have I got a necktie for you! All colors, whatever you

want. Stripes and polka dots. Pictures of girls, of fishes, of sunsets, take your pick. A bargain price, just for today."

"Neckties!" the man screams. "I'm dying of thirst and you show me fucking neckties?"

He knocks the suitcase aside and stumbles on, leaving the little old guy behind. Awhile later, just when he's about to expire from exhaustion and sunstroke, the man sees a mirage. An outdoor café. Right there in the middle of the desert. A mirage—but, no, it's real. The man staggers closer. People sitting in the shade of palm trees, sipping tall cool drinks. The man drags himself to the entrance of this incredible garden and is about to enter when the head waiter appears. Blocking the way. "I'm sorry, sir, we don't allow anyone in here without a necktie."

Joke.

Brenner settled into a chair in the living room. It used to be "his" chair. He'd sit here—and Phyllis would be on the couch. Doing needlepoint or sewing socks or something. That part wasn't clear. TV set on. Mike laying on the floor, staring at the tube, laughing. Or jumping on Brenner when he was trying to read the paper or a magazine. "Don't wear your father out, he's tired." Mike in his lap in the chair, still a tiny guy, Brenner reading him nursery rhymes.

> "Wee Willie Winkie,
> Runs through the town,
> Upstairs and downstairs,
> In his nightgown.
>
> Laughing at the window,
> Crying at the lock,
> 'Are the children in their beds?
> For now it's twelve o'clock.' "

Brenner's father sat in his chair in the house in Bakersfield and watched Westerns on TV every Sunday. Their day of togetherness. Didn't matter who was in the movie. John Wayne. Bob Steele. Sunset Carson. Roy Rogers. Jimmy Stewart. Hopalong Cassidy. If it had horses and posses, the old man would lap it up. His hand hitting the threadbare arm of the sagging, overstuffed chair like he was keeping time to music as the movie nags galloped into black-and-white sunsets. Round and round the familiar phony papier-mâché rocks, the black-hat villains sneaking up on white-hat heroes. Pow! One shot and three of 'em bit the dust. The movies always ended the same way: his father asleep. In the big chair. As much as he loved the cowboy flicks, the old man never made it to the finish. Some people called the tube the Dream Machine; for Brenner's father it was the Sleep Machine.

He snored. A funny sort of reassuring sound. Like a power saw going in a garage a block away, the sound wafting back. Brenner would stay there, listening to his father sleep and watching Gary Cooper shoot it out with the Daltons and it was the best time with his father. When the old man woke up and another show was on, he would ask how it turned out. And Brenner would tell him. At first Brenner just digested what he had seen, but later on he would sometimes change the ending. Lie. Make it come out a different way. If he was mad at the old man for something, he would kill the hero just to see the old man get pissed: "Vot kind of movie is dot?"

They had a phonograph. Scratchy. Lousy tone. A toy really. Brenner had some kid records and a few used 45s he had bought in a swap store downtown. Country-Western stuff that was popular in Bakersfield. The old man hated the records. "But you like it when Gene Autry sings 'em!" the boy used to say. "Ven he sings it's better!" Sam Brenner would answer. There was only one record that his father liked to hear. A thick-lacquered 78 that they had brought out with them in the trunk of the car from Oklahoma. Ravel's *Bolero*. Sam Brenner would reveal the record as if it was a diamond he was unwrapping. A ritual. Wipe it off with his handkerchief. Then put it on the tinny phonograph and sit back with his eyes closed.

The music began softly, an insistent rhythmic phrase that was repeated again and again, each time more fully orchestrated, gaining in momentum and volume. The idea was to go from quiet to loud. But the old man had the volume up as high as it would go at the beginning, so that by the time *Bolero* ended—in a dazzling clash of cymbals —the windows of the musty, desolate rented house were rattling to the music. And his father was humming along to the strident, restated refrain at the top of his lungs:

"Dah-h-h, da-da-dee-da-da-*ump*-da-dah, da-da dee dah dah *dum-m-m-m* . . ."

Brenner could hear the bugler. He was blowing "Taps."

And the row of uniformed men stood with their rifles at attention. The last mournful note was sounded and the officer in charge gave a signal. The men shouldered their weapons and fired a volley of blanks at the sky. Two other dress-uniformed officers of the honor guard stepped forward and took the flag off Ganzer's coffin and began to fold it.

There was a trick to it. End over end, diagonally, making triangular-shaped folds that rapidly formed a compact bundle with the stars facing out. A well-oiled winch was lowering the coffin into the ground. The two Guardsmen marched smartly around the grave site and presented the flag to a small girl. Ganzer's granddaughter.

Brenner held his breath, waiting to see what the little golden-haired girl would do. He had been watching her during the ceremony. She was fidgeting while everybody strutted around and spouted long eulogies. Brenner had

difficulty connecting the descriptions of the departed with
the man he had known. And Ganzer's small granddaughter
obviously had trouble paying attention to it all.

Brass buttons on parade. This was a Class "A" send-off.
Because of Ganzer's long years of meritorious service and
the few weeks remaining before retirement, it had been
decided to award him a police funeral with all the trim-
mings. Why the hell not? If you can do it for a cop
blown away by a liquor store holdup man then why not
for a cop who got it stumbling out of a liquor store in the
middle of his night?

The small girl. Her name was Gloria or Lorrie or something like that. Ganzer had brought her to the house for
an awkward afternoon a year or so ago. Phyllis and
Brenner had been fighting. Mike was off on an outing with
some other kids. And the doorbell rang. They sat around
and looked at each other. Phyllis didn't say anything. She
didn't like Ganzer to begin with. Always felt he was a bad
influence on Brenner when they used to ride together. The
small girl had no toys or other kids to play with so they
all sat around and Brenner and Ganzer tried to talk about
nothing. And Brenner didn't realize then why Ganzer had
come but now that he was a member of the Sunday Club
he did.

She took the flag from the cop who held it out to her.
The small girl didn't know what to do with it. She tried
to give it to her mother, but Ganzer's daughter-in-law
indicated that she should hold on to it, and her father,
Ganzer's oldest son, nodded. So the small girl clasped the
folded flag to her chest.

Brenner glanced around at the mourners. Ganzer's other
son, the law school student, was there. A tall, thin-lipped
kid who didn't resemble his father much. Ganzer's ex-wife
had refused to come. Till death do us part. Brenner spotted
a familiar face standing a distance away. At first he

couldn't place her. Pretty girl, early thirties, crying. He had seen her cry before, Brenner remembered that, but she was younger then . . .

It came back to him.

One of the last things Ganzer and Brenner had worked on together. A slick, slimy Hollywood pimp. Sonny DeBartolo. Drove a Rolls-Royce he bought for cash with proceeds from his ladies. Sonny didn't run hookers, but pigeon droppers. Con gals who bilked little old ladies out of their life's savings. Pretending that they just found an envelope full of gambling money in the street, offering to share with the naïve lonely senior citizens. But first, one of the con gals would say, we've got to prove to my boss, who's a lawyer, that if someone comes forward to claim the money we can repay it. Before they knew it, the little old ladies were emptying their bank accounts to show cash to the imaginary lawyer and when they woke up they were alone again and feeling more like fools than victims. Many of the betrayed suckers were ashamed to report it and some of them took the gas pipe. It was a dirty business. But profitable for Sonny. Street estimates were that each girl he fielded was good for $150,000 a year. He usually had a dozen girls out hustling the con for him.

The only way to get at Sonny, who was very careful to stand off from the actual cons, was through the girls. But discipline was strong in the ranks. Short-changers got their faces sliced up and one gal had disappeared. Then Ganzer and Brenner got a tip. A name. A girl who had been solicited to join Sonny's stable. It took some doing, but they traced her. To her mother's house. A small white house in Redondo Beach with a picket fence around it. And the gal wouldn't tell them a thing. At first. But then her mother had to go out for groceries. Piece by ugly piece, it came out.

She was picked up on Hollywood Boulevard by Sonny.

Wined and dined. Mr. Smooth. A couple days of courtship. And then dead bang into the pitch: a regular Fagin session, Sonny drilling the new recruits, a school for scams. Getting them to memorize the words and moves. And this gal, what was her name? Dorothy. Dorothy Burton or Benton. Called herself Dorry, Brenner recalled. She wanted out. And told Sonny so. He didn't like that and decided to make an example of her.

There were several of Sonny's friends at the house that night. While the other girls watched, Dorry was forced at knife point to strip naked. Then crawl around on all fours and blow each of Sonny's buddies and then Sonny got into her from behind while he made her go down on his German shepherd.

On a sunny day in Redondo Beach, Dorry told them the story and got sick in the middle and managed to finish the telling with tears streaming down her face but not able to look at them. She had not told anyone else. Her mother just knew that Dorry had come running home, shaken and scared, hiding in the house she grew up in.

And after making her go through all that, it wasn't worth a thing. They never got enough to go to court on Sonny. Ganzer and Brenner told the assistant D.A. about Dorry. She could testify about the school for con players that Sonny was running. That was good for conspiracy. But when they told the prosecutor the rest, he refused to go with it. "Can you imagine what kind of credibility she'd have? Pick any twelve jurors you want, nice square citizens from Alhambra or Eagle Rock or wherever—they hear she made it with a dog and we're out of the box." Sonny had won. He was never busted and Brenner thought that was that.

But here was Dorry. Years later.

Crying again. Over Ganzer.

Maybe she read about the funeral in the paper. Or

maybe . . . Ganzer always had a sympathetic eye for ladies with heavy stories. Some guys just gravitated that way. So maybe—but what difference did it make now?

Ganzer's granddaughter was examining the flag in her small hands. Touching the stars. What can a kid make out of all this? Little John-John Kennedy, standing like a tiny soldier, saluting as the caisson rolled by. Enough to rip your fucking heart out. The wirephoto seen around the world.

Kids.

Brenner remembered reading a story about Bobby Kennedy. Christmas week. His first public appearance after the assassination at a party in a Washington orphanage. Everybody walking on eggs. Taking great care not to mention the thing that they all were thinking. Until a little boy stared up at Bobby and blurted: "Your brother died." A moment out of time, all the adults frozen, the little orphan boy realizing he had uttered something terrible. But then Bobby Kennedy smiled and lifted up the boy in his arms. "It's all right," he said, "I have another one."

Slow motion. Like marching through jello.

Ganzer is waiting up ahead. Nosy grin. Head sticking out of the Property Window. His head. Smiling.

"What's happenin'?" Ganzer asks.

"Busy, Marty. See you later, huh?"

Wrong. I'll see you but you won't see me. So why not stop now, take a minute, what the hell's so important I can't spare the time? Here it is again. The Property Window. Coming up. Ganzer. Smiling. This time, make it different. Stop and say—what?

Bobby Kennedy was lucky. With that kid. He knew what to say. But how about later? All of Bobby's kids at Hickory Hill, left with no father, except for Teddy Kennedy, and what does Teddy say when somebody reminds him, "Your brother died"?

The golden-haired daughter of Ganzer's eldest son touched the stars and it was all that remained. In time, the face of her grandfather would blur and probably the only thing that would stay sharp in her memory was this meaningless ritual with strangers gathered around a hole in the ground on a bright September day.

. . . there was a fiddler. No! A man with a golden violin.

The fiddler was bald with the last long strands of black hair pasted across the top of his shiny pate. A waxed Adolphe Menjou mustache stood at constant alert in the center of an amiable moon-face. The fiddler was from Budapest and how he ever wound up playing in a German Hofbrau on the outskirts of Bakersfield no one ever got straight. Brenner and Phyllis used to go there in their courting days.

He had a routine. The early part of the evening was devoted to schmaltzy tunes and comedy turns. His favorite schtick was to play a frenzied "Flight of the Bumblebee" with his eyes soulfully half closed and lean in tight beside an unsuspecting male customer, preferably one on a date with a pretty girl. The fiddler would nimbly entangle the customer's necktie in his bow and pretend not to notice. Just go on playing to a frantic finish. It was always good for a laugh. He had caught Brenner that way the first time they came here. But now he knew them and while he toured all the tables during the evening, he saved his last visit for them. His final selection was a haunting song that Brenner had never heard anyone else play. It was called "Gloomy Sunday." "Schlect Sontag," one of the German waiters translated it for them, which seemed closer to "Bad Sunday" but "Gloomy Sunday" was the title. Once somebody at the next table told Brenner and Phyllis there had been a famous recording of it in the '30s that was banned on the radio. Because somebody heard the song and committed suicide. But Brenner and Phyllis used to hold hands and smile as the Hungarian violinist stood beside their table and without any tricks played the song that was so beautiful and so sad . . .

"Ed?"

Phyllis was calling him.

"Ed?" The song was ending. The fiddler was almost through.

He opened his eyes.

In his chair. In his living room.

Phyllis leaning down over him, shaking him gently.

"Hey, Phyl," he smiled sleepily. "Dinner ready?"

She looked surprised and he didn't know why. Then Brenner remembered. He sat up in the chair and the magazine in his lap fell to the floor. He was embarrassed. "Sorry. For a second I thought . . ."

She nodded. She knew what he thought. The look of surprise was gone, replaced by a softness as she gazed at him.

"How long's Mike been sleeping?" she asked.

Brenner glanced at his watch. Almost eight o'clock. "Since around four."

"And you, too?" She smiled. "You're some pair. Snoozing away the whole day."

"Yeah, dreaming and—well, I better be going."

It stopped between them. But only for a second this time. "How about some coffee?" she said. "Come on, it'll help you wake up."

Without waiting for an answer, she moved off into the kitchen. Brenner stood and stretched and then slowly walked after her.

They were at the kitchen table and the house was quiet. Brenner and Phyllis were talking and it brought back to him other evenings long ago when they sat here and examined their lives or just reviewed the incidents of a day.

"Mike talks about you all the time." Phyllis filled his coffee cup again.

"When I'm not here," Brenner said. "Then when I see him—if I ask a question, I get an answer. It's like I'm at work." He was their son, maybe she knew the answer. "I don't know. Maybe it's me, Phyl, but I never used to even think about what to talk to him about. I'd just talk."

"Sure," she said.

"Now I think about it—and it still never comes out right. We keep running out of conversation."

"Like we used to?" She smiled at him over the rim of his coffee cup and he smiled back, ruefully, nodding.

"I catch him looking at me sometimes," Brenner said, "when he doesn't think I notice."

"Oh, come on." Phyllis put her coffee cup down with a clatter and gave a little laugh. Brenner leaned over the table to get closer to her.

"There's something wrong, maybe he's sick." She was shaking her head. "Something's bothering him," Brenner insisted.

"Wonder what it can be," she said. It was a warning sign, but Brenner missed it.

"Not you, Phyl," he said. "You've been—terrific." He looked up from his coffee cup. He wanted her to know that he knew. "Never bad-mouthing me to him. I been meaning to, you know, thank you. For making it easier, like with missing the birthday party."

"That was to make it easier for him," she said. It went past him again; he rubbed his eyes then smiled wearily across at her.

"Phyl, if only we could've talked like this before. You and me. When we were having our troubles . . ."

She interrupted.

"*We* are not talking." Phyllis sat up very straight. "*I* am listening to *you* talk. You still don't *hear* me! I just told you—I'm not doing a damn thing for you. It's for him. To make it easier for him. The hell with you."

Her voice wasn't loud or angry but it was a sound that he had never heard from her before.

"You don't know what to talk to your own son about? Too bad. But this is the way you wanted it, isn't it? Responsibility one day a week and a couple of minutes each month when you sign the checks. All the time you need to work or go out with the boys—or the girls!" She lingered over the word, then drew a breath. "A nice clean room to sleep in whenever you happen to get there—nobody to bother you. What's wrong with that?"

He kept looking at her. She didn't have any more to say, so now it was his turn.

"Thanks for the coffee," he said quietly. And got up, putting the cup and saucer into the sink as he walked out.

Mike was still sleeping, the quilt up to his chin the way Brenner had left him. But he had kicked one bare foot out from under and Brenner covered his son's foot and stood there with the shaft of light shining in from the hallway. He looked for a long moment at Mike's face.

He was aware that Phyllis was in the hallway watching him.

"Captain Peachfuzz," Brenner said softly.

Behind him, Phyllis heard and moved away.

She was waiting for him near the front door. Brenner pulled on his windbreaker and met her gaze.

"When he wakes up," Brenner said, "tell him so long for me."

"For this week," she challenged.

"Yeah." He wasn't going to play her game. He was cool. She couldn't get to him. He had sounded the alarm and sealed off the nerve centers. He was safe. You took your best shots, lady. Been saving 'em up for a long time, haven't you? He started for the door.

She blocked the way.

"Didn't you know . . . ?" It was the first sign of difficulty for her; she was still talking low, not to disturb Mike. "Didn't you know that everything was going to change? *Didn't you know that?*"

She's shaking, he thought. But not me, babe. I'm okay! He opened the door and went out.

◼◣◤◥◢◼

Caryl Ritchie drew the kitchen curtains shut in the house across the street from the Montroses. She listened to a cough coming from the boys' bedroom. Stephen and Jeff were asleep in their bunk beds. Probably Jeff. His cold had seemed better. She planned to send him back to school tomorrow.

Toys were strewn around the family room adjoining the kitchen, and Caryl began to pick them up. Miniature cabin logs and building blocks with the alphabet inscribed in raised letters. Jeff had pronounced these toys "babyish" several months ago and his little brother, of course, had agreed so Caryl had stored them in a box on a top shelf of the toy closet. Today they had come back into style.

Little Stephen's panda was hiding behind the TV set and as Caryl scooped him up she found herself thinking about what she had been trying to avoid: Bobby Montrose.

It was a day just a few weeks before Bobby disappeared. He had come over to look for the boys. They weren't home from school yet and she let Bobby wait for them in the bedroom. Caryl had gone on about her housework but stopped as she passed the open doorway. Bobby had lined up the panda and a stuffed lion and was playing a game of pretend. The panda was mommy and the lion was the daddy. Bobby was doing their voices as well as his own.

"Look what I know," Bobby said to the lion. "How to count to fifty just like the big boys. Listen, one—two, Stephen teached me, and he can count to a hundred. Daddy? One—two—three . . ."

"Bobby," the lion said, "can't you see I'm talking on the telephone?"

"Isn't that good?" Bobby asked the panda. "I'm gonna know everything that Stephen knows 'cause he tells me all the stuff from kindergarten. One—two—three—four . . ."

"Mommy has a headache," the panda said, "so you mustn't make a lot of noise."

Now Caryl Ritchie put the panda in the toy closet and closed the door. Days into weeks and still no explanation of what had happened to Bobby.

She listened again. There was silence in the house. Brad

would be home soon from the tax law seminar at USC. Her two boys were safe and snug in their beds. The coughing had subsided and it was quiet in their bedroom.

⬛⬛⬛⬛

Brenner roared with laughter. He had his head propped up by his right hand with the elbow resting on the bar and he pounded with the palm of his left hand. God damn, it was funny! Even McKnight was bellowing at the recollection. The Great Stone Face, saloonkeeper of "McKnight's Round Table," laughing. Louder than the fucking jukebox or the noise from the last of the one-o'clock customers.

"You remember that night, Danny?"

"Could I forget?" McKnight chortled from behind the bar. He had a fine head of flowing white hair and the florid face of a man who had enjoyed a lifetime of conviviality. When Brenner joined the Department, McKnight was already a retired cop running a friendly joint on Third Street near Vermont. Cops came here to unwind. Cops and ladies who liked cops.

"Th'night Chris Moran pulled the pin—we closed this place," Brenner told the girl sitting on the stool next to him. Her name was Gwen. She worked as a records clerk at Parker Center. Tall, sensual, with inviting curves, long brown hair and an easy laugh. She had a steady thing going for a long time with Don LeMoine, an Internal Affairs investigator. LeMoine was married and broke it off a few months before but Gwen kept coming to McKnight's in hopes of running into LeMoine, who stayed away to avoid her. She would talk with lots of the other guys and sometimes let them buy her a drink but Gwen usually bought her own and always went home alone at closing time.

"What a night!" The story was legend. A retirement

party. "Pulling the pin" was the slang phrase. As in a grenade. Pull the pin and—boom! "Irv Berman got so loaded, he went into the men's room and then couldn't find his way out."

"Pounding on the wall!" Brenner was choking with laughter.

"Yelling for help—begging!" McKnight guffawed.

"You could hear him all the way out here," Brenner said. "Screaming for somebody to come save him!"

"You're kidding," Gwen giggled. She had heard similar stories before but not this one and she was responding to their fondness of the memory.

"Man, I have been shit-faced in my day, but that night," Brenner howled, "I went home—see, usually I phoned ahead so Phyllis would take the chain off the door. But this time I forgot, till I got there—and I unlocked the door and it'd only open this much . . ."

Brenner measured three inches for Gwen with his thumb and forefinger and a cop he knew down the bar measured a matching distance in the air with his fingers and pointed at Brenner, laughing. Brenner cackled back at him and yelled, "Dirty mind, that's what you got, Garvey!"

Brenner turned back to Gwen, who was tittering and putting a long filtered cigarette between her full red lips with her right hand. Brenner fumbled a pack of "Round Table" matches on the bar but she produced a lighter from her bag and ignited her own cigarette, using her right hand again. Her left arm was not the same size as the other. It was a genetic defect. A ripe young woman's body with a thin little girl's arm. Gwen deftly concealed the fact from casual observers with a wardrobe of full-cut jackets and puffy-sleeved blouses. She usually took a seat with her left hand closest to an available wall; she now occupied the end stool. People who knew her for months frequently were surprised to notice the flaw. To the point that they would say "Hey, what's wrong with your hand?" as if it was something that had just occurred. Gwen would ignore the question and change the subject. Get people talking about themselves and after a while they'd forget. Brenner hadn't noticed. He drained his fifth Scotch and while McKnight refilled his glass, Brenner grinned blearily at this gorgeous groupie:

"This much," he repeated. Three inches. "So I'm reaching in the door with my fingers, trying to unhook the damn chain. Hell, I can hardly stand up and the chain won't come off 'cause it's put on right 'cause I installed it myself. Then it comes to me." He tapped his head, sharing a perception. "With all the noise I'm making, Phyllis is gonna think it's somebody bustin' in."

"And she's got a gun in there!" McKnight yowled. Brenner was coming to the part McKnight liked the best.

"Yeah, she's got the gun." Brenner laughed. "So just then, the front light goes on and I hear her inside and she says, 'Who's there?' I can't believe it! I yell back at her, *'Who do you think it is, John Wayne?'*"

McKnight winked at Gwen. "That's the night Phyllis turned off the porch light and left him standing out there."

"Yeah," Brenner grinned happily. "So I give the door a little kick. Then a *big* kick—and the whole door falls right off onto the floor in the hall . . ."

"Knocked it clean off the hinges, my boy did." McKnight patted Brenner's shoulder approvingly.

Gwen was laughing and shaking her head in mock horror at the craziness of it all. "No, you didn't."

"Oh, yeah, I *did*," Brenner assured her. "Then I staggered in and went to bed."

"Just like that," Gwen said. She snapped her fingers—

on her right hand—to accentuate the casualness of Brenner's absurd behavior. He was bobbing his head merrily, repeating after her: "Just like that . . ."

"Nothing like kicking a door to relax a man," McKnight philosophized. "Tell her about in the morning. When you're sleeping."

"I'm sleeping," Brenner said. "I mean, I need sleep. And Phyllis comes. She shakes me. She says, 'Do you know the door is broke off?' I say, 'Baby, lemme slee-ee-eep!' And she says"—Brenner shook his finger like a spinster schoolteacher—" 'You mean to tell me it's been like that all night? Get up and fix that door—*right now!*' "

"So there he is when I came by." McKnight blew a smoke ring at the ceiling. "With a hangover."

"Like you won't believe." Brenner beamed and held his head.

"And a hammer," McKnight said.

"A hammer," Brenner said. "Knocking in nails and each nail figures like it's going into my head—banging away—bang-BANG! Fixing the door."

Gwen was in stitches.

"That's using your head, m'boy," McKnight hooted.

And they all laughed together and Brenner pounded the bar with the palm of his hand which made McKnight and Gwen laugh louder. But then she caught a flicker on Brenner's face.

He was still gasping for breath, still roaring as he forced the words out:

"Danny? Hey, what am I tellin' this dumb story for? Divorced eight months—*still tellin' this stupid story!*"

He slammed his hand on the bar, making his Scotch glass dance. Gwen saw the distaste and looked away, but McKnight continued to gaze at Brenner as the conversation at their end of the bar came to an uncomfortable halt. Brenner was staring down at the murky reflection of light bouncing off the smooth dull surface of the bar.

McKnight tried a chuckle that didn't make it. "Guess you taught her, huh?" he said in an effort to recapture the lightness that was gone. Brenner poked an exploring finger at a ring of moisture on the bar.

"Yeah. I sure taught her." Phyllis' face was before him: as clear and fresh as the instant they met. "Taught her everything. How to drive a car, how to water ski, how to make love . . ." He looked up and saw no one. "Then I taught her how to hate me."

"Take it easy," Gwen mumbled. Flicking the ash from her cigarette. Unable to watch him.

"Yeah," Brenner said. Words of wisdom. "Sure . . ."

He pushed himself away from the bar and rose unsteadily.

"Easy," he repeated the secret word, swaying, then he moved slowly off toward the door leading out. He lifted a hand and waved good-bye without turning. Until Gwen called after him:

"Hey?"

Brenner stopped and faced her. He was cold sober again. A diligent night of drinking and right back where you started from.

"Need some company?" Gwen asked softly. She was watching his eyes.

He stood for a moment and then he nodded. "Yeah." It was an honest answer to an honest question.

Gwen reached into her bag with her right hand and brought out three dollar bills. She put them on the bar to pay for her drinks, picked up her purse and walked to where Brenner was waiting for her. She took his arm with her child's hand and McKnight watched them go out into the night together.

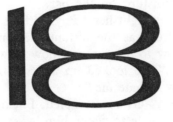

He was a tender lover. Patient. Oh, God he could do fantastic things forever with his fingers and his mouth and—and then take her with an exquisite gentleness that went on and on. She stole a glimpse at the clock on the nightstand. They had been in bed for almost an hour and there still was the best to come. Sunlight was outlining the closed curtains as she made a purring noise. The warm tingling glow that started between her legs now had expanded throughout her body—a rushing, throbbing sensation. She moved her pelvis to the invisible metronome, thrusting her clitoris up at the tongue that had been feasting there for—she peeked at the clock again. At least fifteen minutes. She sighed and he mistook the sound for a signal. Her lover rose up over her.

And Claire Montrose spread her legs for the gardener to plant his seed.

The gardener was an actor. His name was Lance Marshall. There were two smiling, dimpled, dark-eyed curly-haired photos of him in the Player's Directory that the Motion Picture Academy published each year and that all the casting people used as their bible. Lee Marvin and James Mason were on the same page, but there were 791 pages with five pictures to a page. A lot of faces; Lance Marshall was one of the unfamiliar ones. He had worked in a deodorant commercial that ran briefly on local TV and netted him $843 in 1975 and when Mel Brooks made *Blazing Saddles* Lance was one of the tall cowboys for two weeks and a total of $1,254 gross including overtime. He spoke three lines in the picture. "Oh, yeah?" "Watch yourself, stranger!" and "Powerful thirsty!" On the "Watch yourself" line, they did a close-up on him, but it wasn't used in the movie. When he went to see *Blazing Saddles,* he had to sit through it twice to find himself.

Actually, there was no Lance Marshall. He was Stuart Blumberg from Leonia, New Jersey. At the unemployment office on Santa Monica Boulevard, he was still Stuart Blumberg. But after the unemployment checks ran out and between unsuccessful auditions, Lance Marshall, free-lance actor, assumed the role of free-lance gardener.

Some people were born with a green thumb.

He was not one of them.

But Lance costumed himself carefully for the role. Tight bleached and patched denim pants tucked into scuffed knee-high boots. A tapered faded work shirt, red-and-black checkerboard bandana tied around his neck. He had picked up a trunkload of battered mowers and hedge clippers at a garage sale in Culver City. Lance Marshall definitely looked the part.

And as a gardener he was enormously successful.

He modeled his portrayal after Paul Newman in *Hud.* Knocking on the front door of a house, standing there with one hip thrown forward. The center of his gravity in his groin, just the way they had practiced in acting class.

Bashful little boy smiles for the lady of the house, combined with a bold unblinking gaze as he offered a free trial week of service. The money he earned was tax free. At least he paid no taxes on it. And there were occasional fringe benefits.

Claire clutched her fingers tightly around the corner of the headboard. He was the most attentive lover she had ever known and in the years when she was working as a stewardess she had known a few men. She had always gone for older men. Looking for daddy? That was for the shrink to figure out. But then there was Harold. And only Harold. She had been a fairly faithful wife, flirting a bit at parties maybe, but nothing else. Faithful. Not out of choice but by desire. Lack of desire. Knowing that Harold was coming, ready or not, to pounce on her a couple of times each week, usually right after the eleven o'clock news on TV ("It helps me sleep better!") was more than enough, thank you! She turned off on sex. Then when she got pregnant with Bobby, Harold got turned off by her. She didn't carry large, but even before she started showing he would stare distastefully at her belly when she had her clothes off and he started to come after it less and less until not at all. He told her he was being careful about the baby, but she thought it was because he knew he had to be gentle with her and he didn't like it that way. Anyway, he gave it a rest and she couldn't have cared less.

Lance was younger than Claire and she liked the idea. Breaking the habit of going for older guys. Or was it a way of getting it off by feeling younger herself? The shrink would have a long, boring speech to make on that subject. That's why she stopped going to him several months before. He never wanted to talk about what she wanted to talk about. Oh, he'd let her run off on anything she felt like babbling about during her sessions three times a week but he'd never pick up on anything unless it led back to her mother and when she was a kid. Screw him. And don't think she hadn't caught the glimmer in his eye now and then, she knew she had, even though he hadn't made his move yet, but she knew that he wanted it. She didn't need that arrogant old bastard. You could get your hairdresser to listen to you bitch about your husband and he'd do your hair, too.

So she stopped going to the shrink. And she picked up on the signals the gardener was sending. Lance! Can you imagine? Getting jabbed by somebody named Lance. Her knight. Lancelot. It was funny. Lance-a-lot! God, he was good. The lawn looked like shit, but he was an incredible gardener . . . just what she needed . . . needed . . . almost . . . yes, the best! She kissed his sweaty face to reward him for the pleasure he had just given her. He seemed grateful. It was the first time they had been together since Bobby had disappeared.

A week ago she had gone back to the shrink for one more visit. Nobody else had any answers and she thought he might have one tucked away in his desk drawer: Why did Bobby vanish? The one shining thing in her life. This perfect little creature that had sprung from her body. A part of her. But not frightened of the world. Happy. Loving. Her son. She told the shrink that she never realized how much Bobby meant to her, how much she cared for him, how much he gave to her days by simply and quietly being there. Smiling, playing. Looking up at her with his accepting warmth when she would pat his head and smooth his silky hair in passing. Never realized. Until he was gone.

The shrink had no answers. Just the same tired bullshit. He actually tried to lay a guilt trip on her. Make it her fault somehow. She felt a wrenching, ripping sensation in her guts until she understood: He's just trying to hurt me because he knows I won't give him any. Eat your heart out, you dried-up old fart. I love Bobby. And it's not my fault. Not guilty! Whatever happened—it's the police who should feel guilty. For not doing their job, for not finding Bobby. Harold said so.

She walked out before her fifty-minute hour was up and knew that this time it was final; the gardener had the answer: Don't think, just try to feel.

Memories were safer. Memories of Bobby: gorgeous in the little jumpsuits and shorts-and-polo-shirt combinations she bought for him at Saks. Harold complained about the expense, but even he loved the way she dressed their son. A tiny spotless person. She could see him so clearly. And once . . . he had come running in the house. Bobby had been playing in the ivy and slipped and grass stained the outfit he was wearing, fallen on a sprinkler head that had torn a hole in the pants and scratched his knee slightly. He was crying. But not because of the scratch. "I ripped your clothes, Mommy!" Bobby lamented tearfully. And Claire hugged her boy tight and said, "Not *my* clothes, sweetheart, *your* clothes—and don't cry. Mommy loves you and she'll buy you new ones." Mommy loves you . . .

* * *

There had been a shooting.

Elgort and Hyatt were telling Jonas about it in the squad room as Brenner hung up his jacket, pinned the plastic I.D. badge to his belt and walked up to the desk.

". . . so we spent hours creepy-crawling around in the dark, shining our lights around on each other, climbing over fences," Elgort said, "and George tore his pants on a bush."

Elgort pointed at Hyatt, who displayed the rip on the rear of his left thigh; he'd have to pay for a new pair, of course.

■ 220 ■

"We got half the dogs in Bel Air singing a duet with the coyotes." Elgort put his hand to his mouth and let out a yodeling yowl. "But no burglar."

Hyatt laughed at his partner. Elgort shoved a sheaf of paper across to Brenner.

"Your fault," he accused. "If you'd been out there instead of us, George's pants would be alive today. Old friends of yours . . ."

Brenner scanned the papers. Hendrickson. He didn't recognize the name but his gaze darted to the bottom of the page. The signature was his. Brenner went over the report and then he had it. Back when he and Ganzer were still riding. They answered a call at Emerson Junior High in Westwood. Quiet school. Big disturbance. While the boys and girls were in the yard for P.E., a father had driven up and walked out there. He found his teen-age daughter, Mary Elizabeth, who had disobeyed him the night before by coming home a half hour late from studying with another girl two doors away. Now daddy punished her. In front of all her friends. By cutting off all her hair in the schoolyard.

The girl was hysterical, the father was being detained in the principal's office and everybody was looking to the cops to do something.

But there was nothing they could do.

If a stranger comes up to you and gives you a haircut, maybe you could make it into assault. From father to daughter, Ganzer shook his head. "We'll be wasting everybody's time," he told Brenner.

So they went to talk to the father instead. Try to straighten him out. That didn't work either. Hendrickson was a tall, sandy-haired guy with a nice smile and good teeth. "I guess," he said, "I'm about the meanest son-of-a-bitch you've ever seen."

"Sorry," Ganzer said, "but you're not even in the running." No sense letting the asshole enjoy it. Sure enough. The smile faded. Hendrickson was disappointed.

The nurse brought Mary Elizabeth into the principal's office. She was red-eyed, wearing a kerchief someone had loaned her. The girl wasn't crying but she was breathing funny, the air sort of catching in her throat somewhere between a sob and a hiccup.

"Next time you'll listen to me," Hendrickson said to Mary Elizabeth. And he took his daughter home.

That was it. Write up and file it. End of story.

Until last night. Three years later.

Another team of uniformed cops answered the call. A burglar had broken into an expensive house in Bel Air. Nothing stolen. Burglar frightened off. But not before there was some shooting. The man of the house was dead. His name was Hendrickson.

Once it was a homicide, backup crews arrived. Hyatt and Elgort led the search for the burglar, but no trace was found. And then the story inside the house was clarified. It seemed that the family had been asleep, except for the father. He was out late. Drinking, it was later determined by the autopsy. There was a gun in the house; Hendrickson had been an Army Ranger in Korea. The sounds of the burglar were heard by one of the children and she got up and found the gun. She saw the figure in the darkness downstairs and fired. She thought she heard the burglar run off. Then she called the police, but when they came all they could find was Mary Elizabeth with the gun and her dead father.

End of story.

"Makes me glad I didn't have any kids," Elgort joked.

"You ain't even married," Jonas reminded him.

"What's that got to do with it?" Elgort demanded. He

got a laugh out of Hyatt, who was his patsy: Elgort could crack up his partner at will.

Brenner pushed the papers back to Elgort and wondered how long Mary Elizabeth's hair was now and what else had happened in that house during the last three years.

■.■.■.■.

The gardener's car, a tired 1966 Cadillac convertible with the dents pounded out and the original sun-bleached, touched-up aquamarine paint job, was parked in front of the Montrose house. The trunk was open, tool handles protruding and a lawn edger stretched across the sidewalk untended when Caryl Ritchie's station wagon pulled into her driveway and Caryl began toting bags of groceries into her kitchen. Stephen, who had inherited the cold from Jeff and was home for the day from kindergarten, followed her inside.

She was putting away the frozen foods when the phone rang. Jeff was in the nurse's office at the grade school with a slight fever. His cold had returned. It happened this way every September: The kids went back to school and pooled their germs. After a few weeks, they all started missing days. Caryl said she would be right over to pick up Jeff. She piled Stephen back into the station wagon.

On their return, she noticed that the lawn edger had not been moved. Then, after giving Jeff four baby aspirin and settling him on the living room couch to watch TV game shows, Caryl glanced out her kitchen window while she finished storing the canned goods. She saw the gardener loading the edger into the Cadillac trunk with his other tools. The gardener drove off and Caryl remained standing at the window, looking across at the shaggy landscaping that surrounded the Montrose house. The place had been running down for months, though the man would come once a week. But . . . What went on in that house was none of her business. If he was a good gardener or if—none at all! Except—there was that time when she had seen Bobby trailing after the gardener, asking the names of all the flowers, until the gardener, who was apparently running late or simply didn't want to be bothered, screamed at the boy and frightened Bobby off.

Little Stephen came into the kitchen asking for a cookie. One for him and one for his big brother. "I'm taking care of Jeff," Stephen announced proudly. She gave him the cookies and after he went back to the living room, Caryl gazed out the window at the sidewalk where Bobby Montrose and Stephen used to play and now she kept her boys indoors every day or had them play in their own locked backyard, because until you knew . . .

Slowly, she picked up the telephone, dialed information and asked for the phone number of the police.

Ramirez hung up the phone and shifted his attention to the glass wall separating him from the activity in the squad room. Hyatt and Elgort were out there, rolling down shirtsleeves, reaching for their jackets, ending a tour of duty. Brenner and Jonas starting a day. Lucky them. He tore a sheet of notes from the pad beside his phone.

"Montrose's wife?" Jonas said. Brenner was peering over his shoulder at the notes.

"Yeah," Ramirez said. "A busy little household."

"So I'm going bald," Jonas said. "What's wrong with that?"

Brenner shrugged and kept his hands on the wheel of the blue Chevy. "Some of my best friends are bald," he offered.

"Right," Jonas grumbled and looked out the window. "Lots of great men—Benjamin Franklin, Artie Shaw, 'Kojak'—all bald. But not me. I'm not allowed. Connie bought me this blower thing. For my birthday. Says it's from her *and* the kids."

"A blower?"

"Yeah. It makes your hair wet, then dries it, and . . ." Jonas wagged his fingers at his carefully arranged hair style. "Backcombing, they call it. Fluffs it all up."

"Nice." Brenner glanced at him and suppressed a smile.

"What am I gonna do?" Jonas asked. "Connie won't let me out of the house in the morning unless I do it. Doesn't take long but, you know . . ."

Jonas looked at Brenner and caught him smiling.

"What happens when it rains?" Brenner asked.

"Back where I started," Jonas said. They both laughed. Jonas stretched and then studied Brenner. "You look terrible, you know that?" He winked. "Hard night?"

"Who you been talking to?"

"Do I have to be talking to somebody? Don't I know my own partner? One peek at the bags under your eyes, that happy worn-out bachelor drag and I *know*!" Jonas paused but Brenner waited him out. "Besides," Jonas admitted, "I ran into Dave Garvey in the parking lot. He saw you hitting on Gwen at McKnight's."

"You should be a detective," Brenner said.

Jonas grinned at Brenner. "How was it? I mean, you and the lady." Jonas made a fist and gave two short thrusts in the air. Bang-bang!

Brenner shrugged.

"I don't want to get you all excited, Norm."

Jonas leaned back in contented delight, folding his long arms across his chest. "That's what I thought. Those quiet ones. Once you get 'em started, right?"

Yeah. Sure. You had to be there, Norm. A Man and a Woman. Making beautiful music together. For one unforgettable night. Just like in the movies . . .

Two battered survivors clutching at each other on the

springs of his motel mattress. The velvet night broken only by the light shining from the toilet. A voluptuous woman who undressed in the dark and came into the arms of a lover who couldn't get it up. Until. Together, they cajoled and persuaded and inspired and perspired and made it. She said "Yes, yes . . ." and "I love it . . ." and "Oh, yes . . . Don . . ." and Brenner was not disturbed by the moan-mumbled mention of her lost lover because inside his head he was inside Phyllis.

You had to be there, Norm.

Brenner turned the car north off Sunset Boulevard onto Beverly Drive.

"Maybe Gwen can get a friend for me some night and we'll double," Jonas suggested. Brenner glanced at him. "Or I can find my own friend, you single guys haven't got it all sewed up."

Single guys, Brenner thought. That's me. Officially divorced. Joke. A married man who steps out on his wife every now and then. Nothing serious, you understand. Just getting his dipper wet. And then, going without. For eight months. Fidelity. Proving a point—but to who? More faithful to my wife after the divorce than before. Joke. But it was over now.

She was a rainbow of responses. A kaleidoscope of reactions. First, Claire Montrose was gracious and cordial, then surprised and haughty, then . . .

"Hey, you seem to be implying that I'm cheating on my . . ." She laughed and shook her head and her long hair tumbled over one side of her face. "Gossip! You're bringing cheap gossip in here—into my home! Nosy *nasty* goddamn neighbors with nothing better to do than make things up. Hanging out of their windows—I know they don't like me. None of them! Jealous, ugly bitches. Look, I don't even know them, so why do they want to hurt me? Don't they feel sorry for me—for . . ." She was gouging the cushion of the couch with her nails but didn't seem aware of it. "I—I always say hello to them on the street. I smile at them when I see them, but they don't even—I never did anything to any of them . . ."

Like a badly paced runner, she ran out of steam and faltered. They sat opposite her in the white-and-gold living room and watched her but said nothing. The most important part of interrogating someone was knowing when not to ask any questions, to let the suspect do it all.

"I don't have to listen to—who was it? You have no right to do—which *one*? Was it one of them or—? You can't! Please—are you going to tell him? You don't have to tell my husband?"

Now she was still. Unraveled. Quivering. Expecting no mercy, but hoping.

"All we want to know, Mrs. Montrose, is if this could have anything to do with Bobby?"

She looked at Brenner and he could see her withdrawing. The eyes turning inward.

"Bobby . . . ?" He's a good little boy. My good little boy.

"Mrs. Montrose."

The other one was talking to her. She tried to focus on him. She couldn't.

"What can you tell us about this—gardener?" Jonas asked.

"Lance. Lance Marshall is his name." And he was nice to me.

"But what do you know about him? What kind of person is he?" Jonas prodded.

"He—he's also an actor." He didn't treat me like a piece of meat. Maybe he was acting, but I believed him.

"An *actor*?" Jonas snorted. "Look, would he grab a kid? Do you think he could've done something to Bobby?"

"Oh, God, no!" They had brought her back.

"Are you sure?" Brenner asked.

I'm not sure of one damn thing in my whole shitty life, she thought, except that my pretty years are slipping away and my child is gone and for a few minutes I stopped thinking about it all and now they're asking me about the man who helped the pain to stop for a while.

"I'm not sure of anything," she said.

The spacy glaze was in her eyes again. Brenner flipped open his note pad.

"Maybe you better give us his address."

She hesitated, her nails pinching her lower lip. "You—you didn't say if you're going to tell Harold about this."

"Not unless it becomes necessary," Brenner said.

"If that bitch was mine," Jonas said as they drove away, "I'd bust her box! Putting out for the fucking gardener and maybe the postman and the garbage collector—I'd rack her sneaking buns up!"

Brenner caught a glimpse of Caryl Ritchie's face peering out between the curtains as they passed her house. They were heading for Hollywood. That's where Lance Marshall lived.

"Just an itchy cunt," Jonas went on. "Playing matinees as soon as the old man's back is turned."

"No respect for marriage," Brenner said.

"Fuckin' right!" Jonas said. Then he saw Brenner's face. Smiling. "It's not the same thing, Ed. And you know it. Tearing off a piece right in Montrose's own bed! Even when Bobby was there—maybe they had the kid hold a candle! No way any decent woman would ever do that. You think Connie or Phyllis—not in a million years!"

Speak for yourself, Brenner thought. Goldilocks' refrain: "Who's been sleeping in my bed?" Guess. "Hi, I'm

Chet Bowers." The smiling dipshit. Probably making it between my sheets. Ex-sheets. So much for Phyllis. And Connie—your Connie?

Brenner had not mentioned it to Jonas, except casually in passing. "Hey, I ran into Connie in the supermarket." Oh, yeah? Oh, yeah . . .

It was after work a couple months before. He was pushing a shopping cart down the aisle and there was Connie. He smiled and said hello. Brenner had always liked Connie; he and Phyllis had been to their house for dinner, knew their daughters, and the Jonases had spent a number of evenings at the Brenner home. When there was one.

"Stocking up?" Brenner said. Connie was loading diet sodas.

"Trying to knock a few pounds off Norm," she said.

"Want me to keep an eye on him for you during the day?" Brenner offered. Jonas was in the habit of grabbing a few candy bars in the late afternoon. Instant energy, he claimed. Sweet tooth leading to lardass, Brenner always predicted.

"You don't have to bother," Connie said. And instead of bubbling on the way she usually did, she just kept picking sodas off the shelf.

"Prices for food," Brenner pointed. "Really something, huh? I never realized till I started doing my own marketing." They had not seen each other, he realized, since the divorce.

"How's Mike?" Connie said.

"Fine. He's fine. Your girls?"

"Oh, Joan's around here. Some place." She made a smile. "Helping mother shop. Probably at the magazines." She started to roll her cart. "Well, I have to get home and take my dinner out of the oven. Norm'll be waiting."

When he and Phyllis initially separated, Norm had asked

him to dinner one night—alone—but Brenner couldn't make it and it occurred to him that in the months since there had not been another invitation.

Brenner reached out to touch the wire mesh of her wagon. Stopping her. "Connie? You mad at me for something?"

"No—me? Why should I be mad?"

She's so tiny, he thought. Phyllis had often joked with Brenner about how that little woman wound the hulking Jonas around her pinkie. If there was something, better to get it all out now.

"I thought maybe because, you know, the divorce," he said. "Makes it kind of awkward at first, but we've all been friends so long . . ."

She interrupted him.

"I'm not mad at you, Ed," she repeated firmly and he started to smile until he saw her eyes. The eyes have it. Every time. "I'm scared of you. You ride around with Norm all day long. You're with him more than I am—his family—and I—I don't want him to be like you."

She stood there for a moment. Tiny. But shoulders back. Gazing coldly up at him. A strong lady. Certain that he was a bad influence. Leading her Norm astray. He knew that expression. It was the way Phyllis used to look at Ganzer.

"There's two kinds of women," Jonas was saying as they drove down the Sunset Strip in search of the swinging gardener.

"At least," Brenner agreed.

They were approaching Crescent Heights. Brenner signaled a right and turned off Sunset Boulevard. Past the original Schwab's Drugstore, where Lana Turner supposedly was discovered on a soda fountain stool and where hungry actors still thronged to eat grilled cheese sandwiches and scan *Daily Variety* for free. Past a coffee shop next door to Schwab's that changed names and management periodically: When it was called Googie's, a young actor named James Dean hung out there and the jean-clad echoes of that long-dead legend continued to loiter here waiting for the magic to touch them.

Brenner and Jonas found the address. ADULTS ONLY the sign up front read. FOR LEASE—FURNISHED. It was a two-story apartment house built in a horseshoe around a swimming pool. Some of the residents were lounging at the pool. Muscular guys in bikini bottoms. Girls working on their tans. Everybody knew everybody and they only glanced at the two men being led by the manager to a rear apartment. Possible new playmates? But they lost interest when the manager pointed the way for Brenner and Jonas and withdrew. Just visitors.

They knocked on the door.

There was music coming from inside. Loud. Brenner could place the sound. One of those English rock singers. The music blasted their ears as the door was opened by a stunner with a big Pepsodent smile. Form-fitting pants and no shirt. Good chest. His tan was fine. They recognized the description of the gardener.

"Mr. Marshall?" Brenner said. He nodded. Still smiling. "We're police officers." They showed the badges and the smile went away. He hesitated . . . then invited them in.

Lance lowered the volume on the stereo. Catchy rhythm, Brenner thought, good simple melody. He never could understand the words, but he would hear kids singing the songs so they understood the words, or did they just imitate the sounds phonetically the way the British singer imitated the Nashville accent?

"What's it all about?" Lance said.

They were in the living room of what was evidently a one-bedroom apartment. There were bullfight posters on the wall. Empty wine bottles in wicker baskets with drippy candles. Candy-striped beachtowels over one of the worn couches. The drapes were drawn shut.

"We're on an investigation," Brenner said. "Do you know a Mrs. Claire Montrose?" And they put it to him.

The gardener-actor had a deep, trained, phony voice. But the story he told was okay. Admitted his "indiscretion" with Claire Montrose, giving them a debonair "Aren't we all men of the world?" shrug. His attitude was that he considered it his duty: Those lonely ladies needed attention—and servicing. A mercy fuck. He wasn't beating anybody's time, just spreading a little happiness.

"When's the last time you saw Bobby Montrose?" Jonas said abruptly.

"That's what you're after?" Lance seemed to relax. Bobby. Cute little guy. Tragic thing. But he couldn't help them. Didn't know a thing.

They asked him about the time. And he had a terrific answer. The unemployment office. He was down on Santa Monica Boulevard in Hollywood on that morning. All morning. It was the fifth week when you have to be interviewed and tell them all the things you've been doing to find work. Lance showed them his unemployment booklet with the dates and the times, stamped and initialed.

The stud was cool. Free and clear. So why did his eyes keep dancing over to the closed bedroom door? Brenner and Jonas had both picked up on it.

Lance Marshall rose and flexed his tanned muscles.

"Well, I guess that's it," he said.

Bad actor, Brenner thought. The nervousness underneath shows through.

"Guess so," Brenner said, pocketing his notepad. "Except—what's in there?" He pointed at the closed door.

It was as if the vampires had come and sucked Lance Marshall's blood in one big gulp. Beneath the magnificent tan, he went white. The deep voice tried to bluff. "In there? Nothing! Just, you know . . ."

Jonas was moving for the closed door.

"You can't go in there!" The voice had raced high up the scale to a squeak. Lance tried to stop Jonas. But a hand grabbed his arm, spun around and he was looking into the cavernous barrel of Brenner's .38. Lance Marshall trembled and Jonas opened the bedroom door.

The kid stared at them. He was beautiful. Big, wet eyes. Soft mouth. Mocha-toned skin. Delicate. He looked about fifteen years old lying on the bed in his jockey shorts.

"A swinger who goes both ways?" Ramirez said in disgust.

"Takes all kinds," Brenner said. The boy in the bedroom was a parking-lot attendant at a French restaurant on the Strip; and it turned out that despite looks he was eighteen.

"The gardener hears that and he gets pissed off," Jonas said. "He says to the kid, 'You lied to me!' Lance likes his chickens real young."

Ramirez was glowering at them as they slouched in the chairs in front of his desk. Brenner lit up a Marlboro and held out the pack to the squad room's foremost scrounger.

"I quit smoking," Ramirez said.

"Since when?" Jonas asked as he took one of Brenner's butts.

"Since this morning," Ramirez said. "Today is the first day of the rest of my life."

"Who told you that?" Brenner blew smoke at him.

"I made it up. So that's what we've got?"

"A housewife and mother who fucks like a rabbit," Jonas said, "and a double-gaited gardener who wears tight pants with the fastest zipper in the west." He stubbed out his cigarette irritably after two puffs. "Nothing. A big nothing."

Ramirez studied the discarded, smoldering cigarette with longing. Then he shoved the Bobby Montrose file across the desk to them. Brenner picked it up. There was a loose sheet of paper on top.

"Got a good one for you," Ramirez said. "Brand new."

Brenner looked up from the paper. "You gotta be kidding with this."

"Not now," Ramirez said emphatically. "Now we try anything and everything."

The trumpeters came in advance of the procession and proclaimed its presence by sounding a single piercing note. The crowd on the dirt trail parted for the courtiers bearing the drape-bedecked platform on which a wizened, regal being was enthroned.

"Milords and Miladies," bellowed a Henry VIII look-alike, "pray make way for Her Royal Highness, the Queen!"

Maidens tossed rose petals and the Queen Elizabeth I lookalike waved to the horde of commoners. Some of them waved back or held their children up to see the Queen or snapped Instamatic photos of her.

Brenner and Jonas waited for the procession to pass. The jesters, in traditional caps and bells, were still working the crowd but they pushed through.

It was hot and sticky in Saugus. And somehow the weather contributed to the illusion: A mile off the Ventura Freeway and you were in Elizabethan England. Jugglers and tumblers, comedy charades and tented shopping stalls. Most of the year it was just another meadow on top of a hill in the San Fernando Valley. But for a few weeks each year banners unfurled and the Renaissance Faire rolled the calendar back to another time.

The people who worked there all wore costumes of the era and the funseekers were encouraged to do the same. Girls with garlands of flowers in their hair, pushed-up bodices and billowing skirts. Young bearded men in black tights and boots and Musketeer swords. Or Confederate Army caps, World War I spiked Hun helmets. The exhibitionist styles clashed occasionally but overall blended into a happy experience. Those who didn't dress up enjoyed those who did. There were things to see and buy and eat and thousands thronged to the hip Disneyland that like Brigadoon appeared briefly and then was gone.

Brenner and Jonas made their way amid the revelers, crossing a narrow wooden bridge. There was no water under the bridge. Just a couple of teen-agers, cuddling on the dry riverbed, nuzzling, not concerned who saw them. On the far side of the bridge there was a jam of spectators watching a juggler perform in the shade of a big tree whose leaves had been burnt umber by the long summer's heat.

The juggler was clad in a doublet of Sherwood Forest green and he was gleefully tossing three black handballs in the air. "Can't stop juggling," he told his audience, "juggle all day and all night, just love juggling, even juggle when I eat." He added a big red Delicious apple to the balls flying in an arc in front of him. Round and round they went and now each time as the apple came to hand the juggler took a ravenous bite out of it before sending the apple into the air again, chewing the mouthful and swallowing before the next bite was due. He never lost the rhythm and he quickly was juggling three balls and an apple core which he threw away. "Even juggle while I sleep," he announced, starting to lie down on his back in the grass, still keeping the balls going. "I *never* stop juggling."

"Man's got a problem," Jonas said.

They shouldered their way forward and in a clearing near a candlemaking stall they found the tent they were seeking. KNOW YOURSELF, a sign suggested and there was a line drawing of a big hand. *Palmistry, Astrology & Tarot,* the smaller print advertised. Fortune-telling was against the law, but telling people what they are like was legal. The distinction between who you are and what might lie in store for someone like you frequently blurred. Mostly because the shrewd gypsies who ran such concessions recognized the obvious: The future holds far greater fascination than the past and the gypsy will be long gone with the customer's five bucks before the truth of the prediction can be tested.

Usually they dealt in generalities and it was a parlor game, no more harmful than reading the messages inside a fortune cookie. But some of the operators were con artists who would ferret out the vulnerable: the widow trying to make contact with the Other Side or the mother of the leukemia child. These seekers of miracles were easy prey for the gypsy clairvoyant's mumbo-jumbo. Put a fresh egg under your pillow and sleep on it for two days, then bring it to me. Behold, I wrap it in this ordinary white handkerchief . . . now I crack the egg! Inside there was blood or black gunk. Symbolic of the pain or evil being removed. Final phase of the exorcism usually saw the victim bringing large sums of cash for "cleansing." It always worked: The sucker was cleaned out. Some of them without ever realizing what had happened. They simply went home and waited, hoping, for the promised miracle. Those that tumbled would eventually make contact with the Bunco Squad, but it was a hard felony to nail down. If the score was large enough, the fortune-teller usually had moved on and was impossible to trace in the labyrinth of gypsy society.

The tent flap lifted and a young couple emerged. The pretty girl with the waist-length ponytail was staring at her palm, the wonders contained in it still ringing in her ears. Madame Loretta appeared and beckoned to Brenner and Jonas. She was a tiny sparrow of a woman, certainly in her sixties, perhaps even in her seventies, but the face was sharp and alert. She wore a flowing navy blue robe punctuated by white stars. The constellation pattern was repeated on the fabric of her turban. There were wisps of white hair peeping out from the corners of the turban, furthering the image of a wise, all-knowing ancient. If Merlin the Magician had been a woman, this was what she would have looked like.

Then she opened her mouth. And the illusion was spoiled.

"Guess yer next, mister. Y'guys together?"

It was a Bronx accent in Merry Olde England. She gestured for Brenner and Jonas to enter. Inside the tent there was silence and darkness. A table with a globe lamp on a black velvet covering. Two chairs and an outsize thronelike armchair for little Madame Loretta to perch on. A phonograph was playing sitar music. The only decoration visible was a needlepoint tapestry pinned to the tent wall: John F. Kennedy in front of the American flag. On closer perusal the resemblance diminished: The idea was there, but the individual facial features had not been rendered skillfully enough.

"Yer the cops, right?" Madame Loretta smiled knowingly at them. Two points for her—either as clairvoyant or cop-spotting con artist.

"You telephoned a report to headquarters," Brenner said, "that you have some information about . . ."

She held her hand up. There were rings on almost every skinny finger. "I'll show ya," she said.

Madame Loretta brought forth a small wooden box wrapped in a filmy pink silk scarf. She opened the box and took out a deck of Tarot cards. Her fingers began expertly to riffle, shuffle and then deal the cards out face down on the velvet table covering.

"Some people'll tell ya the cards never lie," she said. "But they're liars."

Madame Loretta peered up at them, sharing privileged information.

"Everybody lies," she whispered. "Some of 'em don't mean to, some don't even know they're doin' it. 'Cause there's all kinds a' lies. So maybe I'm not right."

"But?" Jonas wanted her to get it out so they could say they had heard her and then take off.

"It works out the same every time"—she indicated the spread of cards—"no matter how many times I done it."

"Isn't that a matter of interpretation?" Jonas said.

"But it's always me doin' the interpretin'."

Brenner glanced at Jonas. He didn't understand what she had said either.

"Maybe that's why the answer keeps coming out the same," Brenner said.

She knew that she was being doubted. Madame Loretta tapped the Tarot cards impatiently with her fingernails; they were painted navy blue and had small stars on them.

"I ain't tellin' ya to believe me." She glared at Brenner. "All I'm tellin' ya is what I see!"

Slowly, working from top to bottom, she began to turn the cards and reveal their faces. It was stifling in the tent and Brenner felt beads of perspiration on his face. But Madame Loretta seemed oblivious to the heat.

"There, again!" she pointed. "He's alive! That little boy.

Bobby. And he's near his house—home, that stands for home."

Brenner stared at the card she had just revealed.

"He never left—he's there, in the darkness, watching us."

She believed it and she wanted them to believe it. Brenner peered at Jonas: He could tell Norm wasn't buying a word.

Madame Loretta turned up the final card and gasped, showing it to them: There was a drawing of a child and a castle.

"He's under the front porch of his house. In the darkness! He's waiting there—for someone to find him . . ."

The juggler was playing with fire. Three, four—now five flaming torches. Faster and faster until they formed an unbroken flowing circle of fire surrounding the juggler. He ignored the danger, intent on his task: Keep it going, keep it going! Tossing the torches like Indian clubs, effortlessly, inevitably, always catching the safe end of the torch in his fingers, never missing, never getting burned . . .

Jonas nudged Brenner.

"C'mon, he said, "before this schmuck sets fire to the whole Valley."

They walked away from Madame Loretta's tent. She was standing there, watching them go. Brenner could feel her eyes on his back until they had merged with the crowd beyond the juggler. And even after they had crossed the wooden bridge, he was sure that if he retraced his steps she would still be standing there. Wordless. Unblinking. She had shared her vision: The rest was up to them.

Jonas saw the boy first. He was crying. Six or seven years old and his small face destroyed by terror. Surrounded by people and totally alone. A forest of legs topped by a confusion of laughing, yelling, unseeing heads

that looked everywhere but down at him. Brenner saw the
boy through the crowd now, too, on the grassy area off the
dirt trail. There was a game being played nearby: For
twenty-five cents each, two people at a time could balance
on adjoining bales of hay and try to knock each other
off with padded cudgels. Football helmets were provided
to safeguard the fun and insure the management against
damages.

"Mommee-ee-ee?" the boy cried. He was holding a
sand-covered jelly apple that obviously had been dropped
and retrieved from the ground. He knew enough not to
eat it now but he clutched the apple on a stick: It was the
link to his security that had vanished, the world he had
lost.

"The poor kid," Brenner said and he started through
the maze of bodies. But before he could reach the boy, a
frantic-eyed woman appeared. The boy saw her and
beamed through his tears: "Mommee-ee-ee!!" He held his
arms out to her and she rushed toward him, a huge smile
of relief on her face. It evaporated before she got there.
She knocked the jelly apple out of his hand and began to
spank the boy:

"I told you to stay near me! Didn't I tell you? Do you
know how you worried me? *Come on now!*"

The mother grabbed her son's arm and pulled him
away. He was crying once more, but he wasn't scared
anymore. He belonged to someone again.

Brenner and Jonas watched them disappear in the crowd.

"Wow, what a whack she gave that kid," Jonas chortled.

"Yeah," Brenner grinned.

They strolled toward the entrance booths. The parking
lot was on the flatland below.

"What'd you think of the stargazer?" Jonas said. "Some
show, huh?"

Brenner shrugged.

"Bobby's been gone—what?" Jonas said. "Three weeks now?"

"Nearly," Brenner said.

"And she sees him there. At the house. Hiding someplace."

"Caught maybe . . ."

Jonas kept walking but he turned to examine his partner. "C'mon, Ed. You going for that bullshit hocus-pocus?"

Brenner thought about it for another step or two. "Remember with the Boston Strangler," he said finally, "that guy with the powers who told them where to look?"

"Powers?" Jonas laughed. "That dried-up little bird back there only knows one thing: how to shine on the suckers! There's a tall, dark man in your future, honey. And for you, Mr. Fuzz, there's a small boy playing hide-and-seek since last month. Put my face on the TV and my name in the newspapers and make sure you spell it right. Look, I'd like to buy it as much as you, Ed, but . . ."

"Norm," Brenner interrupted sharply. "She sees him still alive." Brenner took a deep breath. "We're going to find him."

Brenner had stopped walking. Jonas gazed at him, surprised at the urgency he heard.

"Hey, man, that's what we've all been trying to do."

"But we are going to do it," Brenner said flatly. He moved on toward their car. It was Jonas' turn to shrug as he followed Brenner.

"We going where I think we are?" Jonas asked.

"The house."

"Okay," Jonas said. "Fine. We're gonna find Bobby. Just like the magic lady says. But under the front porch, that's kind of tough"—he leveled across the hood of their car at Brenner—"considering there ain't no front porch on that house."

Brenner didn't hesitate. He was certain now.

"Then we'll look in the crawlspace under the house—and up in the attic—and under the front porch of all the neighbors who've got front porches!"

They got into the car and Brenner pulled out. He felt good. Better than in a long time. He knew this was how it was meant to work out. They were going to find him. Even days ago when the word came about that kid's body found in the fire, everybody got way down, even Ramirez. Brenner had kept his mouth shut, pretending to go along, but somehow he knew all through it, even before the lab report and the fingerprints, that it was another boy. Bobby was still alive. He had to be.

■.■.■.

It was the barren surface of the moon. With picnic baskets. Empty space. A paved area hundreds of feet wide sloping hundreds of feet down to the water of a man-made lake. Like lemmings, cars and pickup trucks came from all over, towing smallcraft that they backed into the water until they floated. And then parked while they boated.

Phyllis sat cross-legged on a tan cement beach that angled up from the water's edge—a wall of the reservoir. The overflow had been channeled to flood a desolate area off Highway 5 north of the San Fernando Valley. In the shallow coves, bushes that had begun growth in the arid, useless soil now reached branches up through the water. And in the center of the artificial lake, powerboats zoomed back and forth.

Mike waved to his mother as their boat whizzed past. She called "Hi, Mike . . ." and the noise wiped out her sound, but she was certain he could see her lips moving and read her smile.

The boat was a Chris-Craft that Chet Bowers kept in his garage in Encino beside the Oldsmobile sedan that had towed it here. At full throttle, which was the way Chet enjoyed going, the boat could do thirty knots. Phyllis liked the breeze the movement made, particularly on such a hot day, but she didn't like the bouncing as the boat skimmed and sliced, prow lifted high but flopping hard as it cut through the waves created by its own roaring motion.

Lake Castaic was located on a turnoff midway on the road between Los Angeles and Bakersfield. Story of my life, Phyllis thought.

In Bakersfield she had met the first man in her life who she had been taught to believe would be the last man in her life. She had worried about being alone after the divorce. For years. Forever? It had turned out to be hardly even months before she met Chet. And now she had a new worry: Maybe it was too quick. Maybe she was the kind of person who clutches at first chances because she is scared another chance may never come.

She was an organized person. When she worked in an office, she tried to understand the systems and improve on them. When she became a housewife, she organized her work efficiently. As a mother, she went to the Red Cross class during pregnancy and later read the books on bringing up children. When divorce came, she tried to approach it in an organized fashion.

She joined several of the Single Parents groups listed in the L.A. *Times*. It was supposed to be reassuring to find that there were other people with similar problems. As far as Phyllis was concerned, all they did was get together and depress each other.

In those first weeks she withdrew into herself and concentrated on worrying. The only diversion she offered herself was going down to the beach while Mike was in school. She sat and stared at the waves. Then on a whim at the drugstore one day, she bought a sketch pad and some pastels and she began to draw pictures at the beach.

She always went to the same spot, just above Malibu Pier. Twice a week there was a man who came to jog. He stopped once to peer over her shoulder at her picture. It wasn't very good, because she hadn't tried to draw anything since high school when she was an "A" student in art. The jogger didn't say anything and trotted away up the beach. The next time he appeared, he nodded at her. A week later, they had a cup of coffee together at Neeny's foodstand. And then she wasn't alone any more. Unless she wanted to be. Her choice.

He was a design engineer working at a think tank in Malibu Canyon and he would jog on his lunch hour. Twice a week. Organized. He had been places she had only read about and he got enormously enthusiastic about technical processes that she didn't find interesting, despite his explanations, but maybe that was because she really didn't understand them. When they went to bed, he was a considerate lover, solicitous of her feelings and excitements, helping her to achieve maximum pleasure before taking his own. Organized. And with a little time and a little effort, she might be able to love this man.

But it would never be the way it was between her and Ed Brenner.

Ed was disorganized and unpredictable and she loved him for it. Bed for them was a wild, joyful, nonthinking, delicious, laughing and devouring closeness. They had been young lovers together and the bond they shared and the times they had were sweet in her memory. Songs they had heard together, places they had walked and talked about their world, planning and dreaming. At the end of each day, she waited for his return. But he stopped coming home. It wasn't the other women. She believed that they never mattered to him, and after the pain of her discovery turned to numbness, it really hadn't mattered to her that much either. It was that even when he was there, he wasn't.

His excitement was out somewhere in the streets, being a cop. That's where he lived. Their home and their life together was simply where he came to catch his breath. Rest a while. Doze in the living room chair. He was tired, but he couldn't wait to go again. That was the whore waiting for him out there. Her unbeatable competition: his job. It turned him on and wiped him out but kept him coming back for more and he really didn't need anything else. She knew her marriage was over on the day she realized that she was lonelier when he was there than when he was gone.

"Mike!" she yelled as the powerboat raced by. "Hi!" Chet was letting the boy handle the wheel now. Standing beside him. Chet waved to Phyllis as they made another pass and pointed at her son's accomplishment. Mike was having a ball.

■.■.■.

The gold Cadillac was pulling into the garage at the front of the Montrose house as they came plodding through a break in the hedge. Brenner and Jonas were dirty. They both were carrying their jackets, and their shirts were streaked with sweat and dust that reflected the trail they had followed: through backyards and over fences and under cantilevered patios on the sides of hills and trudging through ivy where small brown rats scurried to escape them and plowing through spiderwebs that clung invisibly to their flushed, perspiring faces as they shone a long five-battery flashlight everywhere they could think of and found nothing.

"I hope you're satisfied with this crazy stuff," Jonas was saying. "You can't go getting emotionally involved in these things, Ed." And then they saw the gold Cadillac.

Harold Montrose slammed the car door and sauntered toward them. Behind him, the garage door lowered electronically. Despite the heat, Montrose wore a dark blue three-piece Carroll & Co. suit with every button fastened. He carried an attaché case with the Gucci stripe running around it and gold clasps with a combination lock.

"Well," he said disdainfully, "I heard you two were back here. Poking around. Find anything interesting?"

"Nope," Brenner said. He wiped at the grime on his forehead with the back of his hand.

"What brought you back?" Montrose asked. "I mean, after all this time."

"We had some—information," Jonas said. Why tell him what kind? But it was as if he had guessed.

"As reliable as your usual sources?" Montrose was rubbing it in and testing at the same time. He had not heard from them after the abortive ransom delivery. They had never come to ask again about the pills business. "Seems like we've heard from every crank and crackpot in the Western world, and you people go running around each and every time exactly as if . . ."

Montrose made a weary, dismissing gesture and turned his back on them. He moved toward the front door.

"Yessir," he heard Brenner say from behind him. "That's what we do. Serve and protect the citizens."

Montrose detected a note of challenge. He stopped and looked at Brenner and Jonas. He wasn't about to let these piss ants get away with anything now.

"Slogans and promises, that's all you're good for. Weeks go by and you come up with nothing. Where's my son? What does it take to find one little boy? Maybe some— oh, forget it!"

Montrose was about to go inside, but:

"Forget what?" Brenner called belligerently, stepping toward Montrose. Jonas moved up behind Brenner, as if to restrain him. *"Forget what?"*

Montrose looked at the dirty, sweaty, glaring detective and then his gaze went beyond to the driveway. Get out of there! Go on, Bobby, get back in the house! If only the boy had listened. If Montrose hadn't been running late that morning and had the time to stop—to take his son inside to safety.

"Been like this every day," Montrose said. What the hell was he telling these idiots for? He could never let them know what happened that morning, never let anyone know that if he had thirty seconds to spare . . . "That kid was trouble to me from the day he was born," Montrose mumbled, reaching for the door handle.

"What did you say?"

Montrose spun around. The big cop was coming for him. Jonas. Throwing his jacket on the ground, lifting the heavy flashlight like a club. Not Brenner, whom Montrose had been watching carefully, gauging. But Jonas. Shrieking at him:

"You lousy fucking asshole!"

Montrose shrank back in fear against the heavy front door, rattling the handle. It wouldn't open. Jonas was swinging at him. But Brenner was suddenly there. Blocking. Preventing Jonas from reaching Montrose. Jonas was out of control, but Brenner's movements were trained and precise. He hooked Jonas' arm, knocking the flashlight out of his hand. Then he wrapped his arms in a bear hug around Jonas. The momentum of the big cop's rage dragged Brenner with him . . . closer.

"Watch that guy," Montrose begged. "Watch him, he's . . ."

Brenner, his face ashen, had stopped Jonas' forward movement. But Brenner didn't loosen his grip on his partner as Jonas screamed at Montrose:

"You ever say anything bad about that kid again—and I'll . . . ! You hear me? *You hear what I mean?"*

Trembling, Montrose nodded. He had the door open now. Just enough to slip inside and slam it on them both.

Twist the bolt lock. And lean against the door. Sons-of-bitches, who did they think they were talking to?

Outside, Jonas was still glaring at the closed door. His hair was matted with sweat and dangled limply, revealing his baldness. It made him look older. Brenner went to pick up their jackets and the flashlight from the ground. Then he took gentle hold of Jonas' arm.

"Norm?"

Jonas looked at him. "He—he just shouldn't say things about Bobby," Jonas said.

"I know," Brenner said.

And he guided Jonas away from the house to the blue Chevrolet. Funny, Brenner thought. That it should be Norm. Another second and they might have been playing reverse roles. He and Jonas. Or it could've been the two of them together. Pounding the shit out of that germ. Bad. Not professional. Worse yet, they had given Montrose the chance he had been hoping for to get the whip hand over them. After what had just happened, all Montrose had to do was dial the station and make a complaint. He had them both—Jonas particularly. It could be a lot of trouble. An I.A. investigation. Conduct unbecoming. Attempted assault. Even Ramirez couldn't stop it. All Montrose had to do now was complain.

But he never did.

20

For years there had been talk about tearing down the Santa Monica Pier, but so far no one had gotten around to doing it. On a sunny Sunday, they still drew a crowd. Cars lined up on Ocean Avenue to make the turn onto the bridge that led over to the pier. There was parking on the side of the road with all the amusement rides, game stalls and food stands, but those few free spaces were always filled. Behind the rides, there was more parking but they charged by the half hour.

Down at the end of the pier were the docks for the all-day fishing boats that left each morning to troll the waters off Malibu. And there were benches along the rails where the fishermen who couldn't afford the boat would bait their hooks, cast their lines and try their luck. There were two kinds of fishermen here: sportsmen and survivors. The sportsmen were usually kids who didn't depend on catching anything but came for the fun of it. The survivors were old people, social security pensioners, who looked to the sea for free food to offset the nibbling inflation. Occasionally a teen-age boy would finish a day of reeling them in and give his catch to one of the senior citizens, rather than carry the smelly fish home on the bus for his mother, who preferred to buy at the supermarket where the scaling and cleaning had been done already. As a result, there was a spirit of camaraderie between old and young on the fishing pier.

Brenner and Mike walked all the way out, pausing to watch a girl in a baseball cap, gray sweatshirt and stained jeans tug a big one out of the ocean. It was a flat-nose shark, about three feet long. Such catches were not uncommon, but since *Jaws* they attracted interest. Passers-by and other fishermen gathered around to stare at the fish floundering on the tar surface until an older man stepped forward helpfully to start clobbering the shark with a wooden paddle. A tall boy and his cute girl friend had been observing. Now she turned her face into his shoulder and he laughed and protectively led her away. An old woman watched them and grinned toothlessly.

"We brought you out here on the Fourth of July once," Brenner told Mike as they continued on. "There was some big U.S. Navy destroyer or battleship anchored there. And they were ferrying people out to go on board. You know, a tour."

"I don't remember that," Mike said.

"You were maybe four or five," Brenner said. "And we didn't get on. We were too far back in line and by the time we got up front they stopped taking anybody else."

They stopped again. There was a small octopus floating in a pail of salt water beside another fisherman. Two kids were watching, but the sea monster wasn't doing anything.

"Gettin' hungry?" Brenner asked. Mike shrugged. "Then

maybe we ought to go on some rides before we eat, huh? You know, have some fun."

The car was heading straight for him. Brenner swiveled his wheel as far as it would go and flattened the accelerator, but it was too late to avoid a crash. The bumpmobile driven by Mike slammed into him broadside and Brenner's electric car skittered out of control and smashed against the rubber tires in the center of the rink. Brenner put his foot out the opening on the side of the car and shoved off from the buffer of tires. When he looked up, Mike was bearing down on him again with a big smile. Brenner pressed the floor button turning on his juice, and the pole scraping the metal screen on the ceiling crackled sparks as Brenner's car lurched and Mike's car missed him and hit the tires instead. Brenner was waiting for Mike as he caromed off and Brenner rear-ended him. The boy howled with glee and Brenner laughed.

They were locked together now, side by side, their two cars pushing against each other as they glided like dancers around the bend in the circular course. Brenner thumbed his nose at Mike, who giggled and let go of his wheel to shake his fists in mock rage at his father. Brenner roared with pleasure and they were slammed apart by other riders. Their heads snapped back and they raced on down the slippery floor—down . . .

. . . down—from the crest of a three-story height. They called it the Superslide. From the top you could see the full sweep of the coastline looking south. Venice, Manhattan and Redondo beaches, the green curve that was the Palos Verdes Peninsula. There were ten narrow polished metal paths leading to the bottom. The idea was to sit with your legs together on a burlap bag and shove off. Brenner and Mike started next to each other, but Mike was lighter and more experienced: He seemed to fly ahead of Brenner and then Brenner lost sight of Mike in the blur of the descent. The horizon rising as the wind rushed at his belly like a rollercoaster ride and then the midway point, the dipsy-doodle, as he left the track briefly —coursing through the air with the burlap bag now a flying carpet—until he bounced on his tailbone and slid to a final halt at the base of the Superslide. Around him, kids were springing to their feet and Brenner was regaining his balance, trying to get up, when there was a hand extended to him. A small hand. He took his son's outstretched hand and Mike helped his father up . . .

. . . up and down—and all around—the hurdy-gurdy music oompahing as the merry-go-round turned in its endless circle. Horses chasing horses they would never catch. The riders on the outside galloping in place but also up and down. Mike was shaking the reins, urging his steed to greater speed as he whirled past Brenner, who waved from the sidelines. The boy hadn't seen him so he didn't wave back.

The music was very loud. Brenner didn't know the name of the merry-go-round song and when he was away from here he couldn't recall the melody, but while he heard it playing he knew the tune as well as his own name and he hummed silently as it triggered memories. The Playland on Pico near the house. Torn down to make room for a department store. The amusement park on Beverly Boulevard near La Cienega. Shuttered and dismantled. Replaced by nothing. Just a shell left standing—the echo of children's laughter quieted by time. Unless you were willing to make the trek to one of the major amusement parks—Disneyland or Knott's Berry Farm or Magic Mountain—this one on the pier was just about the last of the first-rate merry-go-rounds left in the area. No small thing. A generation was in danger of losing their chance at the brass ring. They might grow up not being able to hum to the oompah music.

Mike was riding toward him again on the tallest, whitest mount of them all. Brenner spotted him early this time and called his name over the music and waved both arms. This time, Mike saw him and waved back.

Beneath the boardwalk was a midway with delicacies for every palate except the gourmet's. A United Nations of junk foods: breaded hot dogs on a stick, corn on the cob, knishes, taquitos, burritos, egg rolls, stuffed grape leaves, slices of pizza, steamed clams, French custard, submarine sandwiches and chocolate-covered frozen bananas (sprinkles extra).

Brenner munched popcorn and Mike worked on a whirl of pink cotton candy while they watched the gymnasts flexing and levitating on Muscle Beach. It was a symphony of rippling biceps as the narcissists tumbled, glided, soared and flipped on the rings and parallel bars.

They strolled on past the playground area where mothers in bikinis guided tots down the slide and fathers pushed youngsters high on the swings and triumphant kids climbed alone to the topmost rung of the monkey bars. "Want to play a little?" Mike shook his head. And they walked on. The beach-front neighborhood had become a blend of the old and the new. Retired folks in sweaters and coats sat on benches in the warm sunlight while teeners in swim suits ran by and scruffy hippies with transistors clamped to their ears ambled along the pathway facing the beach. There were chess games being played by bearded opponents who were twenty-two *vs.* seventy-two. Low rents for the delapidated accommodations had broken the age barrier, but urban redevelopment threatened them all: Steel and concrete condominiums loomed in the background, the shape of things that real estate speculators hoped would come. So far, the neighborhood was holding its own. Some chic salons and fashionable restaurants had taken hold a few blocks away on Main Street, but they coexisted beside the swap shops, cafeterias and corner bars that still serviced the beach people.

Brenner led Mike to the electric tram that rode on hard-rubber wheels along the beach path between Santa Monica Pier and Venice. The boy was licking down to the white cone in the center of the cotton candy as the tram dodged breaks in the pavement and slow-moving pedestrians. Soon they were out in the open, away from the people and the houses, passing wide clean beaches that were deserted because the waves were not the kind that attracted the surfers and the increased distance from the sand to the nearest street made them difficult to police, so they attracted muggers who preyed on children and old people unwary enough to come here.

The tram's route traveled all the way down into the heart of Venice, but Brenner took Mike off at Pacific Ocean Park. An amusement park built on another pier, P.O.P. as it was called, never quite succeeded. Perhaps it was that the weather had changed over the years: Brenner had seen photos in a beach-front restaurant of huge crowds along the Venice walkway on a summer evening in the 1920s. But the Japanese Current had shifted and the evenings in the 1960s were cooler and the crowds were fewer and P.O.P. was forced to close at a tremendous financial loss. Various plans were announced to reopen but they never were realized.

"You like the rides we went on before?" Brenner asked.

"Yeah," Mike said. "They were good." He was peering through the wire mesh fence at the blackened, rotted pilings and the skeleton shell of the Fun Palace that once operated. "What was it like here?"

"Like Disneyland almost."

"Why'd they close it up? Because of a fire?"

"No. The fire came later. They closed it 'cause—not enough people came."

"I'm sorry it's gone," Mike said.

"Yeah, well—you know. Things change," Brenner said.

The sun was in the wrong place. It comes up in the east and goes down in the west, but not around here. As they carried their shoes and walked barefoot with rolled-up pants along the water's edge, the sun was beginning to settle where it always did: on the horizon somewhere north of Malibu. It was not an optical illusion, just a zigzag of coastal configuration. The Pacific Ocean was still on the west side of North America, just like on the schoolbook maps, but the sun was going down where it wanted to.

"Want to sit?" Brenner said.

"Yeah." The boy was tired. They went to where the dry sand started and sat next to each other and watched the long waves rolling in. The beach was almost empty. A tanned boy and girl still breasting the breakers a distance away and a jogger passing—an elderly man, thin, with skin like parchment from the sun and an incredibly firm physique. There was a dripping-wet black spaniel trotting along with the jogger, staying a couple of paces ahead but constantly glancing back at the runner. Who's the leader, Brenner wondered, and does it matter?

Mike was digging in the sand and it didn't take many scoops of his hands to reach damp soil. Now he began to shape a castle. More of a ditch around a mound, but the boy was adding refinements that he wasn't capable of the last time they had been to the beach. Something about the beach, Phyllis always used to say, the salt water and the sound of waves, the clean air and openness. It always seemed to have a calming effect on kids; they'd run around a lot at first and then become relaxed and tranquil.

But not today.

"China," Brenner said.

"What?" Mike looked up at him with a handful of mud.

"When I was a kid, we used to make a hole and say we were digging to China. It's on the other side of the world. So if you dig deep enough . . ."

"Can't," Mike scoffed. "Nobody can."

"Found that out," Brenner smiled. The boy didn't smile, just went on digging. Brenner gazed off at the water. There was a pathway of shattered diamonds shimmering off the ocean and leading to the waning sun.

"Can I ask you something?" Mike said without looking up.

Ask me anything. Just talk to me.

"Sure," he said. "I ask you enough stuff all the time."

"Why'd you and mom get divorced?" Mike was still leaning over his castle, patting, shaping.

"Hey, we talked about that already . . ." Brenner said. He made a sound that was supposed to be a little laugh.

"No, we didn't," Mike said. And he looked up at his father. "Didn't you love each other?"

The eyes. The eyes always have it. Something was there, but Brenner couldn't label it. Nervousness, maybe. What the hell do you tell a kid? What do you tell yourself?

"Sometimes," he began slowly, "people start out loving each other. Then they stop."

The words were simple enough. Honest enough. Even a kid could understand. Don't ask me why, but that's how it is and . . . The look in Mike's eyes was changing. Like a veil lifting so Brenner could see inside—but only for a flash: It wasn't nervousness, it was terror. Mike turned down to the digging again, scooping rapidly, speaking almost too low to be heard over the waves even though they were sitting so close.

"Does that mean," the boy gasped, "that sometime— you're gonna stop loving me?"

Brenner was drowning. His lungs filled and he couldn't breathe. He reached out, clutching at life—and embraced his son, who was too scared to look at his father while he waited for the answer to the question that had been festering for so long.

"No, Mike"—he hugged the boy, his voice choked—"never gonna stop." Mike's face was pressed to his chest. "Goofy kid like you—couldn't stop loving you."

Mike gazed up at Brenner. There were tears in Mike's eyes, but they were tears of relief. And he was smiling.

"You promise?" he asked.

"I promise," Brenner said.

The tide overran Mike's castle and after a few waves there was almost no trace of it left. But Brenner and Mike had walked away by then. The sun was an orange crescent on the edge of the world but the warmth of the day remained and the cool water came up to their ankles and receded only to find them again a few steps farther down the beach with the next gentle wave.

There was a sound.

Brenner looked around to find its source. On the walkway up ahead, framed against the sky and backlit by the last dazzling slivers of sunlight, a young black man, handsome and well developed, barefoot and barechested and wearing cut-off white sailor pants, was riding a bicycle nohands while he played the trombone. Gliding the long platinum slide gracefully in and out, sending a strange haunting call across the emptiness and the endless vista. It wasn't exactly a song, but it touched Brenner deeply with its melancholy glow and sad knowledge of promises that might only be hopes. He knew that the yearning, lonely sound of the man on the bicycle would be locked to this moment and always be a part of it.

Brenner held Mike's hand and this time his son didn't let go or pull away and they walked on together . . .

■ ■ ■

It was a dream but his eyes were open. Each time it reached the end, the dream started over again like a film playing inside his head on a continuous loop.

The street. A Western street. Clapboard buildings. Courthouse. Blacksmith & Stable. General Store. Church. Bar. Barber Shop. Jail. A dusty, deserted street. Henry Fonda as Wyatt Earp in the brush mustache might come around the corner in another moment for the final shootout. And all the townspeople were indoors, hiding from the flying bullets. But Fonda/Earp never came; nobody came.

Only the boy.

Running alone down the Ghost Town street. Rattling knobs that were locked. Entering a hallway that was open. And finding roughly furnished turn-of-the-century rooms that nobody lived in with panes of glass on the doorways so that he could look but not touch.

In the street again. Calling. Listening. Hearing nothing except the pounding of blood in his ears. The rasp of his own breath, his throat and tongue dry, unable to swallow as he gulped air and ran on—searching . . .

The boy was Ed Brenner.

And Ed Brenner, the man, lay on his back with his hands folded behind his head on a bed in a motel room staring up at the ceiling. Still fully clothed. Staring across the years at the boy.

There was a well under a huge oak tree at the end of the next street and the boy raced to it and stopped. There was nowhere further to go; a fence blocked the way beyond. He looked down into the well, but it was only the stone façade of a well that had been transported here so there was a shallow hole where the water should have been. I will turn now, the boy thought, and look where I have been—and he is going to be there. But when he looked the streets were still deserted. Brenner, the boy, was still alone.

And Brenner, the man, tensed and waited for the boy

to run again, knowing what came next but this time it would be different.

Run, he willed, and the boy he once was ran . . .

Black windows with no one behind them. Whitewashed wooden walls. Cracked and rotting. He's here. I'm looking for him and he's looking for me. I know he is! Is he hiding somewhere? Watching me? Come out, come out, wherever you are. Please! I need you!

The sky was gray when they came and now fat juicy warm raindrops began to fall. Making puffs of dust as they struck the ground in the center of the dirt street. The face of the running boy became splotched by the raindrops; not tears, no tears, raindrops. He licked his lips and tasted the rain and his salty sweat and now he could swallow and cry out again. Da-a-a-d-d-d! Daadd-dd-ee-ee!

The place was called Pioneer Village and it had been brought from somewhere else and put here on the outskirts of Bakersfield. He and his father had come on an outing, but even in good weather the transplanted street of preserved memories rarely drew many people. An occasional busload of schoolchildren on a weekday, but on an overcast Sunday the place was theirs alone.

Sam Brenner had led his son into a warehouse. There were vintage cars on display and crude tools—drills and cranks and pumps—that had first been used to suck the oil from the great fields. Beside the outmoded chunks of steel, there were old black-and-white photographs blown up to poster size showing the early wells and the grimy, bandy-legged roustabouts of another time in action.

In his guttural German-accented English, Sam Brenner explained the use of each piece of equipment and described the improvements that had come with the years. His son did not share the father's interest in the evolution of the oil company's profit-making prowess and his attention wandered. There was a faded photograph of a family in front of a small wood frame house built on a slope. The sky was behind the house and emptiness all around it. There was a mother and a father and three children. Two girls and a boy. The boy stood closest to his mother and father and the father had his hand on the son's shoulder.

Sam Brenner moved slowly from one piece of equipment to the next, while Ed Brenner went faster. Looking at only the photographs. Hoping to find another glimpse through the window of time at that long ago family. But there was no more. And he found himself near an open door. He stepped out and saw the Ghost Town streets. Ed Brenner, the boy, began to explore and soon he was lost in the weave of the past. He tried to retrace his way, but could not find the building from the present that he had come from. The place where his father was waiting for him. He'll be mad. He'll yell at me for getting lost. I have to find him.

And the boy began to run.

Around another corner and another corner and—he suddenly stopped, with his rain-soaked face and his pounding chest. Because here at last was his father!

Waiting for him. On this street. The boy had been searching and the father had been searching. Missing each other. Round and round. And now they had found each other. They stood and looked across the space between them. The father's face was flushed, his hair matted by the rain. The boy waited. He'll hug me. Or maybe he'll hit me. Because he cares! And I'll tell him how scared I was. He'll say, I love you. "I loff you." *Say it!*

Ed Brenner, the man, screamed soundlessly across the expanse of years to Ed Brenner, the boy: Don't wait for him. Not this time. You do it: *You* tell *him! Make it be different this time!*

But the boy couldn't hear. He did what he always did. Just stood there. Silently. Waiting. And his father stood there. Silently. And when at last Sam Brenner spoke it was to say: "Vee go home now."

They walked without touching and disappeared around a corner—and now the street was empty again—empty until . . .

. . . a boy came running . . .

Brenner made the dream stop by sitting up on the bed and looking around the motel room. Green, gold and brown, flying the colors of the Land of Noontime Checkouts. The lamps on both the nightstands were lit. So was the bathroom light and the fixture over the sink and the floor lamp and the lamp on the bureau beside the yellow telephone. Lots of light on the subject. There was a hairline crack that Brenner had not noticed before over the door leading to the nighttime street. How long had it been there? Since the last earthquake or as a result of some subtle shifting and settling of the building today? They don't make motels like they used to. The TV set was switched off: Ask me no questions, I'll tell you no lies. It stood there like a milky blinded eye. He looked away— to . . .

. . . the telephone . . .

He moved to the phone and dialed without thinking. A familiar voice answered.

"Brenner. On the Montrose thing?"

The voice of Lipton, the night-desk man, told him there was nothing new.

"Just checking," Brenner said.

He hung up but didn't let go of the receiver. What the hell? He lifted it again and dialed.

"Hello," she said.

"Phyllis?" he said. "Hi . . ."

"How are you?" she said. Warm. Friendly. Not the same. Not ever again. But friendly. Polite.

"I—wanted to find out, you know, how Mike . . ."

"He had a wonderful time today," she said enthusiastically. "Can't stop talking about it."

"Yeah? He had a good time? So did I—I mean, we had a beautiful day."

"That's what he said."

"Really did, huh? Can I talk to him, is he there?"

He could hear her handing the phone to Mike "It's your father," she said.

"Hello?"

"Hey, big guy—how ya doin'?"

"Good, Dad. Watchin' TV, goin' to sleep soon, you know. What'd you call for?"

"Nothin' special," Brenner said. Don't wait for him. Tell him! "Just wanted to—to tell you—I love you."

There was a pause and then Mike's voice came back to him through the phone:

"I love you, too."

"Thanks," Brenner said. Thanks? Yeah, thanks. "I'm glad. Sleep good . . ."

Brenner eased the phone back into the cradle and stood up in front of the bureau in the silent motel room.

His father in the hospital bed, gurgling sounds that Brenner leaned forward to hear. Sounds he couldn't decipher. Waiting to hear him say the words he couldn't say any more. I should have told him. He couldn't talk, but maybe he still could hear me. Not like Ganzer, beyond hearing or seeing or being—too late! It just keeps repeating and repeating. For as long as we let it.

Not this time.

Not with Mike. It was going to be good. Not the way it was or the way it would have been between them. But good. Good. Different. The best it could be.

He looked at the face of Ed Brenner, the man, in the mirror over the bureau. And then his view widened as he gazed with detachment: The man gripping the back of

the chair tightly with both his hands was lifting it now . . .
Brenner smashed the mirror.

A cascade of silver glass leaped out at him, but he rushed through it. The follow-through of his swing sent the lamp on the bureau careening into the wall. Brenner pivoted and shattered the dead watching eye of the TV set. A chair leg crashed through the looking glass into the picture tube. The chair got stuck inside but he yanked hard and it came loose with a spray of gleaming shards that covered his pants legs. Brenner ignored the bits of glass and struck at a framed print on the wall near the door: birds taking flight over a marsh. The frame exploded and jumped off the wall and the chair was splintering but he took out one of the nightstand lamps with a backhanded bash and went at the floor lamp, kicking it across the room into the sofa. He demolished the light fixture above the sink and the mirror below and shrugged off the glass in the air, scrunching onward. The chair was just broken pieces of wood in his hands, but he clubbed at the lamp on the other nightstand, rocketing it into the wall and then took care of another crappy glass-framed picture of a ballet dancer. The room had been dimming with the destruction of each pool of light and was now illuminated only by the bulb shining in through the partially open bathroom door. Brenner dropped the last chunk of the chair and stood there panting in the near-darkness of the demolished motel room. It took a moment for him to realize that the pounding he heard was not all inside of his head. Some of it was coming from the outside door.

"What's going on in there?" demanded the voice of Mr. Atkins, the prissy proprietor. "Open up! Are you all right? What's the matter in there?"

"*Nothin'!*" Brenner yelled at the voice and the pounding. "Nothin's the matter. Everything's okay. Everything's all right!"

Dr. Irving Riskin had a secret life. He protected it through subterfuge and deception. Everybody assumed he was still a Wednesday golfer and he encouraged that belief. He made casual comments to his wife about the weather on the links that day or dropped mentions of how he ran into an old colleague in the locker room whom he had actually encountered at lunch on Tuesday. To his office, he was vague about precisely which course he was playing, but indicated he could be reached in an emergency by car phone or beeper. Actually, he couldn't, not right away, but so far no one suspected. It had been going on for seven Wednesdays.

He liked his work and he loved his wife, but he needed the release and the feeling of youth and wild abandon that he had found. In a very short time, it had become vital to him.

The rest of the week he was on call. Constantly. He was not only a doctor, but a corporation. There were five partners in the medical group. They had been his junior associates. But the tax laws had changed and the benefits of incorporation were now available to doctors and they were considerable, the accountant had explained. So they filed the papers with Sacramento. Nothing was supposed to change, except on paper. But it did.

Dr. Riskin had been in demand for twenty years, since he first opened his office on Bedford Drive. Orthopedic surgeon. He had mended bones for ski casualties and knees for the L.A. Rams. Whiplash necks and aching backs. The office had grown to include a therapy wing. A brisk, steady but sensible practice.

Until they became a business.

Then the tempo increased. More and more patients, filling the outer office like the lobby of a hit show, people twisted with pain and delivering their hopes: Heal me! Some he could help, others he could only soothe. But there was an endless line beyond. And the office had been rebuilt to accommodate a volume operation. It was like the stage set for a French farce. Lots of small cubicles along long hallways where half-dressed supplicants who had waited in the waiting room now waited again. White-coated doctors, the principal players in the comedy, raced up and down the halls, opening doors and closing doors, opening and closing, in and out, keep 'em moving, keep 'em happy, how are you, *who* are you? Smile and act like God and pretend you know the name, which you just scanned on the file folder as you walked in—and how've you been getting along? But not really remembering most of the patients until he was about to leave their cubicle. By then, it would come back, but it would be gone again before they returned for their next appointment.

The practice of modern big city medicine.

Dr. Riskin had gone over it any number of times with his associates and the accountant. Wasn't it possible to

simplify? The answer was no. Rental in good medical buildings had risen sharply. The X-ray equipment would have
to be replaced next year and equipment costs had soared.
The office staff was so large they were tripping over each
other, a hefty payroll, but the amount of clerical work
needed to run the office was staggering. Not only individual billings, but an intricate blizzard of paper perpetually
being exchanged with Blue Cross, Medicare and the countless other health insurance programs that seemed to require
three forms from the doctor for every check they issued.
Then came the capper: malpractice insurance. The sky-
rocketing cost to doctors for protecting themselves against
litigation sealed off any possibility of slowing the pace of
the office's activity. They had to keep going, faster and
faster, in order to stand still—a treadmill to where?

Wednesdays.

He felt guilty the first time. Lying to his wife, mislead-
ing the office. But the joy he found in his secret life was
so satisfying. He had to keep on doing it. For a few hours
each week he was free.

He would drive through the early morning streets. Away
from his Bel Air house. Away from his Beverly Hills office.
Into Santa Monica. Through a mesh wire gate on Clover-
field. To the Santa Monica airport.

Irving Riskin was a pilot. On Wednesdays.

The Air Force had trained him to fly for the Korean
War, but he never got closer to the Orient than Pensacola.
After his discharge, there was college to finish, then medical school, then internship and residency and then . . . All
those years. Never at the controls of a plane again. Until.
He was on the freeway rushing from the hospital to the
office when he looked up and saw a light plane. Probably
one of those radio station guys reporting on traffic. But
it gave him the idea.

He kept that Wednesday open, turning down two golf

invitations. He went to the airport instead. They checked him out, tested him. He flew with an instructor that day. Three weeks later, he soloed. And now he went up once a week. Alone. Away from the phones and the beeper and the pressure. For a little while.

The plane he had been renting was a Pitts Special biplane. Other guys might long to handle a Lear Jet, but for Irving Riskin this was flying. Up there over the city, before most of the world down below was even awake, performing Cuban eights, hammerhead stalls and vertical rolls. Thinking of nothing but the indicators in front of him and the pedals beneath his feet and the stick in his hands and the roar of the nose prop and the air rushing at his goggled face. Like a graceful, lackadaisical bird he would drift and float.

From on high, the world was a patchwork. Places were small and people were invisible. Cars on a freeway could be seen for what they were: streams of ants on a conveyor belt. A strip of greenery that looked as wide as a lawn was running from Hollywood to the ocean. It was the mountains and Irving Riskin swooped lower to marvel at this enormous green belt. How much undeveloped land was still left in the heart of this city. Some of it had been scorched by a recent fire below. He flew past the desolation and it was fertile again, wild and untouched, but only for a moment. Then there were houses again. He kicked the rudder and banked. As he rolled on his side and turned, he looked down and saw a house and a yard and a pool. There was a swimmer in blue.

He pulled up on the stick and the horizon dipped as he lunged for the sky. I can fly so high. I can fly forever! There are no limits up here.

Irving Riskin leveled the plane and executed a turn and then pointed his craft downward so that the sensation he so enjoyed of the wind tugging at his clothes and hair and cheeks would begin again. Down, down—the earth reaching for him. Now ease up, pull out—he was low, almost too low; somebody might complain about him buzzing the area—better get a little altitude. But as he passed over the top of a hill he saw a street below him. And a house. And a pool. The same pool he had seen before. Because it was the same swimmer. In blue. Irving Riskin felt drops of water on his face and realized that it was raining down here and yet there was someone swimming anyway. Takes all kinds. He looked off toward Catalina Island, the sun was shining out there. Be fun to go over to the Catalina field for breakfast, but first, out of curiosity, he would take one more pass at the street. Have another look at who would go swimming in the rain.

▰▰▰

They were arguing when Brenner walked into the squad room. He hung his jacket on the rack near the filing cabinets and poured himself a cup of coffee as Elgort shouted at his partner:

"Look, I'm telling you, it was him!"

"Uh-uh," Hyatt said. A man of few words and all of them obviously were bugging Elgort this morning.

"You don't know what the hell you're talking about," Elgort said and he welcomed Brenner, who was passing with steam coming out of his coffee cup. "Hey, you tell him—set him straight, huh?"

"What's the hassle?" Brenner asked.

They surrounded him. An impartial referee.

"Caught the end of the Late, Late Show," Elgort explained. "That old gangster show, *Dillinger?*"

Brenner nodded. "Where he carves the gun out of soap."

Elgort beamed and flicked Hyatt's shoulder. They had come to the right person with their question. Hyatt didn't smile, just gave Brenner his Indian stare.

"So tell him." Elgort pointed at Hyatt, as if indicating a retardate. "Who played Dillinger? Lawrence Tierney . . ."

"Or *Gene* Tierney." Hyatt poked Brenner with his forefinger in absolute certainty.

Brenner looked from Elgort's smiling, expectant face to Hyatt's intense glower. "George," he said to Hyatt, barely suppressing a grin, "Gene Tierney's a woman."

"Told you so," Elgort crowed victoriously. "Five. You owe me five!" He wiggled his fingers in the air, each one demanding a dollar bill. They were moving toward Ramirez' office and Hyatt shoved his partner irritably. "Next thing I know, you'll be tellin' me fuckin' Spencer Tracy's a broad!"

Brenner balanced his coffee and settled into a chair near the door. Jonas was already in the office, leaning over the desk. Ramirez was showing him a folder. Now as they all assembled, Ramirez looked around:

"Okay, first, there's still no smoking in here. That includes you." Ramirez jabbed his finger at the offender. Elgort stubbed out his cigarette. "It's a dirty habit," Ramirez pronounced.

" 'Specially since you quit," Elgort said.

Ramirez clapped his hands. Team huddle.

"All right, gentlemen. Where are we?"

"It's still a smorgasbord," Hyatt said. "Little of this, little of that."

"Okay," Ramirez said. Take charge. "We have had seven new sightings. People spotting kids who could be Bobby." They all perked up. "Unfortunately, in seven different places, but that's how it goes." A weary collective sigh. "We'll divvy 'em up as usual and . . ."

The light on the second line of his phone winked. He scooped it up. "Ramirez. What? Yeah, put him on. Hey, Frank, what're you doin'?"

As the voice of Sgt. Rybicki came over the line, Ramirez'

jaunty smile faded. Even before he knew, Rybicki's tone chilled Ramirez:

"Thought I ought to call you, Ben. We're back at the Montrose house . . ."

The station wagon that was a mobile command post was parked in front of the house. The B&W squad cars were in the driveway and an ambulance was double-parked in the street.

Rybicki was in the backyard talking softly into a white Princess phone on the redwood table. The patio overhang protected him from the drizzling rain that was dotting the surface of the pool. His dark-blue uniform was damp from when he had been standing out there with the others.

"It's kind of hard to explain," Rybicki said into the phone. "We sent scuba crews everywhere—except here."

From across the pool, a siren sound began. Like a thin version of the Friday 10 A.M. air raid warning test. But this wasn't as loud and it was human. The sound was coming from inside Claire Montrose, as she crouched on her knees beside the small, bloated form in blue pajamas lying on the pool decking. Claire was all dressed up in a cream-colored Italian pants suit from Giorgio's that was being soaked by the slow, light rain and discolored by the chlorinated water she was kneeling in. She had been on her way out to meet an ex-stewardess friend for some shopping and lunch.

Rybicki wondered to himself if Ramirez could hear her sound over the phone.

"It was an accident," he said to Ramirez. "Just some kind of freak accident." As he watched and explained, one of the uniformed cops poked at the pool bottom with a skimmer pole. Something was stirring, rising to the surface. From the depths of the opaque water, the object took form. It was a floppy-eared stuffed dog with buttons for eyes and a silly grin. The doll broke the water and bobbed around.

Across the pool, the uniformed cops stood back while the paramedics lifted the misshapen blue form onto a stretcher and covered it. Claire's lament hit a new high note. A doctor who had been summoned from his home on the next street turned his attention to Claire, offering her medication. She didn't seem to hear him as her hands worked upon each other, her expensive nails scratching and tearing the skin of her hands. Phone calls to her husband's office had so far been unsuccessful in locating Harold Montrose; he was out at a business meeting somewhere. The doctor prepared to give Claire Montrose a mild sedative shot. She didn't resist his overtures; she simply seemed unaware of them.

"Yeah," Ramirez said into the phone. "He's *sure*? The whole time? But we—uh-huh, yeah—right."

The men in the office didn't know what he was hearing so they were bored, waiting for him to get off the phone so they could finish their meeting and get on with their day. Ramirez drew a deep breath. "Okay. Let's get it written up. Thanks, Frank."

Ramirez put the phone down in its cradle on the desk and kept his hand there as if that somehow maintained contact with the other end. "They found the kid. Dead. In that shitty swimming pool."

It stunned them all. The way it had stunned him.

"But we . . ." Jonas managed to get something out. "That was the first place . . ."

"Yeah, yeah, I know." Ramirez slapped at the phone, pushing it away. "We looked—we all stood there and—it's some kind of optical illusion. The pool's got a funny bottom. It falls off sharp." He thrust his hand, plunging down, describing a shape in the air. Dipsy-doodle. "Bobby must've tumbled in—slipped down under that layer of silt and drowned."

"But I could *see* the bottom," Elgort challenged.

"You thought you could," Ramirez glared at him. What the hell am I getting mad at him for? We all thought we could. God damn it! "They're out there now, they checked it."

Hyatt advanced on the desk with a crafty gleam in his eye. "Maybe he wasn't there when we first . . ."

"He was there!" Ramirez said loudly. "No tricky stuff, just straight shit. Medic says it's so. Want me to tell you about water decomposition and the fucking body gases that accumulated in three weeks. *He was there the whole time.*" Ramirez pulled in a chestful of air. "Until he popped to the surface this morning."

They sat there and didn't look at each other. Nobody else had anything to say until:

"Who spotted it?" Brenner asked quietly. And what difference does that make? But maybe if we add enough details it will seem real. Over. Finished. And then I will feel something.

"Some amateur pilot spotted it," Ramirez said dully. He picked up the Montrose file and looked at the 4 x 5 jumbo-size color photo on top of Bobby in knee pants and polo shirt. The slightly out-of-focus picture his mother had given them. Ramirez closed the file. "Guy buzzed the neighborhood. Noticed something floating in the pool . . ."

"Bobby," Jonas said. "There was Bobby . . ."

"The zipper," Ramirez added. "On his pajamas. The end of it got stuck in the drain on the bottom and kept him from comin' up before."

"After all the . . ." Hyatt began over: "After everything we . . ." He trailed off again.

Jonas leaned toward Ramirez. There had to be something. Something.

"Can we still put the pill case together against Montrose?" he asked.

Ramirez shook his head and shoved back his chair. "No, no—I don't think so. That's it."

He came around the desk.

"Okay. There'll be new assignments for all of you. Elgort, you and Hyatt'll move over onto that firebug thing, they can use a little help."

Dismissed. That is it, Ramirez thought. Next. Go on, move it. They filed out and closed the door behind them. Ramirez looked down at his desk. Elgort had forgotten his pack of cigarettes and a book of matches. McKnight's Bar & Grill. Ramirez took a cigarette, lit it and filled his empty chest with smoke.

In the squad room, Elgort snatched his jacket off a hanger. He looked at Hyatt, who was staring off. They hadn't spoken since they walked out of the office; they were supposed to check in with the guys who were working on the arson case.

"Gene Tierney was in *Laura*," Elgort said as he pulled open the door to the hallway.

"The one who was the cop," Hyatt said.

"The *broad*!" Elgort said angrily as they went out.

Brenner straightened his desk. There were files and folders. Bits of paper and phone messages. Weeks of work. And she was right. The fortune-teller. He was there all the time. In the darkness. At the house. Waiting for them. He felt a tickle at the back of his mouth and Brenner cleared his throat. Jonas was on the phone, talking to his wife, but not telling her about Bobby. Just shucking about what's gonna be for dinner. Brenner walked past Jonas out into the hall. He coughed but the tickle wouldn't go away.

The corridor was empty as he bent his head over the water fountain. Cool clear water. "I'm dying of thirst and you give me neckties?" Wash it all away. He drank again and the tickle went down into his belly. It was a bubble now but it was still there. Bobby was still there. Bobby Kennedy on the floor of that stinking hallway with his eyes opening and closing like a semaphore signalman. Still there. And Bobby Montrose deep in the water you couldn't see through. The bubble was rising. Ganzer in the ground and Sam Brenner's accented Sid Caesar voice no longer heard. Doesn't bother you now, does it? Not a bit. Not now. It's all a game, right? Win a few, lose a few. But why couldn't we win this one? Why not? Just one. It really would have meant—what? A lot. For how long? For right now. To who? To all of us—we all needed this one. *To who?* Say it! *I* needed this one. The bubble was a burning sensation and it was in his throat. He sipped water from the fountain and choked. The overflow ran from his lips down his chin. Things change. Didn't you know that? Bobby's gone! But Mike's still here! For a while . . .

He coughed, trying to clear his throat. His right hand came up to wipe his chin and he heard a pulsing sound. It was being made by the water fountain. It was shaking on the floor. He was holding it and shaking it with his left hand. Why are you doing that? He tried to let go of the side of the fountain but his left hand remained fused, gripping, quivering. The back of his right hand was frozen in the air near his mouth and from the corner of his eyes he felt tears trickle down his cheeks as the sour burning bubble burst in the back of his throat. He began to cry. Brenner turned his face deep into the alcove where the water fountain was so that if the elevator or one of the doors along the hallway opened, no one would see. But for the moment it was all right. He was alone in the empty corridor.

Brenner wept for all of them and for himself.

In the mountains that divided the city, the rain was absorbed as quickly as it fell onto the parched brushland. The wildlife that during these months had been creeping closer to civilization for survival could now retreat to temporary safety.

In the streets of the Valley, the drainage began to clog and flooding would start soon. In the hillside areas, particularly those that had been badly scorched by sun or flames, mudslides were only hours away. Traffic was slowing everywhere and the people of Los Angeles adjusted resentfully to a dreary day.

Outside the building without windows, the light drizzle had become a steady rain. Butler Avenue was slick and the shiny surface of the wet gutter reflected the signal light at the corner and the small neon sign that had been turned on in the grayness of the morning by the liquor store proprietor.

The prediction had been 90 percent chance of showers in the only city that gives daily odds on the weather. A nine-to-one shot had come in. The rain would last all day, the radio voices were telling motorists, and possibly into tomorrow. The fire season was over.